CRUSHED TRACHEA BLUES

BRADLEY VANDEVENTER

THIRD-EYE LASIK PRESS

Crushed Trachea Blues, First Edition.

Copyright © Bradley VanDeventer (2024). All rights reserved.

ISBN

978-1-732028-24-1 (Paperback)

978-1-732028-23-4 (E-Book)

Publisher: Third-Eye LASIK Press

Cover design: Stefan Prodanovic

For inquiries regarding this book, contact:

bradleylvan@outlook.com

No part of this book may be reproduced in any manner or by any electronic or mechanical means, including information storage or retrieval systems, without written permission from the author, except for the use of brief quotations in critical articles or book reviews.

This is a work of fiction. The characters, dialogues, and incidents are products of the author's imagination and are not to be construed as real. Any resemblance to actual persons, living or dead, is purely coincidental.

Other books by Bradley VanDeventer

Our Lady of the Hypercube

Angels With Engine Failure

For Criseida

Life's the study of dying
And how to do it right
__Queens of the Stone Age, *Song for the Dead*

CRUSHED TRACHEA BLUES

CHAPTER ONE

It was shaping up to be one of those gift-wrapped-from-God LA sunrises that made you instantly regret having got drunk the previous night.

The marine layer ionized the smog just enough to render it charming, officially making it the best time and place to be on earth. The line of palm trees on both sides of the boulevard confirmed it, as did a fit twenty-something who held the door of the high rise open for me before passing me to dart up to her yoga class.

Instead of chirping *Namaste*, I offered her the international thanks of nodding with a smirk. Her smiling back over her shoulder cracked the shell of my hangover somewhat. Two minutes remained for me to make it up to the ninth floor. A sprint up the stairwell would have been optimal, but I did not know where to find one.

Just as I was about to reconfirm my atheism, the leftmost of the three elevators open-sesamed. I slid in. An oversized cell phone spun in midair a few times before landing face first on the threshold. "The hell," erupted a blonde in a power suit and one of those nondescript faces that looked either twenty-five or fifty. "Why not watch where you're going, dude?" she snapped as she bent to pick up her phone. I pressed the button corresponding to my floor. It lit up orange-red. She trailed away toward the main entrance, stuffing her phone into a lavender handbag that matched a rolled-up yoga mat tucked under her other arm.

"*Namaste*," I blurted out, craning my neck so that she could see me until the elevator doors sealed us off from each other for all eternity. I thought I saw a middle finger begin to form, but wasn't sure. My vision was blurry and my head throbbed just one notch under migraine status.

Praise the lord and all his alternate *noms de guerre*, I made the class on time. I swiped my timecard on the time clock whose digital readout read 6:59.

Commotion at the door erupted behind me. I turned to find three people vying for first entry into the suite. Much to the two men's detriment, their chivalry had them insist the lady go in first. The tall redhead took the timecard from her teeth and performed an impressive standing broad jump, the end of which had her swipe the card through the time clock upon a graceful landing. She smiled at me, shook her head, and wiped the sweat of despair from her brow.

The clock switched over to 7:00. The two gentlemen at the door didn't bother to fuss about who went in second, both of them instead about-facing and waddling away.

The redhead and I entered the salon to take seats at the large circle of chairs. Not a few of those present were in the middle of serving themselves drinks from the array of bottled spirits that cluttered the coffee table in the middle of the circle.

"How about a bartender?" I proposed to Rebecca Murphy, the counselor.

She rolled her eyes, twiddling her pen against her clipboard. "Step eleven of Functioning Alcoholics Anonymous. 'Never outsource your own dipsomania to someone else.' You will continue to make your own drinks."

I shrugged and looked over at the redhead as I took the seat next to her. "Worth a shot."

She toasted me with a shot glass full of whiskey, which she then threw down the hatch.

Rebecca did roll call. To my delight, detective Hector Sandoval answered, "Present." I looked three chairs down at him. He acknowledged me with a jutting of his goatee.

The coffee table had a cluster of high-end tequila bottles, in and of themselves works of art. They stood bunched together like skyscrapers, dwarfing the whiskey bottles and cans of IPAs and craft stouts that most of those present opted for.

I fixed myself a *paloma*—two fingers of tequila, three fingers of mineral water, the rest grapefruit soda. A lounge chair and parasol would have been ideal.

Rebecca cleared her throat. "Let the marked number of empty seats today be admonishments to you. Punctuality is not only crucial. It is everything. All else is procrastination, and therein lies sloth, and ultimately death. To be on time is to stay alive. Truancy is one of many enemies to responsible alcohol abuse."

These meetings were meant to be anonymous—and mostly they were—but I knew the detective's name because he was an old high school buddy. He found me work from time to time. Attending FAA was his idea. It was, in fact, a splendid way to stay on top of my dipsomania. At the end of class, having perused my hour-by-hour log for the previous few days, Rebecca would give me the green light to drink up to the next class—a literal green light, as the app on my phone would read out the alcohol content via the stint in my arm. If I missed class or failed to provide the hour-by-hour log, or came up short on the multitasking activities that Rebecca's diabolical mind had whipped up in the interim, a notification would go to her phone showing that I had attempted consumption when all along I hadn't procured the right to responsibly abuse it.

She didn't suffer any slipups. She was severe. A first-time violation was a last-time violation. Zero tolerance. Banned for life. It made sense. Attending the classes helped me find that sweet spot between inebriation and productivity. It meant that I could drink no more than three times a week, not including anything consumed during class. Getting absolutely hammered meant that I had to pull up my bootstraps the following day, hangover be damned.

Glutathione helped. A candy dish full of the supplements sat among all the liquor and beer. They looked like liver-saving roly-poly bugs.

"All right, gang," Rebecca said, peering at me over her reading glasses. "You're going to read the first ten pages of Kant's *Critique of Pure Reason* while performing burpees. You have forty minutes. At the end, your quads should be screaming for mercy and you should know the difference between *a priori* and *a posteriori* reasoning. So stretch out, take a hearty swig, and get ready."

"Dufuq," the redhead to my left chirped, removing her green pumps.

I took a sip of my drink and set it down under the chair.

Rebecca handed us printouts of the German philosopher's impenetrable masterpiece. We began stretching in front of our chairs.

"Earn your hedonism," the redhead said to me, her head upside-down and at her knees as she stretched out impressively, touching her toes with her palms.

So it turned out that *a priori* reasoning was deduced, whereas its *a posteriori* cousin was induced. Through a complex labyrinth of *a priori* deduction, I was able to knock out perfectly executed burpees while realizing that Kant was a kook.

"Ok, ladies and gentlemen," Rebecca said after blowing a whistle that she kept slung around her neck. "Time's up. You'll have twenty minutes to write your thesis. It must be between 100 and 400 words. Please don't let the music distract you. Oh, and mind your apps. BAC should be .11."

She produced a Bluetooth speaker the size and shape of an overgrown bratwurst, fiddling with her phone. 90s gangsta rap oozed into the room. The music dated her. The whistle dangled delightfully between the pronounced protuberances of her tight cable-knit sweater. She glanced at me; did a double-take; lowered her reading glasses and peered over them at me. "Get to work, you," she barked. "And finish your tequila. You're slipping."

Fortified with the rest of my *paloma*, and a second one, I went to work with the pen and notebook, trying to dodge drive-bys and pimp-slaps.

Once the curriculum was over, Rebecca allowed us free time for the rest of the class. Hector had beat me to the conference room. A lineup of empty beer cans barricaded the bottom half of his face as he sat slumped in his chair. "Marathon," I said, "not a race."

"No," he said, sitting up, "it *is* a race. Marathons are for excuse-makers and slowpokes. The Jamaican gets the girl, not the Kenyan."

I plopped into the seat facing opposite him, the hydraulics in my left arm keeping my drink from spilling as I gently lowered it onto the glass table.

With a Luciferian goatee and slicked-back hair, my college buddy resembled a high-ranking cholo from Boyle Heights. In fact, he had been so entrenched in East LA drug stings that, in order to guarantee his safety after a nasty coke sting, they moved him out of RICO and sent him into the more affluent areas of the San Fernando Valley. On the north side of the Hollywood Hills, a saturnine Latino like himself would come across as intimidating enough to scare the yuppies straight.

Hector furtively looked behind me. "Check it out," he said, producing a manila envelope and nudging it toward me.

Before opening it, I fortified my guts with a drink. I sat up in my chair, propped my elbows onto the desk, and opened the folder. The first thing I saw was a photo of Charles "Blitz" Volkenrath, welterweight champion of UMMA (Ultimate Mixed Martial Arts). I was a big-enough fan of MMA to know who he was. UMMA was the feeder league to the biggest game in town, the UFC. In the photo, Volkenrath held the belt around his waist with one hand while the other remained aloft by a referee. Charles beamed a glorious smile. Handsome fella. Eight-pack abs. Boxer's delts. Wrestler's quads. All of it.

I slid that photo to the side to find the next photo of Charles "Blitz " Volkenrath. He lay in the middle of a cage, belly up, eyes closed, his face a shade of blue not found on the spectrum of the living.

I had seen it on the MMA news websites. The crux of the story, besides the untimely demise of the rising combat athlete, was whether it had been accidental. He had died from a collapsed trachea, and ultimately an inability to take in oxygen. What remained to be determined was if the person with whom he had been sparring had willfully held onto the choke for too long or if it had been an unwillingness on the champion's part to tap out of some sense of pride—which was unlikely, because even the most hardheaded fighter had enough self-discipline to tap out and live to fight another day. No reason to risk one's life over a meaningless sparring session.

"What could I possibly do with this that you foul play fellas can't handle yourself?" I took a nifty sip of my *paloma*. "My specialty is hiding out in dirty laundry hampers and knowing the best parking spots at fleabag motels." I took an even niftier sip of my *paloma*.

Hector moved the beer cans out from between us and tapped on the manila folder. "The dead dude, Volkenrath, left behind a wife. She's been a real nuisance at the department. In desperation mode, which is understandable. Still, she threatens us with nonexistent injunctions and harasses our secretaries with cockamamie reports. We'd like to yank her off our backs for a good while and keep her off. Figured you could use the work. My boss remains impressed with that Winnetka gig you tied up for us. I don't know why. I still maintain you got lucky. Plus, you're a combat sports aficionado. Are you not? Boxing and karate and jiu-jitsu?"

"You esteem me so lowly, my friend. You're not the only overachieving alky in town, you know. I worked my ass off on Winnetka."

"And I told my boss the same. Hence the manila folder under your chin. I still think the stars cut you a break. Nothing wrong with that. To an extent, we create or own luck." He upended a beer can and slammed it down on the table; wiped his goatee clean. "We won't cut you a check, but the girl will. I cornered her outside a few days ago and mentioned you. Said she was open to it, provided it got finished quickly, what with her limited budget. Apparently, being a mixed martial arts champion doesn't back up the Brinks truck."

"You know," I said, raising an eyebrow, "you should take up a martial art. You'd do some damage, what with your build."

He shook his head, twirling an empty beer can. "The gun range is my dojo. It's enough for me. I take one of my girls to TaeKwon Do twice a week. I want nothing to do with other peoples' feet."

I shrugged. "Numbed by all the mayhem. I get it."

"You could call it that." He drew a fresh can of beer from somewhere near his feet and cracked it open. "The girl will show up at your place tomorrow, if not today. Be patient. She's a mixture of hysterical and melancholy." He held his can up to me. "*Salud.*"

I bumped his double IPA with my glass. "*Salud.*"

I thought I had made the mistake of hiring a blowhard as a bodyguard/assistant, but it was more of an Aristotelian argument that Mazagon held against colored belts in Brazilian jiu-jitsu. "True ninjas recognize no colors," he said. "Not even black. The only worthy color would be that of clear." He explained this to me over lamb kabobs downstairs from the office on the sidewalk. We had convinced each other to eat healthfully for once.

Mazagon actually hadn't trained in a dedicated BJJ gym in over three years, preferring to sneak up on people from behind and choke them out. Being a high-level black belt meant nothing, he maintained, if the person wasn't stealthy and didn't employ smoke bombs or other chicanery to sneak in the hooks and squeeze.

I originally offered him work because my cleaning lady, Araceli Sanchez, happened to be his mom. She wanted to get him out of the house. He was twenty-three and showed no signs of wanting to find work. He spent his days playing first-person shooter games for money and watching BJJ YouTube tutorials. When he couldn't practice moves on cannabis-addled girlfriends, who got fed up with his contorting of them, he practiced his moves on a makeshift grappling dummy. Araceli said he dumped a cute blonde, "a keeper," because she had small feet, which didn't present for easy toe holds or heel hooks.

I had to keep a close eye on him because he intended to choke out or submit everyone who came into my office, including his own mom. This included clients as well, both prospective and existing.

Sure enough, back up at the office, when a young woman came up the steps, he was crouched behind the water cooler, ready to strike. He was likely going for an Imanari roll, a sweet technique that ended up with him toppling over his victim and snagging a heel hook.

I dove at him. Fully aware of the stairs behind her, the woman pivoted out to the side, as if delivering a check left hook. Her arms went up to shield her face, elbows in tight. She had a good guard.

Mazagon, blown away by the pint-sized Valkyrie invading our sweat lodge, dismissively shook me off and stood up as if he were the one in charge. "Sorry," he muttered. There was no excusing his shock of coarse black hair.

The young woman frowned and gazed down at a business card she held in her hand. "Do I have the right place? Paisley Fuentes's Investigative Services?"

I stood up. "I am he. I mean, yes you do. My overzealous assistant doesn't trust a single person in the world. Probably the weed. He was looking to get you in a heel hook, which is this very painful, possibly debilitating—"

"I'd have slipped my heel and done it to him," she said, her oval face serene and severe.

We found ourselves in an awkward, nonverbal standoff. I always lacked an opening line for prospective clients. I figured if I played it close to the vest, they would divulge more than they initially wished to and would therefore make for a somewhat easier case.

She eventually stirred, raising an eyebrow. "Aren't you going to ask 'What can I do for you?'"

"No," I said, "but I will insist with, 'What brings you to this, the seventeenth level of Dante's Inferno, where only alcoholics and socially awkward grapplers dwell?'" I nodded over to Mazagon, who on cue fell back onto the floor and once on his side performed hip escapes—or shrimps—out of sight.

She pointed at him, left with a finger indicating nothing once he disappeared into the copier room.

"I've decided on calling it eccentric," I explained.

She twisted her head back over her shoulder, perhaps toward the door.

"Please," I said, "Please take a seat, Mrs. Volkenrath." I pulled out the chair facing opposite my empty desk. She obliged me, patting herself down while I walked around and sunk into my executive chair, the most expensive item in my office, second only to a bottle of Don Julio *añejo*.

She slumped in the chair. "Name's Moira," she said. Once we established eye contact, she gazed down into her lap and took a deep, silent breath. "Mr. Sandoval sent me here. He said you could help me."

"I can't imagine what I could do for you what Reseda PD can't. I'm just a gumshoe who has a knack for going unnoticed in a town were unnoticing is a skill on equal terms with overpaying for coffee while burying one's nose in one's phone."

"I don't want you to solve a whodunnit. More like a *whydunnit*. Charles had no enemies, Mr. Fuentes. He was the golden boy of UMMA. He prided himself on being the good guy. Captain America to a fault."

"The suspect turned himself in two days after, did he not?" I asked her. "I take it you're not convinced it was an accident?" I crossed my legs and reached for my bag of sunflower seeds in the side drawer to my right.

"No way it was," Moira said, shaking her head. "The autopsy results showed a deep bruise across his throat. Forensics guy maintains the choke was held for a very long time. Very on purpose."

"Did Charles ever mention this Facecrusher cat?"

"Never," Moira said, sitting up and for the first time staring me directly in the face. Her eyes were a breathtaking emerald. They smuggled more light into them than they should have. "I sifted through Charles's social media posts. The guy shows up in all those post-sparring photos, usually standing in the back row because he's on the taller side."

"Taller than Charles?" I unfurled the bag of sunflower seeds and realized to my dismay that it was empty.

"A lot taller. The guy was 6'4". Charles was 5'11". Not even close to being the same weight class. Meaning there could have been no beef as far as title opportunities or promotions go."

I had seen Facecrusher fight a few times. He was a dangerous striker, a high-level specialist, with over thirty muay thai fights before transitioning to MMA. He was one of those striker prodigies who hated to go to the ground, preferring to stand and bang. "Do you know Facecrusher's jiu-jitsu rank?"

"How the hell would I know?" Moira shot at me. Her squinting didn't make the eyes any less effulgent.

I balled up the empty sunflower seed bag and bank-shot it into the wastebasket in the corner. "Pardon me for asking," I said, standing up, ready to usher her out of my office if she insisted on more acidic coyness. "There are these things called questions. They get posed in order to garner information. I may be a smartass at times, but I'm not stupid. And I'll never ask a stupid question, at least not intentionally."

Remorse froze her face. If it thawed just a tad, it would collapse in despair. "I'm sorry, Mr. Fuentes. It's just that the DA is dragging his feet. And I can barely feed my boy. I had to sell the house, give up training, and move into a studio apartment."

I shifted gears. "Do you know who Facecrusher trains his jiu-jitsu with? Or where?"

"I do, as a matter of fact. Legion MMA. His social media profiles have been shut down. But through the accounts of other fighters, I was able to find that out. Isn't much of a grappler, from what I've gathered. A striking specialist whose ego probably couldn't take the burden of once more being a white belt. It looks like he did at least minimal grappling work for his fight camps. He was such a good knockout artist that he could get by on that alone. The heavier divisions are easier to do that in."

I nodded. Seeing the heavier weight classes bang it out was always exciting because the margin of error was so small. One tiny miscalculation, and night-night. There were a few heavyweight jiu-jitsu black belts, though.

"How was Charles's jiu-jitsu?" I asked, looking around the office for anything to snack on—potpourri, mulch in the orchid pot, whatever.

"Underrated," Moira said. "Brown belt in gi. Purple belt in no-gi. His top game was exceptional. Not saying it because he was my husband. For him to stick his neck out like that, even during a friendly roll, would be insane."

"Have the cops assigned to the case asked this kind of information from you?"

"Not at all," Moira said, sitting back in her chair. "Which is why I'm here."

"Are you currently pressing wrongful death charges?" I asked.

Her eyebrows bunched together. She ironed her face out with some deep breaths and eventually said, "Yes. Yes, I am."

"Against Facecrusher?"

"Yes."

"You might want to hold off," I said.

"How dare you suggest such a thing. Charles had a life insurance policy, though not the best one around. I don't know how well you know the business side of MMA, Mr. Fuentes, but you'd be shocked to learn that there's little money in it. Despite his championship belt, Charles barely made six figures. That's not after paying taxes, coaches, blood and doping tests."

What an enterprise: get kicked in the head for something a starting UPS courier could make schlepping cardboard. "I get it, Mrs. Volkenrath. It's just that you may be barking up the wrong tree. Said tree might yield little to no fruit if you gave it a generous shake or two. I'm convinced there's more behind this than a meathead like Facecrusher. From my experience in foul play, it's either passion or money that's the motivating factor. Sometimes the two are not mutually exclusive."

"Are you suggesting I drop the case?" She sat up in her seat again.

"No," I said. "I am not. I'm suggesting you let the police drag their feet a little. That will give you more time to zoom back and see what's really cooking. Like, who were Facecrusher's sponsors when he fought? What other mutual contacts did he and Charles have that could have resulted in friction? Trigger warning, because I'm about to ask you another silly question. If you want to kick my ass, then do so. My only request is that you leave me alone in my office to nurse my concussion and never come back. Did Charles fool around on you?"

"No," Moira said. I sighed relief. Her attitude was improving. "And before you say that groupies are part of a pro athlete's life, I get it. But he and I spent so much time together training that I'd be hard-pressed to know when he could manage such a thing time-wise. I get hit on all the time, and I'm actually too busy to act on any of it. Not that I would."

"So, what exactly are you hoping that I can unearth about your husband?" I heard Mazagon fumbling around in the bathroom. No matter how stealthy, a guy desperately having to take a leak made enough noise to wake a slumbering newborn.

Moira stood up from her chair. "Well, as you said, maybe letting the cops drag their feet on this would help me figure out who to go after. My counsel assumes that Facecrusher has nothing worth going after. I'm not about vengeance. I have my boy to take care of."

"How old is he, your boy?" I stood up as well.

"Six," she said. "Certainly old enough to suffer the loss of a father. It's been hard. I'd go to the ends of the earth to make him happy."

"I take it you have not been training? Any fights coming up for you?"

"Fighting is the last thing on my mind. After a violent act is perpetrated on your soulmate, the last thing you want to do is train. I hate jiu-jitsu now. I can't stand the idea of wanting to choke someone unconscious."

"What about MMA in general?"

"A cruel sport. Maybe even the cruelest. It's only obvious. Funny how people coming up justify it with the whole samurai code of ethics bullshit, the whole 'I compete with myself' line. Martial arts and honor and all that. I'm at the point now where all those techniques don't mean shit compared to a Glock 9mm. Best self-defense technique ever is to get your ass to a shooting range."

I made my way around the desk and got up close to her. She was shorter than I initially thought. How much damage could a girl her size unleash on me? I was athletic for a forty-year-old, but my repertoire was limited to boxing. She'd probably beat me up in under two minutes. "I don't suggest taking the law into your own hands. It never ends well. You'd be no better than Facecrusher."

She guffawed. "Mr. Fuentes, I don't need you to remind me how to be a responsible mother. I pack heat at home and would only use it if they broke into my house."

"Doesn't the Volkenrath residence have a home security system?" I heard the toilet flush from behind the closed bathroom door.

"It does," Moira said. "Complete with a response team that leaps into action minutes after the fact. The alarm will merely serve as a cue for the criminals to make a speedy exit."

I chuckled. "Hence the Glock."

She shrugged. "As far as payment goes, what are we looking at?"

I walked over to my desk and from one of the side drawers withdrew a card. "Give Tricky Goodsilk a call. She takes care of my billing. She's offsite. If you wish to talk to her in person, she's probably across the street on the first floor, at the cafe."

"May I ask how long you getting to the bottom of this will take you?"

"I must admit, I've only worked on two foul play cases. I usually camp out between bird-of-paradise plants and Silver Lake bay windows."

"Are you saying you're not up to the task?"

"Not saying that at all. I'm saying that the time frame and price reflect the proximity-to-danger ratio. Hazard pay, if you will."

"Well, I'm not sitting on a heap of diamonds, but I'd be willing to foot the bill required to figure out why this happened. Once the why is found out, my counsel and I can move forward."

"Don't ever call me. Email me instead. I check my account all the time."

With downcast eyes, she exited the office and closed the door.

I exhaled deeply. I preferred non-violent cases. The upside would be the pay. But with a kid involved, I couldn't in good conscience charge the normal hazard rate. I called Tricky and told her to give Mrs. Volkenrath the bro deal.

Meantime, Mazagon had been back to practicing his hip escapes back and forth across the office floor. "You know," I said, opening my drawer and fishing out my ledger, "you should work on your stand-up game as well."

Mazagon froze on the floor, on his right side, arms T-rexed, and gazed up at me. "If I have to kick or punch, or elbow, or knee, I've already lost. That just means that the element of surprise has been absent in my strategy. One should never depend on the knockout."

"Boxers do it all the time," I said, maybe a bit biased about my love of the sweet science.

"Yeah," Mazagon shot back, "against other boxers."

"Either way, homie," I said, "best at least work on your clinch game. The very first place we're going to visit is an MMA gym."

"White belts, all of them," Mazagon retorted, flipping over to his other side and shrimping out of sight.

Chapter Two

It turned out that Moira Volkenrath was a fighter herself. She was a journeyman (journeywoman?) with the less-than-stellar record of 10 wins, 6 losses—a record that renders one a realist, I imagine—the taste of victory being offset by the abysmal depression of defeat. The kind of record that keeps one from being a blowhard. Tough cookie either way. Her fight name was Shrapnel.

Going through the manila envelope she had left me made me feel like a kid who gets all those cheesy cutout membership badges and frameable accolades when he joins a superhero's fan club. As if to erase the darkness left by the crime scene still shot, what followed were photocopies of Charles Volkenrath's NCAA wrestling championship plaques, Brazilian Jiu-jitsu belt rank promotion certificates, and honorary recognitions of his charity efforts.

I struggled to find a reason to dislike the guy. While certainly good-looking, he didn't possess the waifish runway model aesthetic that most men envied but ultimately scorned. He was a man's man who happened to be a dime piece. Blue eyes, chiseled jaw, Adonis body—good looks worked for and maintained, not just born with.

One curious photo was that of a banged-up Volkenrath posing with one Derek Federspiel, President and CEO of Berzerk Fight Gear, a major manufacturer of combat sports equipment—board shorts, rashguards, shin guards, boxing gloves, you name it. Berserk Fight Gear had been Volkenrath's main sponsor. Mr. Federspiel stood at Volkenrath's left, arm slung around the champ's sweaty shoulder, other arm bent forward and forming a fist—one of those awkward fists that non-fighting fight fans insist on performing even though the lack of technique is telling.

I picked up my phone and dialed Tricky. She picked up on the first ring. "Tricky. Do me a favor, yeah?"

"Wouldn't be a favor, boo, since you be paying me to do these things." Her special blend of sarcasm seeped up through my phone's speaker like talcum powder, causing a cloud of choking dust.

"Look," I said. "Can you please text me Mrs. Volkenrath's contact info? Phone number, email? I forgot to gather all that when she was here."

"A little flabbergasted, were we?" assumed Tricky, perhaps correctly so. "I can see where a virile dude such as yourself would lose track with pertinent information with such a knockout in the vicinity. Homegirl's gorgeous." My hacker secretary, a Tongan beanpole with bewitching eyes that excused everything else, loved poking at my heterosexuality.

"What's that got to do with it?" I fired back. "Look, just get me her email, please. No leaked nude photos. Girl's been through the wringer. Last thing she needs is a creep breathing over her."

Tricky laughed. "Didn't seem shaken up by tragedy enough to not dish out attitude every chance she got, that's for sure."

She was right, of course. "Could be a defense mechanism in order to cope. Also, try to find out who MMA fighter Charles "Blitz" Volkenrath's sponsors were during his entire pro career."

"How do you propose I go about finding that out?"

"I don't know. Those magical things called search engines?" I ran through the same routine every time. Prodding Tricky Goodsilk into doing her job was like starting an uncooperative leaf blower: full of laborious yanking, but once you got her going, she more than got the job done. "Start with his manager. I doubt he'll clam up. That would make him a suspect. Unless, of course, he deserves to be, in which case, bingo."

"Okay, but it's going to take all day, probably."

"Good," I said. "That would mean I didn't pay you in vain on this fine Thursday."

She hung up.

Handling a case like Moira Volkenrath's required police contact. It was a matter of limboing under the red tape that hand-tied the detectives. I turned to the one person who could help me: Hector Sandoval.

I texted him to see if he was free. Would I like to meet him at a brewery in Van Nuys? There was a triple IPA he was dying to try out called Turbo Teabag, a thrice-brewed New England blend with Simcoe hops and a musky aftertaste.

I headed west and drove straight through the metal teeth of Downtown LA, figuring I'd do some bum-watching and forcibly appreciate my own threadbare existence by comparison than deal with the northbound 101, which at that time of day would nearly disqualify as being a conduit of transportation and be nothing more than a free parking lot.

When I got to the brewery, Hop-A-Razzi, I found Hector sitting on a barstool, knees against a barrel. He was working on a jigsaw puzzle and a tall glass of what must have been that Turbo Teabag. Odd for a family man to be spending a day off alone at a brewery.

"How's the triple?" I asked, doffing my fedora. What with all the surrounding hipsters, I could have kept the thing on and not provoke a trace of irony-hating disdain. I pulled up a stool.

"Meh. Try the double IPA instead, called Screw Your Peanut Allergy. The only IPA in the world to provide a protein boost. Fiber, too, if I'm not wrong."

"No thanks," I said. "Not an ale guy to begin with. Even less a pale ale guy. Too hoppy. You should try a pilsner or something. You know, a cruiser beer."

Hector's hands let go the two jigsaw puzzle pieces, a crane letting go of an I-beam. He looked at me with dead earnestness. "I'm not here to cruise, son. Cruise. I need to get from point A to point B. Ain't no damn cruising."

"What's Point A?" I wondered, bouncing my fedora on my knee.

"Life-negating sobriety," Hector said, going back to the puzzle.

"And Point B?" I asked, trying my hand at the sea of puzzle pieces, a lot of which hadn't been overturned.

"Floating aloft within the beautiful ether of inebriation," he said, finally looking up at me with his customary friendliness.

"Unsustainable," I said.

"Don't you take the glutathione?"

A server came by and took my order. I settled for a Kölsch.

"Cruise." Hector continued. "If I wanted to cruise, I'd smoke weed or something similarly stupid. Cruise. Not here to cruise."

"How can you manage a jigsaw puzzle while buzzed? Seems like the dizziness would make it extra hard."

He took a giant gulp from his triple IPA. "The point is to enjoy it. Have no expectations. I haven't connected two pieces in at least ten minutes. The key is to jump around and not focus on any portion overly much."

"In other words, cruise," I said. The server came back with my beer. I took a sip. It was quite good. "What are you currently working on?" Despite the recreational alky he lapsed into being on Fridays as part of Functional Alcoholics Anonymous, he was actually a stone-sober go-getter throughout the week.

"Some insurance fraud up in Canoga Park. Not even close to a challenge." He downed his glass of beer.

"I've got a challenge for you. Procuring some stuff on the snuffing of the MMA fighter last month. The gym's in Reseda. Near to here, in fact."

"You know I'm up in Simi/Canoga on a semi-permanent basis, right?" He motioned our server to come back.

"Wouldn't need much. Just a transcript of your guy interviewing the perp, or the gym owner. I'm going to visit the scene. Not far from here at all."

"I'll be honest. There's a slim chance I can get you anything. My boss made it crystal clear to not intervene in my colleague's work. Bad for interdepartmental morale." He ran a hand down his goatee, which was starting to show a little gray. "The place isn't cordoned off?"

"No. It's an MMA gym. Dude got done up right in the practice cage."

"I know that part. What I didn't look into closer was the method of death. Kick? Punch? Elbow?"

I shook my head, took a sip of my Kölsch. "Choke."

"Choke? As in with both hands on the throat?"

"No no. Choke. Jiu-jitsu choke. Grappling technique. Forearm, I imagine. There are way more methods of taking someone out than two hands to the throat, which, believe it or not, is far from ideal when it comes to chokes. You're open to armbar counters. Triangles, guillotines, rear-nakeds, anacondas."

"The fuck you talking about?"

"Jiu-jitsu chokes, man. C'mon. Haven't you caught any MMA? Don't they show that stuff at places like this?"

"No. They usually just show baseball. That's about enough cis-male culture they can handle. Why don't you just ask the gym owner? What is it you're after, really?"

"He's a prominent cornerman for many pro fighters. I want to know why it happened there and what the suspect was even doing there. If I interview him, his story might not be a carbon copy of his original."

"There might be footage."

"Maybe. Maybe not. That's my first entry point." I took a swig of my beer. "Turns out that the widow's a fighter herself. Has a six-year-old boy."

"Didn't know that," he said. "Sorry." The server brought him a nitro-infused stout. It looked tasty.

"She wants to cast a wider net," I said. "Suspect appears to have no assets."

"Probably just a hotheaded overreaction. Fighters."

I jutted my chin at the mess of jigsaw pieces. "Where's the actual picture of this thing? You know, from the top of the box?"

"Nope," he said. "Brought it in with a large Ziplock. Need to assemble it to it see what it is. Threw away the box. Part of the charm. Say, this could be considered cross-training for my work. For yours, too."

I gathered some of the border pieces.

"Amateur move, Paisley," he said. "I bet you spin the rods when playing foosball, too."

"I do, yeah." I finished my beer.

"Pathetic," he said. "You should move around. Keep your perspective fresh. Sort of like a centerfielder."

"So, what's the word on you getting me that transcript? Or even just a file? I know you're still buddies with a few of them over there."

"On one condition," he said. "You help me finish this puzzle while we get comatoasted."

It wasn't the hardest bargain in the world. It took a good three hours to assemble the jigsaw puzzle. It was hard to say if it would have taken more or less time if we hadn't been imbibing. I switched back and forth between the Kölsch and a Mexican lager called Nalgas de Nogales. When we got down to the last piece, I let Hector pop it in. He relished the opportunity like a little boy. It was the scene of Christ the Redeemer overlooking Rio de Janeiro.

Back at the office the following day, I had Tricky make some calls at truck rental companies. I needed a van that I could throw a plumbing snake into. I dragged two magnetized signs out of the office closet only to find them rolled up so much that they wouldn't stay flat against the van's sides. So I called the sign company a few blocks away and put in an order for two new ones. They should be done by tomorrow, which worked out perfectly.

Also back at the office, Araceli Sanchez, Mazagon's mother, continued to harass me into getting her a green card. "You know, Paislito, if you married me in holy matrimony, not only would you have to no longer pay me to keep this place clean, but I would cook for you every day and perform other wifely duties."

I looked up at her as I sat at my desk. "Araceli," I said, placing my fedora on my knee, "while flattered, I would never subject you to my lifestyle. Guns and crowbars and all."

"*Gabacho*," she scoffed, "I'm from Santa Ana. The hood. Don't think I can handle myself?"

"Honestly? No, I don't. No offense. You're what, a buck-ten?"

She put her hand on her hips, presenting her peanut of a body at me. "I've lived by my wits my whole life. How do you think I raised that boy all by myself, without his good-for-nothing *fracasado* father in the picture?"

"Guns," I reiterated.

"Forget the trajectory of a single bullet, Paislito. Try dodging backhands from *la abuelita* your whole life."

"Buck-twenty, being generous?"

"What's known in the industry as a spinner," she chirped. I had to sit up in my chair and cross my legs. The fedora snapped off my knee.

Petite and pretty, she looked great in jeans and a T-shirt, the usual uniform she wore at my office. But I had seen her attitude in action. She had been engaged to a good friend of mine. It didn't work out so well. She had honestly tried to choke him in his sleep.

She liked to bend over as I stood or walked behind her. My drawn-out divorce had taught me the tough lesson of not mixing business with pleasure.

"*Gabachito*," she said, setting a circular box down onto my desk. "I made tamales. They're warm, so eat them right now. Microwaving later is not recommended. Trust me, they won't taste the same."

"Why not?" I wondered, opening a bag of sunflower seeds. "They're mostly *masa*. With what inside? Carnitas? Cactus? Corn?"

"Yes, yes, and yes," she said, slinging her purse over her shoulder and jangling her car keys. "But trust me."

I was starving, actually. Once I heard her steps echo down the stairwell, I made for the circular wicker drum she left behind. I removed the lid. Delicious steam rose to my face. I inhaled deeply. My marrying her would add fifty pounds to my frame. She had even included a fork.

The fork cut deeply into the *masa*. I figured I'd let my taste buds decipher the tamale at hand. I chewed and swallowed. Pork. So tender. It was cold outside. The office was cold. But the tamale made my entire world warm. You could always turn to comfort food to warm your frigid soul. I knocked the pork tamale down in four forkfuls. The next one was of *elote*, corn. A little sweet for my taste, but swigging the *elote* around with the masa in my mouth made for a life-affirming mush. I obliterated that tamale like a lumberjack hacks away at a prone log.

The third tamale was tough to cut. By the fourth attempt with the fork, I decided to carve around the filling, Probably cactus. *Nopales*. I wasn't a fan, but with Araceli's dough around it, I'd eat anything.

I cut the dough away and found a folded-up piece of paper. I dropped the fork and unfolded it, not bothering to clean my hands. It was a picture of Araceli Sanchez wearing crotchless lingerie.

I let it fall on the paper plate alongside the hollowed-out tamale and chucked the whole thing against the wall.

A five-o'-clock shadow usually appeared on my face by noon. So after three days of not shaving, I got the dark thickness of sprouted chia, coming up just under my eyes. I consulted the mirror and slicked back my hair; donned a fitted LA Dodgers baseball cap.

Before Mazagon and I set out to Legion MMA, I sent him to pick up a two-pound bag of concrete mix at the hardware store. Mazagon never learned how to drive, but the store was three blocks away. He was more than happy to bear the load in his backpack. On our Uber ride to the gym, he performed hand-fighting maneuvers used to stave off a rear-naked choke. The driver peeked a glimpse into his rear-view before inching lower in his seat.

"Don't pour too much in there too fast," I explained to Mazagon, "or else it will solidify right there in the bowl. The gist is to get it deep down into the pipes."

"Roger that," he said, strong-arming his imaginary opponent's choking arm and spinning around to do, I don't know, whatever the hell he thought he was doing.

Legion MMA sat in the far-right corner of a strip mall, next to a massage parlor and a pizza joint. Orange-lettered offerings of "Boxing," "Muay Thai," and "Strength & Conditioning" made the storefront windows impossible to see through.

I entered first. The door jingled with one of those Christmas-bell deals. There was a boxing ring to the right, a large mat space and a rack of heavy bags in the middle, and the ominous cage in the back left. An MMA sparring session was in progress on the mats. The four pairs of individuals were too engrossed in their work to acknowledge us. We took seats at a wooden bench, facing the mats. "See that guy?" Mazagon whispered, leaning into me.

"What guy?" I wondered. There were eight guys there.

"The guy in the brown rashguard. It means that he's a brown belt."

"I do," I said, adjusting my Dodgers cap.

"His technique sucks," Mazagon whispered. "He has the other guy high in his guard, but won't go for a toplock."

"Maybe he's working on something? Or helping the other guy work on something? Situational stuff, you know?" I knew nothing of jiu-jitsu, but understood enough of the fight game to be an effective contrarian.

Mazagon shook his head. "When you got a guy high in your guard like that and his head is over your bellybutton, you go for it. Triangle, kimura, flower sweep. No excuses. Brown belt, my ass."

"Can I help you gentlemen?" came a voice from over to the left. A tall, muscular, fifty-five-year-old with close-cropped salt-and-pepper hair and a thick beard approached us. He had on a red tank top and black satin muay thai shorts, ankle supports, and red wraps around his hands.

"Yes, good afternoon," I said, standing up.

"Good afternoon," he said, offering out his hand first to Mazagon. "Name's Pete Branford." He was the owner and head coach of Legion MMA. Besides touting an impressive kickboxing record of 38-3, he was a black belt in jiu-jitsu and a Golden Gloves boxing champ. I had seen him on some of the televised fight cards cornering his pro fighters. He was a lot taller in person.

"Marcus," I said, shaking his hand. "And this is Bryce. We were interested in lessons?"

"Oh yeah?" Branford wondered, hands at his hips. "You guys have any martial arts experience?"

"No," I said.

"Yes," said Mazagon. Goddamnit.

"Such as?" Branford asked.

"Tae Kwon Do," Mazagon said, adjusting his backpack. "When a kid."

"We're fight fans," I said, redirecting Branford's attention meward. "I'd like to learn some techniques. Would hate to live this life not knowing how to throw a flying knee on a fool."

Branford chuckled. "I get you. It's a great skill-set to have, that's for sure." He pivoted out and with his left arm showed the class in progress. "These guys were drilling double-leg takedowns off of overhand rights. Now they're working ground-and-pound from the closed guard. Class is about to end in ten minutes. We have open mats on Saturday mornings. Competitive prices, no contracts. I detest contracts. If my product is good, I figure, the students will keep coming back."

"Flat rate for all classes?" I asked, "Or packages for each martial art?"

"Excuse me, sir," Mazagon interjected, "Can I use your bathroom?"

"Why, sure," Branford said. He pointed beyond the rack of red heavy bags of all shapes and sizes.

Also beyond the heavy bags was the MMA cage where Charles Volkenrath had met his maker. Up in the far-left corner of the room was a camera that should have provided a splendid view of the entire incident.

"I'm mainly into the hands," I said, "having boxed when younger. But I'd like to try grappling. Get into some of that jiu-jitsu."

Branford sighed and scratched his chin. "Unfortunately, we discontinued our jiu-jitsu program. As of a month ago. We've always chiefly been a striking school, anyway. Not enough people attending to justify paying the jiu-jitsu coach. Too much nearby competition. There are three jiu-jitsu gyms within a mile radius from here. Not to toot our own horn, but we have some of the best kickboxers and striking MMA fighters in the world. Middleweight Muay Thai Pros champion Burton Taylor. IFC bantamweight champ P.J. Atkinson."

"Bummer," I said, looking purposely woe-struck. "All fights end up on the ground."

A look of irritation crept over Branford's face. "One, that's not even statistically true. Two, last time I checked, all fights start standing up."

Deep down I agreed, but ever the devil's advocate, I pitchforked him in the ass. "Can't depend on a knockout to dispatch an opponent. If it happens, nice, sure. But headhunting can get you hurt." Mazagon's philosophy had crept into my subconscious.

"Point taken. Look, our MMA fighters get their jitz elsewhere, anyway. We're a striking academy. And like I said before, we'll work with you on pricing. And we do month-to-month. Never believed in contracts."

I mulled it over, finger to chin.

"Would you like a free class?" Branford asked, shadowboxing lightly. "You say you boxed before?"

"I can handle myself, yeah. Been a while. Had a few amateur bouts. A gnarly left hook scared me straight, not going to lie." I adjusted the brim of my cap.

Branford chuckled. He turned around to look at a line of equipment leaning against the wall, under the shadowboxing mirrors. He went over and pulled out a pair of black community boxing gloves and chucked them at me, saying, "You said that you had no prior martial arts experience, but that you used to box. Sorry, but boxing is certainly a martial art. And a tremendous one at that."

I turned my Dodgers cap backwards. As I strapped the gloves on, he went into his office. He returned with his hands webbed into focus mitts. "One!" he barked, holding the left mitt out to me.

I pumped a jab. The pop from the impact sounded like heaven. It had been so long.

"Two!" he commanded, and I darted my right arm straight into his right mitt.

"One-two!"

I jabbed-crossed.

He held the right mitt facing the floor.

I dug into it with a rear uppercut. That had been my go-to move. I had it down pat back in the day. Slip the opponent's cross and counter with a clean shot to the chin, sending the guy's head skyward like a Pez dispenser ejecting a sweet tablet of victory.

"Three-four."

Left hook, right hook.

"Not bad, man," Branford said. "Not bad at all. What are you looking to do? Just stay in shape or maybe fight again? You're in your what? Mid-thirties? Never too late."

"Stay in shape, mainly. Ain't looking to sell out The Forum. Besides, I make enough money as a Web developer."

Branford held the mitts at his hips. I really wished he'd kept going. "So would you like to try a free class?"

"How much would a month of straight boxing set me back? I've got a bad right knee, so I'm not looking to go muay thaiing anytime soon."

"I can do one-twenty a month. Our boxing classes are an hour-and-a-half. Monday through Friday."

"Let's do it," I said.

Ever the astute business owner, he didn't ask me to think it over. He motioned me to follow him into his office. I took the guest seat opposite him as he swiped his computer awake with the mouse. "Alrighty," he said. "Boxing it is. Sorry, what was your name again?"

"Marcus. Marcus Dunlop."

As he entered my contact info, the wall to my left shook.

"Dufuq?" he cried, hands out over his head.

"Regarding the payment," I said, getting his attention back to the task at hand. "Will this month be prorated? Or is it a rolling month?"

"I'll give you these next, what is it? Ten days? Free. Then you'll be billed on the first."

"Thanks, man," I said. "Appreciate that."

The wall thundered again, this time louder and longer. Mazagon must have flushed the entire bag down in one go. I'd have hoped he'd done it incrementally. Again, Branford wondered what was going on.

I gazed out through the glass window, out toward the gym, as if the ruckus had originated therefrom. Branford stood up and scanned the premises. I felt a tremor at my feet. "So who's the boxing coach?"

Distracted, Branford shook his head and looked over at me. He established a smile. "Ernie Reyes," he said. "The best. Used to spar with Chavez."

"No shit," I said.

"Yep."

"Dope."

Chapter Three

I now had two inroads to Legion MMA. I would attend the boxing classes for at least a few weeks. Why not? I long missed it. Snapping the mitts reminded me of how gratifying knowing at least a little of the sweet science could be. May as well get back into shape. Running was becoming boring. I could at least earn my day-drinking. I'd start on Monday.

The second inroad, however, wouldn't manifest until the following Saturday. The concrete had worked. I got hold of Branford's computer's IP address from having signed into my email while filling out the gym membership registration. I had Tricky spam Branford's internet browser with pop-up ads for a plumbing company. He took the bait.

I answered the phone with a low-register voice. "Gluten-Free Rooter. How can we help you?"

Branford went into detail on his plumbing woes: toilets backed up, water not emerging from sinks, a possible slab leak under his boxing ring.

I showed up with the minivan. The decals said in bold green letters:

GLUTEN-FREE ROOTER
Because Even Your Plumbing Should Be Paleo

Pete Branford had a different attitude with my plumbing company than he had with prospective student Marcus Dunlop. Some of it may have been out of frustration with his facility's plumbing. No one likes backed-up toilets. Even less than no one likes having to fork over cash to fix said backed-up toilets.

It would be an easy fix: run a 100-foot plumbing snake down the toilet (I already knew which one was clogged, for Mazagon had told me), followed by running the snake through the clean-out from the roof vent out to the street. I got there at eleven. I dicked around on my phone for a while, at least enough to be there at the gym while pro class started at noon. The best method to kill time was to cyber-stalk Moira Volkenrath.

Once the little Christmas bell at the front door jingled repeatedly, I knew pro class was ready to get underway. Branford darted into the bathroom and knocked on the stall door. I turned around.

"Bro, what's the prognosis? About ready to finish?" He looked eager to get me out of there.

I ran my hand down the side of my clean-shaven face; adjusted the bill of my Gluten-Free Rooter beanie. "We at GFR take a holistic approach to doing away with a clog. This can take some time."

"Holistic?" wondered Branford, annoyed. "You kidding me? What's so holistic about it? You find the blockage and you punch through it."

I shook my head. "I understand your frustration. However, 'punch' would be an improper word. That would imply male-dominated violence. We at GFR espouse a more integrated approach to treating clogged pipes and looking after their well-being into the future, for years to come."

Branford ran his hand through his salt-and-pepper hair, frustrated. He pointed behind his shoulder with a thumb. "My class is about to start. I can't have my guys running over to the Jack In The Box to take a shit. What's this talk about integrative?"

"Well," I said, removing my gloves, "pipes can't simply be cleaned out. They need to be cared for. As our company name implies, we advocate a clean diet for those using the facilities. This doesn't just mean gluten-free food, but toothpaste without fluoride, assuming people brush their teeth here."

"Of course, they do," Branford said. "They also shower here. I have two full shower stalls."

I held up an admonishing finger. "Aha. Another pathology. Using bars of soap that contain lye, which thickens into a froth upon contact with water, is known to clog pipes. It's not just about clean eating." I turned around to fiddle with the snake; jiggled the line. "I have a bit on the end of this thing that cleanses fecal matter containing gluten. After another half hour or so—"

"I don't need to know the details," Branford interrupted. "Please. Just fix it."

"Are the karate practitioners known to consume refined wheat?"

"We don't do karate here," Branford said. "Karate is for eight-year-olds. That and pussies."

"Corn products? Refined carbohydrates?"

"Bro," went Branford, actually turning red. "I have world-class fighters here," again with the thumb over his shoulder. "They eat very healthfully, at least mostly. If they want to shit anvils down the tubes, I don't care. And if it takes you eight hours to finish up, then so be it. I'll throw in a T-shirt when you're done."

"Roger that," I said, all seriousness. "I'll get to it posthaste."

"Thank you," Branford said, finally placated. "What size?"

"Medium," I said, drawing my shoulders in.

He left the stall. I finally exhaled. I could hear him getting the fighters' attention out on the mats.

Ten minutes later, I emerged from the bathroom with the wound-up snake and went to the minivan to get the ladder. I caught a sidelong glance at the ten or so fighters, all in headgear, boxing gloves, and shin guards. They were doing sparring drills. They ranged from featherweights to middleweights, with two sturdy girls paired up, their ponytails flailing at the motion.

As I hauled the snake up the ladder to the roof, I could hear hip-hop conducive to bloodlust blaring from the speakers. Curious acoustic guitars strummed over the heavy beat. More curious lyrics concerning jiu-jitsu moves and being a pimp on the street rapped over the track.

I descended the roof and went inside to get my gloves left purposefully in the stall. Branford saw me for a quick second as he oversaw the girls duking it out. He paid me no further mind. As I headed toward the door, I activated my phone's Shazam app to capture the music. I looked beyond the MMA cage, up in the corner. The camera appeared to be the only one in the gym.

I would later task Tricky with hacking into Branford's surveillance system through his computer. Assuming he hadn't erased any incriminating footage of Volkenrath's deadly sparring session—otherwise, he'd be a person of interest—I could dissect the scene denied me by the Reseda PD. Tricky said that even if pertinent time stamps had been deleted, they likely existed in Branford's cloud storage, should he have an account.

I timed the draining of the clogged cement to the dispersal of the fighters. There was no pure grappling during the entire three-hour-long MMA class. "Ladies and gentlemen," Branford said, pointing at me. "Fresh meat." Happy that I had fixed his plumbing, he had completely changed his attitude. We all have bad days. Some more than others.

Too exhausted with lactic acid buildup to take the bait and punk me out, a few of the fighters acknowledged me with lazy nods as they left the sweat-drenched blue mats, their headgear askew to where their eyes poked out at me from odd angles. Other fighters sat hunched over on the bleachers and unwound the wraps from their hands.

I charged Branford $300. He beamed in delight at the low cost. I pocketed the check and made toward the door. "Yo," he said. I turned around just in time to catch a black, size M Legion MMA T-shirt.

I made the same amount of money as a bona fide plumber in four hours than I made in a full day as a detective.

From the time the indictment commenced, and the suspect was in custody, to the time that the prosecution ended deliberation, the defense had decided to counter-sue.

This was baffling. Reading remorse or any other emotion of Face-crusher's inscrutable visage would be impossible. Moira called me in a weeping panic to tell me she was coming over. She sounded so shaken up, I didn't bother to tell her not to.

"Mazagon," I called.

"Boss," came a voice from behind the copy machine.

"Stand down," I said, sliding my feet off my desk and sitting up.

"No problem, I'll just roll—"

"Stand," I insisted, hammer-fisting my desk, "down."

"Boss."

A more-effeminate Moira entered the office. Gone were the marked deltoid and chest muscles from photos of her in action—the kind of chest muscles that turned womanly breasts into pecs on some of the more conditioned female fighters. It was an understandable change, since she hadn't fought in four months. All her time was now used up in mourning and taking care of her little boy. She wore a simple get-up—jeans, spaghetti-strap purple blouse, and brown sling-backs. No purse. A hot tomboy. Just my style.

"I just don't get it," she said, once she saw me.

As I made toward her, she withered into herself, slumping so unlike a combat athlete. She had said that the violence enacted on her husband had all but obliterated the urge in her to maim and bruise. It was an obvious cue for me to embrace her. I did. I heard Mazagon stir behind my desk.

She settled her chin on my left collarbone. "I need to eat something. Something unhealthy. Comfort food. You hungry?"

Over a Chicago deep dish the size of a spare tire, I drew out probable reasons for the defense team's countersuit. I doubted Facecrusher had gone soft—unless some soy-based steroids made him suddenly grow a set of feelings. The prosecution team wanted her to bring her son in to pull on the juror's heartstrings, but she wasn't having it.

She shifted gears. "This cheese is sensational," she said before taking a deep bite into a slice. Her eyes widened. Pure joy. In-the-moment joy.

"Have to wrap it around your forearm a coupla times and pull to cut it," I said. Her eyes widened as she chewed.

I ruined my dinner jacket by wrapping some cheese around my left arm and yanking. I stood up for effect. She cackled.

"You're funny. Charles wasn't very funny. He was sweet, kind, upright, but rarely ever funny. He was so romantic, though."

"Unfunny but romantic?" I wondered, slurping a carcinogenic dose of high fructose corn syrup through a straw (because eating pizza should never be cancer-free). "Is that possible?"

"Of course," Moira purred, slouching in her seat. "Very possible."

"Anything without a touch of humor comes across as forced, wouldn't you agree? A little blowhardy?"

"You're too flippant, Mr. Fuentes. That's your problem. Yes, you're clever and funny, but your very existence seems to be kidding. You live as if it were a pun to do so."

I slammed my knife and fork down and sat up straight; patted down my tie. "I. Don't. Know. What. To say. Is that what you like?"

She laughed, helping herself to a fourth—a fourth!—slice. "Not what I'm saying at all. Just saying, a little dash of tough seriousness wouldn't look that bad on you. Your bone structure's too good to be that of a clown."

We comforted-ate so much that we called it a night. There were too many roadblocks for me to navigate my way into her Silver Lake flat. She could still be emotionally hobbled to shack up with a non-fighting man like me, let alone present me to her little boy with a shiny bow. Plus, all that cheese led to acid reflux and constipation. I was in no hurry. If nothing happened, that would be okay. The universe had torn a part of her to shreds, and I wasn't confident that I could sew any of it back up.

On the drive home, I got my brain into a Bavarian pretzel trying to figure out the reason for the countersuit. Point scored for team insomnia. By four in the morning, I slammed back six shots of Don Julio and plummeted into the arms of Morpheus until two pm the next day.

I'm an ardent supporter of responsible alcoholism. My little brother, Jake, not so much. He showed up banging on my door with two semi-cute girls in tow. Mazagon was absent, attending an IBJFF tournament down in Anaheim.

"Yo, big bro! Place stinking of agave. Why'n'choo share? The girls here are thirsty, and water, recent studies have shown, causes gingivitis. Brother, meet Mia and Jessie."

There was a lot of background noise, dimmed to a low-volume setting by my encroaching migraine. Jake and his two girls were trying to get my attention as I threw on my workout clothes and opened the box that contained my brand-new 14-ounce boxing gloves and red wraps. I slung the gym bag over my shoulder and headed toward the door. I turned around. "No way am I having an orgy with my own brother. Get it together, guys."

Hisses and boos followed me down the steps toward the street. I hopped into my car and drove toward Legion MMA.

I was ten minutes late to boxing class. I hated being late, but my cloudy head didn't permit me the usual ability to dilate time and deftly maneuver through afternoon gridlock.

The siren song of swiveling heavy-bag chains rang out as I entered the gym, cleaning up my consciousness a little. The victorious perfume of sweat smacked me wide awake. In the middle of the boxing ring to the right was a bald, stocky Mexican guy with glasses and a mustache, holding focus mitts for a teenage boy who had a devastating right hand but leaned a bit forward while throwing it. The coach addressed the flaw, countering him lightly on the forehead with the right mitt before stopping the drill to demonstrate proper form. The kid paid close attention, a gob of sweat plopping from his chin every time he nodded.

I set my gym bag on the outside edge of the ring. I pulled out the red wraps. As I bound my hands, I scanned the premises. The rest of the boxing class attendees were skipping rope. Over to the left was a cardio kickboxing class. The cage to the back left sat in dimly lit silence.

"Sir," called a voice to me. I looked up into the boxing ring. Ernie Reyes was gazing down at me with those glasses whose frames make them look like they're suited more for welding than for improving poor eyesight. "Get your gloves on and get up here."

I nodded and fished out my brand-new gloves from my bag. I ducked between the first and second ropes, which almost sprung me back to fall ass-first back down to floor-level had I not hooked my left arm under the second rope just in time. Should I ever take a fight, I would not be having Don Julio in my corner, unless it was as the towel guy.

"*Como te llamas?*" Ernie Reyes asked, holding out a hand.

I shook it before slipping on the gloves, discarding the tedious wraps and chucking them into the corner. "Marcus," I said.

"A good boxing name," Ernie said, "especially for a white guy."

I chuckled. He chuckled back. The gym was eighty percent Asian and Latino, and there was no way of avoiding its obviousness.

I pumped my gloves together to signal I was ready. "*Vamonos.*"

He held his left focus mitt out at me. I jabbed.

He held his right focus mitt out at me. I crossed.

He held them both out. I one-two'd.

"See?" he addressed the kid, who nodded from the corner. Ernie was referring to my form. "See how he sits low? Bent at the knees, but not leaning."

Ernie Reyes turned out to be a great boxing coach. Over the course of the hour-and-a-half class, we had all taken turns individually hitting mitts with him in the ring, working the bags, skipping rope, doing body-work sparring with Philly shell guards, working the slip line strung up from opposite sides of the bag rack, doing box jumps, and returning to the ring to individually work with Ernie on the punching shield that was used for power shots.

At the end of class, I was exhausted. My hangover was completely gone, but my arms cramped up. I had become so enamored with the boxing that I hadn't paid attention to any other activities going on inside the gym. I figured that my homework that day comprised slowly becoming a familiar face around the gym and getting a bit of life-affirming fun in, something I direly needed lately.

When I got back to my flat, Jake and his two sidepieces were gone. The bottle of Don Julio was empty. For once my wayward little brother had done me a favor.

I hopped in the shower and was ready to crawl into my Gluten-Free Rooter uniform and go fetch the minivan to return to Legion MMA when Tricky texted me the name of the musical artist whose song had been playing at the gym the day I had shown up to fix Branford's plumbing. Ronnie Parrish. Multi-instrumentalist. Tricky had also provided me his home address.

In a way, I was relieved. I always felt comfortable in my disguises, knowing how well I could shift into various personas with my voice-changing abilities and feigned mannerisms, but Pete Branford intimidated me. He seemed like a real hothead. Tomorrow, then.

I drove up Laurel Canyon and turned right onto Mulholland Drive. Every time I took that route, I marveled at the houses—not for their size, but for the display-like quality they possessed. Driving by the countless split-level art pieces on stilts made them resemble a moving parade float.

I'd done business in these houses half a dozen times. Every time provided a bigger headache than anything on offer from the common folk down the hill. The longer I had to wait in the high-ceilinged foyer for the interviewee to traipse down the staircase, wine snifter in hand, the more unsettling the silence became. All that whiteness. All the minimalist living rooms and playrooms and vestibules, with not a molecule of décor out of place. Yet somewhere behind one of those white walls, someone was bleeding miserably from the throat. It was like ancient Roman statuary cursing the echoing halls of a colonnaded building, threatening the white uniformity with an accusatory tsunami of blood. All the money in the world could not banish away the fact that man was an incorrigible sow.

A strikingly handsome woman, maybe in her mid-twenties, darted soundlessly down the stairs, cotton socks taking the steps like a CrossFit girl's feet dotting the spaces on an exercise ladder. Her auburn hair was pulled back in a ponytail. She had a yoga body, but a face that looked too pleasant to deal in that discipline. She had a bookish sexiness that a pair of glasses would conspire with to cause me to fall in love. "He'll be right down," she said to me.

"He?" I wondered, pulling off my fedora.

"My brother, Ronnie." She extended her hand. I shook it. The sensation of her pleasant fingers combined with an apricot-scented deodorant. I fell in love immediately. She smiled. "Would you like a glass of water?"

I kept enough cool to say no.

"Okay, then. He'll be right down." She about-faced before zipping up the steps three at a time.

After ten seconds of silence, I heard a spanking sound, then a playful yelp from the voice that had just addressed me. Right after, a gaunt man naked but for a pair of jeans came shooting down the stairs. He lacked the stealth of his sister—was noisy, actually, reminding me that for all its alabaster sterility, the mansion was still merely timber and plaster.

The man walked up to me, brushing chin-length bangs from his face. Eyes, bloodshot. Though very good-looking, he was unwholesome as his sister was vibrant. "Bro, would you like some water?"

"As a matter of fact, yes," I said, tipping the brim of my fedora.

He froze. He brushed bangs away from his face again. "Eunice!" he yelled, pointing his head back up to the steps while eyeing me with suspicion. "Get your ass down here now!"

"Coming!" came his sister's voice, muffled by a room likely jam-packed with carpet flooring and throw pillows. Again, she zipped down the stairs. She shot up to us. "Yes?"

"This man here would like a glass of H 2 O. All I have here is a fuckload of O, but nearly no H. So make it happen, Cap'n."

Eunice looked back and forth between us, not sure of what was expected of her.

Ronnie looked at me in disbelief. "*Agua!*" he yelled into her face. "A glass of fucking *agua*! For my man here." He calmed down and humored me with a smile.

I smiled back.

"Oh," went Eunice, who zipped out the vestibule.

Awkwardness spread like maple syrup over a stack of dilapidated pancakes.

"How about that weather?" Ronnie mused, bloodshot eyes wide.

"Freaking hot."

It was uncharacteristically cold for June—outside as well as in. Hence, I guess, Eunice's thermal workout wear.

She returned, balancing a glass full to the brim with water. Quite a lot of trouble could have been saved by having left it an ounce or two empty.

"Why, thank you," I said.

She curtsied, smiled, then glared at Ronnie for approval, patting her hair back.

Ronnie nodded at the staircase and spanked her on the ass. She silently zipped back up the stairs.

Before I could contend with Ronnie, I had to slurp a few inches from the glass of water. He eyed me suspiciously as if witnessing me partake of an illicit substance. When I finished, he smiled and motioned me to sit down. I was about to take a seat on a sofa upon which rested a beat-up acoustic guitar when he insisted that I trade places with him and sit on the loveseat facing opposite. "Of course," I said, placing my glass of water on a coaster on the coffee table in the middle.

"It's just that I like to have it by me at all times," he said, nodding at the guitar.

"What about up there?" I asked, nodding at the room where the staircase led to.

"I have two there already, one on each side of the studio," he explained, brushing bangs back from his face.

"So you were recording some stuff?" I wondered. "You have a full-blown studio up there? Pro-Tools? 64-channel console? The works?"

Initially surprised at my knowledge of recording equipment, he then shook his head. "No ProTools. All analog. Like back in the day. Reel-to-reel, floating ceiling." He fished a can of tobacco from under the coffee table and set to work on rolling a cigarette.

"What do you do for the drums? Ten mics? One for the cymbals, one for the snare, one for the—"

"No drums, man," he explained, pinching tobacco into the paper.

"Really? So what exactly are you recording? Music, I presume?" The sight of tobacco made me thirsty, so I took a large sip from the glass of water.

"Of course, music," he said, looking up at me with a sign of contempt. "Just not corporate, grocery-store music. Not that there's anything corporate about drums in particular, but there's no need with my percussive strumming. It's just me and a guitar. No electricity, save the recording stuff. Are you a musician? Or should I say, do you play any instruments?"

"I've dabbled in drums," I said, "but that was a lifetime ago. Used to jam in a hardcore band back in Detroit. Now I'm just an avid listener. What kind of music do you write, then?"

"Toxic folk," he said, twisting and licking the ends of the cigarette like those of a spliff. He lit up with a Zippo lighter that had sat tucked between the sofa cushions.

"Anti-establishment anthems and such? Angst-ridden choruses and tongue-in-cheek verses?"

"You peg me too easy, detective man," Ronnie said, sitting back and smiling. "I'll have you know that I detest hippies and folkies as much as I do squares and cops. I'll also have you know that I'm not a drug user. I caught you peering at my eyes. Yeah, they're bloodshot. No, it's not because of glass or angel dust or some shit. It's because I'm an insomniac and all I do is record music, day-in-day-out."

"Guilty as charged," I said. "I'm relieved to hear it. I'm pretty libertarian. If someone wants to shoot into outer space on PCP, it's their right. Don't recommend it, though."

"I must confess," Ronnie said. "I wasn't always clean. I've been clean for a little over a year. I was lucky to come back full circle to the music. Funny, that circle. Music got me involved in the scene, which chewed me up so much that the music became an afterthought. Imagine getting high every day and being balls-deep in some nineteen-year-old former homecoming queen from Calabasas."

"Glad to hear you're clean, kid. So what are your songs mainly about?"

"A bit of everything. I'm not the best lyricist in the world, I admit, but I don't get too lost in social justice. It's about the music in the end. I don't know. Rebellious homecoming queens going into downward spirals." He chuckled, coughing on the nicotine. "The dangers of thinking you have it all figured out. The hypocrisy of the hippie movement. Of all movements in general."

"You remind me of Frank Zappa," I said. "Dude didn't drink or do drugs, but smoked like a chimney and recorded over 60 albums."

"Nothing wrong with Frank," Ronnie said, blowing out smoke, "though the 80s stuff was horrendous."

"No one survived that shitty decade," I said. We shared a laugh. "Martial arts was in a weird place, too."

The kid saw my changing of the subject and smirked. He was brighter than his strung-out aspect led on. "Ninjas," he said. "That was pretty much it. Kumite. JKVD and Seagal were coming up. Crane kicks and other shit that doesn't work."

I went straight to it. "Have you trained Brazilian Jiu-jitsu?" I twiddled my fingers.

Ronnie sat up and put his hands on his knees. He looked like one of those rangy fighters who could throw up a triangle choke with ease, what with those long legs. Could get me, in fact, right from where he sat. "So what exactly is this about?"

"You wrote a song. With drums, I might add, called *From Bell to Bell*. I'm paraphrasing here, 'What's a line of coke/When you sink in da choke/On that punk-ass lil' bloke/Who got you with da eye-poke/He be tapping hard/When you got him in yo guard.' Unless that's someone else singing? Or someone else wrote the lyrics, and you just wrote the music?"

"Where did you hear that other than on Bandcamp? That's the only platform I have that song on."

"I'm not going to hide anything from you, Mr. Parrish. This song can be heard on a video recording of Legion MMA in Reseda, about a month ago. It was playing on the Bluetooth speaker system right after a fighter had been allegedly murdered in the cage. We've searched through the victim's playlist and music library and your song is nowhere to be found. Nor was it found on the gym owner's phone. This leads us to believe that the killer's phone linked to the Bluetooth while he arrived. He may have even intentionally played the music while he committed the crime. Do you know Craig "Facecrusher" Farrell?"

"I do not," Ronnie said. He looked worried. I had no reason to think it was because he was directly involved. He may have just been aghast at having been associated with a murder, however marginally. "Maybe just a fan? I've gotten some viral marketing going. Been pleased with the numbers, actually."

"He was a fan indeed, Mr. Parrish. He had that track of yours as his walkout song for his last two fights."

"What?" Ronnie hurried and stubbed the cigarette out in a pewter ashtray in order to deal with the implication. "I never got a call or email or anything requesting permission. Plus, I didn't release that song until two months ago. An Australian guy with a jump rope YouTube channel used it in one of his vids and it kind of hit."

"Toxic folk?" I mused. "It's pretty urban for folk. Drums, horns, rap?"

Ronnie sunk back into the sofa. He held his hands up at his temples as if airing out his brain to let it properly work. "Horns? There were no horns in the final mix. I took them out. Thought it made the song too ska, which I loathe."

"There are horns in that song," I said, downing the glass of water and setting it on the coaster.

"No," Ronnie said, "not on the final mix. But there were on the demo. I recorded a demo of the song right before I moved back in with the folks and got clean. Out at Sadistic CGI, I recorded the demo."

"Sadistic CGI?"

Ronnie said nothing for a good minute. I had all the time in the world. He obviously was mulling over what further divulgences would implicate him in, but he seemed more than anything perturbed that his song had been used for walkouts and murders without his written consent.

He scooted back up and placed his elbows on his knees. "It must have been the Family," he said, staring off into space. He leaned over and reached for the tobacco can on the coffee table.

"The Family?"

Another long silence. Ronnie looked straight at me. "I'm so glad I cut those fucking degenerates off. I trained a little BJJ. For two years. Then things went south."

"Which degenerates?" I asked, grabbing the pack of rolling papers and fishing two out for his cigarette. I handed him the sheets.

He took them and nodded thanks. "Charlie and all those freaks. Disaffected homecoming queens and all that. Up at the ranch. Sadistic CGI."

"Sadistic CGI?" I asked again.

"Yeah. Like Spahn Ranch. Newer version. Reboot, what have you. A digital movie set over in Studio City. Up on the fifth floor of a high-rise. New-era CGI. Still looks like shit, if you ask me."

Spahn Ranch had been a movie set out near Simi Valley. Charles Manson and his "family" hung out there doing nothing before the media storm of the Tate/LaBianca murders. Two years later, the ranch burned down.

"What went on at Sadistic CGI? I take it not all-night grappling sessions or seminars from *de la riva* specialists."

"Not quite," Ronnie said, lighting up a new cigarette. "Vegan orgies."

I laughed and shook my head. "Come again?"

"Gangbangs in tubs full of lentils. Quinoa *bukkakes*."

"Not exactly movies special effects."

"No, all that was after-hours. The plant-based Kraft food service leftovers got incorporated into things once Charlie showed up."

"Charlie?" I asked, twiddling the pack of rolling papers through my fingers. "Charlie who?"

"Charlie, bro," Ronnie said, exhaling a cloud of smoke my way. "Chuck. Charles Manson."

"Charlie's been dead since 2017, Mr. Parrish. I don't follow you."

"Charlie has been uploaded, bro. Into a stack of servers on the second floor of that same Studio City high-rise."

"You mean, like, AI Charles Manson?" It sounded stupid when I said it.

Ronnie shrugged, eyebrows raised.

I remember having heard some of the psychopath's music a long time ago. It wasn't half bad. It had promise. It was earthy and unsettling at the same time. Like *toxic folk*.

"How do you think the first mix of your song got out there? Was there anyone at the ranch who expressed admiration for the song?"

"I couldn't tell you, bro. I was stoned out of my gourd and balls—"

"I know I know. Balls deep in a disaffected, nineteen-year-old homecoming queen from Sylmar."

"Calabasas," Ronnie corrected. "I don't know. I guess a few people did. Lots of people came through there, looking to party."

"Why was everything so decidedly plant-based?"

"Pure coincidence. We used to mooch food from the studio. The catering contact was one of the original family members."

"From back in the late 60s?"

"Yup."

Jeez. Not even cold-blooded, cowardly murder of innocents or five decades of aging could keep some people from wanting to live the hippie life.

"Any name you can offer on this person?"

"Afraid not. Other than him being the food guy, an old cat cool enough to kick us some grub, he was of no consequence."

"Did he ever take part in, you know, the orgies?"

"He may have beat off in the corner or something. Can't imagine any of the girls looking to ball with him. At least not voluntarily. At least not unless Charlie commanded it, which I don't recall him ever doing. Though I wouldn't put it past him. He liked to get creative with the configurations, Charlie did."

"I don't follow," I said. "Charlie? AI Charlie?"

"Yes, bro. Who else?"

"Charlie interacted with you guys in real time?"

Ronnie flicked cigarette ash into the ashtray. "Yup."

"The technology doesn't exist yet for consciousness uploads, Mr. Parrish. Not even close. It's still theoretical at this point, despite Kurzweil and other singularity cheerleaders."

"Bro, them CGI boys could do weird shit. Neural network shit with EKG and 3D-printed silicon brains. Who knows? Homeboy out in Kern County Jail may have offered himself up as a guinea pig all the time he was incarcerated."

What better way for a megalomaniac to deal with the impossibility of parole than to undergo digitization for the sake of possible eternal life? "Mr. Parrish, what did you guys do out at Sadistic CGI, other than yahoo it up?"

"Record music, listen to music."

"The Beatles' *White Album*?"

"I'm afraid so," Ronnie said, shaking his head.

"Why afraid so? Sounds like a good time. Listening to the Beatles during your refractory period."

"I hate that fucking album. I hate the Beatles."

"Wow."

"Yes," Ronnie said, looking to back up his vehemence with another rolling of a cigarette, though he hadn't finished the lit one. He fetched the tobacco can again. "Overrated musicians, overrated songwriters, under-produced studio albums, chipmunk voices. They were really nothing more than a boy band, as far as I'm concerned."

I was blown away—not by his opinion, but by his iconoclasm, his willingness to go against the grain. I sort of liked him.

"And when they went all quote psychedelic unquote," he mocked, "with their yellow rubber walruses and strawberry submarines, ooh, how profound." He mimed masturbation before lighting up the new cigarette.

"So did Charlie and the family dig the Beatles?"

"Oh, big time. That was an issue of contention for me. You might say that music saved my life. It was the deciding factor on me leaving and getting clean."

"So in a way, the Fab Four saved your life," I said.

Ronnie brushed bangs back from his face and gazed at me. "Checkmate," he said, smiling.

"Was it hard for you to leave the family? Any blowback? Life threatened, et cetera?"

"Not really. They're all too gone to really care."

"That could change, you know," I said. "What with this investigation."

"Might as well tell you," he said. "They moved out to the desert a month ago. Death Valley, in fact."

"How come?" I asked.

"Trying to simulate the original family. Barker Ranch and all that jazz. Without the murder, of course."

"Of course?" I asked, an eyebrow raised.

Ronnie considered this for a moment. "Who hired you, by the way?"

"A fair question, Mr. Parrish. But for reasons of confidentiality, I can't say."

"Wasn't them, was it? The family?"

"I don't think they could afford me. So, no."

Ronnie briefly smirked. "I want to know how the fuck they got hold of my song. Not that I care from a monetary standpoint. I feel slighted more than anything. The song was drivel, but it was still mine."

"If I find out, Mr. Parrish, who got it and how, I will certainly let you know."

"Would you?"

"Yes."

I stood up. Ronnie stood up to see me off, probably eager to do so. I could see on his face that the can of worms I had opened up on him had included not a few corpse-consuming maggots. "Thank you for the water, Mr. Parrish, and good luck with your music. Stay safe, yeah?"

Once the front door got closed behind me I heard him shout, "Eunice, get your ass down here and wash this glass!"

Chapter Four

The goings-on of the desert largely evaded internet capture. All that vast emptiness left ample room for the waves to disperse so far apart that they tore into silent nothingness. So, the best way to gather data or get a beat on some tawdry activities up in Mohave National Preserve or on a drifting daughter hiding out in Salton City with dune-buggying meth-heads was through old-fashioned gossip. For this, I turned to my acquaintance Tutmoses Ochoa.

Tutmoses Ochoa was a pseudo-neo-Luddite—meaning that he preached about the evils inherent in gadgets and rampant technology but unabashedly indulged in every one of its benefits. It was a cognitive dissonance I truly didn't think he was aware of. He lacked the necessary irony.

He lived off of Figueroa on the third floor of a walk-up. I paid him a visit. I stomped up the dark stairwell leading to his door. Lots of dirt always caked the steps. It had to have been him since he shared the stairs with a Mexican family that I didn't take for being the gold-prospecting sort. Traffic going out there was oddly light. Sure enough, as if having spent all my luck dodging gridlock, I found him not to be at home.

I couldn't wait for him to get back into town. No telling how long that would take. He liked to go prospecting for three days at a time. He felt it made the trip out to the foothills worthwhile. I was too antsy to sit tight, so I made a straight shot on the 261. I laced up through the Cajon Pass and made my way to his favorite haunt: Lytle Creek. After a two-mile rocky dirt road that cut my car's struts' life in half, I found his maroon Silverado parked at the end of the turnaround. After a 45-minute wait of listening to the serene flow of the creek, I sighted him shambling out of the trees, carrying a bucket of sand in one hand and an aluminum sluice with the other.

"Howdy," I yelled, sitting on the front bumper of my car.

He stopped and leaned his head down, squinting in order to make out who was waiting for him before approaching. He recognized me and shook his head.

"Any luck?" I called out.

"Luck has nothing to do with it," he called back.

I met him halfway and relieved him of the bucket. It was incredibly heavy.

"Quite a few pickers," he said, as if justifying the bucket's weight. Sunlight bouncing off his aluminum sluice spanked me in the face. Dealing with him always became a chore.

"Why don't you get a real job like everyone else?" I asked, not kidding.

"To join the workforce," he said, "would be to call it quits on independence."

"You call your studio apartment independence?"

"Low overhead, wake up when I want, not enter a turnstile. Yeah, I'd call it independence. I don't do half bad prospecting. You'd be surprised." Aside from digging for gold, he donated plasma once a week and traded Topps and Lear baseball cards.

"Figured that Lytle Creek would be all used up by now," I said.

He stopped in his tracks, making me stop with the heavy bucket and turn around. "See that?" he said, pointing at the mountain beyond the creek. "When that gets used up, I'll call this place quits. Rained like cats and dogs all last week, you recall?"

I nodded and continued walking.

"So, when are you going to get an honest job yourself?" he quipped. I could feel the acerbic comment nip at my Achilles' heels.

"I've been self-employed going on ten years, bud."

"You call snooping on behalf of paranoid *hausfraus* employed? How do you live with yourself?" He caught up to me and took a cigarette out of his flannel shirt pocket and lit it with a tiny Bic lighter.

"There's always some assholery somewhere that makes me out as semi-heroic to someone," I said.

He chuckled smoke. "Thanks," he said as I plopped the bucket of dirt onto his tailgate. "What brings you away from the anthill? Want to help me sift through this?" I was about to answer, but he interrupted. "Say, give me your honest opinion." He took a cell phone out from his back pants pocket and showed me a picture of a tatted-up Betty Page-looking rockabilly chick with a good face and a great bosom. "Is she right-swipeable?"

I took my index finger and swiped right.

"Hey, man! What gives?"

"Sounded like you needed me to confirm the obvious. Plus, you should swipe anything that's willing to be swiped by you."

"She has two kids, man! I really had to think it over."

"Set the bar high much?"

"Aim for the stars, and you'll brush up against the moon. Or is it the other way around?"

"In love myself."

"Yeah? What's his name?"

"Moira Volkenrath," I said. "Recently widowed. MMA fighter."

"Not my type," Tutmoses scoffed.

"If you saw her, you'd see that she's everybody's type."

"Widow? You're like a German Tiger blitzing through the Ardennes. Wasting no time."

"Husband got choked to death by a renegade jiu-jitsu cult or some other. Absconding to the desert. Possibly Death Valley."

"Death Valley's an awfully big place," he said.

"Figured the happenings there could be squeezed down to the size of a reception hall. Heard anything about this wannabee Manson family? Sadistic CGI?"

"Dufuq?"

"Bunch of neo-hippies too chickenshit to kill on their own, outsourcing their helter-skelter to trained fighters."

"Dozen or so good-to-go hotties?" he asked, an eyebrow arched.

"Likely," I said.

"Nice," Tutmoses said, tucking his phone away. He gazed off into space while plopping down onto his tailgate. "Fellow prospecting buddy of mine, name of Unethical Ted, digs borax out of the Panamint Mountains. Western side of Death Valley. Heard of a group of kids fetishizing Barker Ranch. That's where Charlie and company got busted after their murder spree. You need a four-by-four to get up."

"I thought it burned down, that Barker Ranch?"

"Did," Tutmoses said. "I guess these folks refurbished it. Suited it up like the good ol' days."

"So your buddy mines borax? In the twenty-first century?"

"You'd be surprised."

"Don't think I would. How'd your buddy hear about this?"

"Said some girls hanging around Panamint Springs were prone to harassing diners at a steakhouse while on acid. Railing on about meat consumption. Vegan terrorist types. Panamint Springs is a ways away from Barker Ranch, but not really. Like you said, chop down the distances and everything fits inside a reception hall. You can talk to him, my buddy. Might take a week to get hold of him. Hates technology like yours truly."

"Where can I find him?"

"Make it out to Ballarat, right off the 395. It's a ghost town, but the guy at the general store will key you in on him. Say you're looking for the Borax Guy. The mine is straight from Ballarat into the mountains. If he's not out there, he's likely down in Ridgecrest."

"Doing what?" I asked.

"It's where he lives. Doing whatever one does with money. In his case, hookers and ribeyes. I don't know."

I elbowed the bucket of dirt behind me. "How much gold do you figure you'll get in there?"

"Immaterial," Tutmoses croaked.

"Meaning—"

"It's not about the gold."

"If it's not about the gold, what's it ever about?"

"Enjoying the journey," he said. "Ever sift through paydirt with a pan? It's a very calming experience. Never been one for TM."

"They have apps for that. Guided meditations."

"Another abomination. Apps."

"Yeah, not quite as wholesome as a hookup forum for facilitating fornication."

"It's always consensual," Tutmoses disclaimed.

"Are you saying there are gold-prospecting groupies?"

"You'd be—"

"Surprised? Yeah, ok."

"To extract ore from the earth is no small feat. Equivalent to fixing those atrocious contraptions called radios."

"Radios?" I cried, incredulous. "Radios? Those things barely exist anymore."

"Had one in my truck. Yanked it out and tossed it. Regardless, all I'm saying is a good girl digs a dude who can mine a bit. Show 'em a nugget and they drop to their knees."

"I didn't know chauvinism was part of the anti-tech syllabus, Ochoa."

"I don't hate. I penetrate."

"You wrap up, I hope?"

"Never enjoyed making love to latex. I pull out in time."

"Anything else out beyond the 215 I should know about?"

"Let's see. Other than the customary black magic orgies out in Nyland and a serial groper in Furnace Creek you should be on the lookout for, nope. Oh, the Mongols biker gang have a meth monopoly out in the Coachella Valley."

"Is this like in Elizabethan times, where by the time a story reaches one's ears, it has completely changed?"

"No chance," Tutmoses said. "Things happen out here as slowly as their news gets disseminated. It's why I come out here."

"Where's the rockabilly chick from?"

"Orange County. Huntington Beach."

"Of course. Better act fast. She might be hooking up with a dude as we speak."

"If she's worth a dime, she'll take her time."

"Nice motto. Got one for a nickel?"

"Low-hanging fruit."

"Never stopped you before. Well, thanks, pal. Good luck on the bucket."

He was about to enunciate the fallacy of luck, but said, "If those neo-Manson girls are right-swipeable, you'll let me know, yeah?"

I doffed my fedora and headed toward my car.

If I was to drive out to a ghost town out in the middle of nowhere, looking for a guy by the name of Unethical Ted, with no law enforcement for a fifty-mile radius, I was going to need protection. I returned all the way home from Lytle Creek. I got lazy once inside and decided to leave first thing the next morning. I put together a 500-piece jigsaw puzzle and took apart my brain with some Centenario *reposado* mixed with Coke.

I had Araceli drop off Mazagon the following morning. For the second day in a row, I was met with light traffic. I could feel the logistics gods smirking down upon me as if saying, *Invite terror into your life, dumb-dumb.*

It took three hours for us to get out to Ballarat. The ghost town consisted of nothing save a gift shop and a strange tombstone with a cage around it. The grave belonged to one "Seldom Seen" Slim, the town's last official resident. There were a few building foundations lined up in two rows. The wind and heat had seen to the withering of whatever once thrived there, if thriving were the word for it.

It was still some distance to the Panamint Mountains. What kept the town's founders from creeping ever closer for convenience's sake was a mystery. Maybe they consulted a fortune-teller before surveying the land. Wouldn't want to get up too close to a place called Death Valley for a reason. Plus, Ballarat was within sight of the 138, which shot up and down to civilization—Panamint Springs and Trona, respectively.

When we pulled up to the gift shop, the car kicked up enough dust to blind the windshield. Once the dust settled, standing there was a squat man with gray lamb chops and greased jean overalls. "Hey," I nicked Mazagon on the left arm, "be ready to suplex this guy. I think he's clutching a monkey wrench."

"Not being a takedown guy that gives up my back, I'd prefer to pull guard."

"Whatever," I said, annoyed by my bodyguard's martial arts pedantry. "Spit on him and hit him with chlamydia if you must."

With a pace between non-threatening and not-intimidated, I opened my door and stepped out. "Morning," I said, perhaps overly chipperly.

The man stood his ground, as tentative as I. "May I help you?"

"My friend and I," looking at Mazagon, who was no longer there . . . "I'm looking for my friend. Goes by the moniker of Unethical Ted."

The man looked to ruminate on the name. "What makes him unethical?" he demanded.

I wasn't about to give up a litany of crimes that made him out as a saint or a monster compared to who he actually was. "You know, known to perform this. Guilty of participating in that. Nothing too disreputable, and certainly nothing unforgivable, lives by his own code, is all."

"That's all a person living under the broad sky can do," said the man, his bulging eyeballs concurring. "Sorry, no. Don't know anyone by that name. To go asking a man in a ghost town that's barely even a ghost town at this point seems like pure folly if you ask me."

"Didn't mean to intrude upon your business," I said, tipping my fedora. "Just looking to get to the bottom of a wrongful death. I only care because a widow has to struggle to feed her six-year-old boy."

"Sorry to hear about that," the man said, "Where'd it happen?"

I pointed toward the west.

He shrugged and smiled. "Figures. Other than up in Skidoo, a long time ago, we don't get many murders out here. Everyone's too busy contending with the elements to be a pain in each other's asses."

"Alrighty, then, sir. I guess I'll be on my way."

"You good on water?" he asked.

"Yes," I replied. "Yes, I am. Kind of you."

"Listen," he said, lightening up, "you look like a strapping fellow. Mind helping me load my alternator into my Tacoma? I've got bad wrists and the angle's awkward and deep. Buried beneath the air filter housing."

My solicitude for the water backfired. Oh, well. "Sure thing," I said, and shut the car door.

I followed him out behind the gift shop. A late 90s Tacoma sat with its hood popped open. The alternator sat on the radiator. "See?" he said, pointing at the cavity where it was meant to go into.

"No kidding," I said. "Like joining the final corner piece of a Rubik's cube into place."

"Heh heh heh," the old man went. We cradled the alternator, which was heavier than it looked, and tried plopping it into place. The man's wrists gave way, causing him to drop his end. "Son of a—"

"You okay?" I asked, still holding my end.

"Yeah yeah. Sorry. Don't mean to be a temperamental bastard. It's just that I've been trying to get this installed for a couple of days now." Despair crept into his face. Even in the twenty-first century, Death Valley was giving folks problems.

"Only vehicle?"

He nodded. "Runs like a teenage boy's wet dream, though, when she's in commission."

"Mazagon," I shouted out.

"Boss," came a voice from behind a rock.

"Get out here."

The old man, startled, scurried about like a surprised cockroach. "What the—"

"My assistant," I explained. "Don't worry. He's harmless. Well, not exactly. He's a trained killer. But his Bushido code wouldn't allow him to hurt a fly." I looked at Mazagon, who approached on his tiptoes. "Stop it," I said. "Stand down. Come help me here."

After quite a lot of jiggling the alternator, we got it into place. The old man beamed a crooked-toothed smile and attacked the alternator with a socket wrench. "Give me a jump?" he asked.

"Of course," I said, and headed toward my car.

After driving around back, parking the car, and popping the hood, I got out to find Mazagon holding the old man in a head-arm squeeze.

"He'll be here by lunchtime," the old man croaked, holding Mazagon's forearm with his two hands. Mazagon squeezed tighter and engaged his hips. "Promisssssssse," the old man hissed.

Mazagon let go. The old man stumbled back, holding his neck.

I stood there, speechless. I didn't know whether to fire Mazagon or give him a raise.

"All you had to say," panted the old man, his voice but a hoarse whisper, "was it was the Borax guy you were looking for."

We waited until lunchtime after giving the man's Tacoma a jump. Right at noon, as if riding on the waves of a desert mirage, a man appeared from out of nowhere with two mules in tow. Unethical Ted looked like he was all but twenty-five years old—clean-shaven, blue-eyed, fine-featured. His well-parted and combed matinee idol blond hair was dusted with borax. The two mules pulled a cart upon which had been bungee-strapped a blue tarp.

"Didn't they stop mining out there over a century ago?" I asked.

"Them bastards at Rio Tinto would certainly have you think so." Unethical Ted seemed too cool to evince any alarm at two strangers waiting for him. Perhaps Tutmoses had keyed him in on our eventual arrival.

"Sturdy creatures you got there," I said. "What do you feed them?"

"Hay," Unethical Ted said. "Exclusively hay."

"Nice," I said, patting one of the mules on its hind legs. The animal didn't stir. "Would hate to think they consumed meat."

Unethical Ted let go the reins and sauntered toward me. He was quite short, not much taller than Charles Manson had been. "Enough of the charade," he said. "I know why you're here."

"It's just that one can get a full amino acid profile on plants alone. No need to eat anything with a face or a mom."

Unethical Ted shook his head. "Please." He fished a twenty-dollar bill out of his jeans pocket and handed it over to the old man, who disappeared into the shop.

"Are you saying you're a meat eater?"

"Proud one," said Unethical Ted. "Please don't tell me you're a haybreath." He reached into one of the mule's saddlebags and withdrew a stalk of beef jerky.

"With dietary knowledge at our disposal this day and age," I said, "I'd struggle to find a reason to go for a steak. Unless, of course, I was seeking inflammation." At this point, he knew I was merely egging him on. Had to admit, I got a rise out of annoying him. Something about his punchable face I didn't like.

"Look, man," Unethical Ted said, "I'm hungry. Been slogging away in the mine all day. I know why you're here. You're going to take the 178 to Wingate Road, then Coyote Canyon Road, to Goler Wash Road." He ripped open the beef jerky wrapper and took a bite. A look of revulsion overtook his face before he spat it out and chucked the rest of the stalk over his shoulder. He gazed scoffingly at my car. "You'd be better off with a jetpack."

"Tutmoses sold me on your availability as far as conveyance goes," I said, nodding at the mules. The two animals, indifferent to the acrimony burning between their owner and the dick from the city, stared straight out toward Trona, probably hungry enough to lick some of those salt pillars down to the ground. "Are they available to rent?"

"That depends," he said, obviously meaning the price.

"So they'd make it up the wash?"

"They'll do anything," Unethical Ted said, "short of trigonometry."

"C-note each?" I offered, my finger wagging between me and Mazagon. "Assuming currency's not anathema to your way of life. What do you do with the borax, anyway?"

"Undercut Rio Tinto," Unethical Ted said. "Most of my customers are down in Searle Valley. Cleaning dirt from the windstorms is one of their chief pastimes, behind filing for unemployment. No, I'm not against greenbacks or other analog, fiat-based currencies. I won't take credit cards or that abomination known as cryptocurrency."

I had two-hundred bucks. Exactly two-hundred bucks. I long since figured *baksheesh* into my monthly overhead. "Today a possibility?"

"Absolutely," Unethical Ted said, "right after I eat."

The old man, whose name turned out to be Spinnaker, came out with four one-inch-thick porterhouse steaks marinated in a mesquite dry rub. Divine. None of us held back from scarfing down the meat with nary an exchanged word. Whatever gratitude he had had for us in helping install the alternator and giving his truck a jump had been killed by Mazagon's tight D'arce choke. He turned away without a word as the three of us headed toward the mountains on mule-back, me and Mazagon atop one mule and Unethical Ted on the other.

During the hour up the wash, Mazagon and I took turns dismounting to remove large boulders from our steep path up. One was so large and couldn't be lifted that we had to let gravity get them out of the way by pushing it. This involved some dodging and hurdling from the mules that, despite their lassitude, leaped into action with surprising agility.

From his saddle, Unethical Ted said, "You're on your own from here on out. I can't afford to be seen leading strangers up. And don't tell them how you got up here, or who told you about them. Good luck and good riddance. And here." He snatched the wad of twenties from me, handed Mazagon a bundle of individually wrapped beef jerky sticks, and about-faced with the two mules and was gone.

Chapter Five

All sonic traces of life left with Unethical Ted like he had sucked away all the sound waves with him down the wash. From Vincent Bugliosi's famous book, I recalled that Charlie had posted sentinels along Goler Wash, and had only been raided by the police when one or more of his acid-heads fell asleep on the job or saw too many open-eyed visuals to notice any out-of-place intruders.

All the same, I told Mazagon, "We may as well not dissimulate. I think simply walking up there would be our best bet."

"Under what pretext, though?"

"Dunno," I admitted. "We'll think of one. So, how does jiu-jitsu work with multiple attackers? At least with boxers, you can lace a few dudes with straight one-twos."

"You take a hostage," Mazagon said, panting in all-too-mortal fashion as we climbed. "An elbow on the carotid is as good as a barrel to the head."

I wiped sweat from my brow and barely looked over at him with doubt. "They're not going to take a rear-naked choke as seriously as a gun," I said. "They'd just wait for you to choke him unconscious and eventually let go."

"That's when you don't eventually let go. You choke him unconscious to the ground and tell them that if you continue, he will die."

"Then you're left with a limp corpse. Then what? Now you're standing there alone."

"Same thing with a gun," Mazagon said. "Think about it."

I couldn't think about anything in the blistering heat. He had a point, kind of.

"You could also use the corpse as a human shield," Mazagon added.

I guess he would say what he had to in order to defend the merits of jiu-jitsu to the ends of the earth. "Calm down, bin Laden."

We ate up all the beef jerky Unethical Ted had given to us. Once the fire road widened with tire tread tracks that shot both ways, we knew we had made it up to Barker Ranch. Three red hawks soared in the air, right above a brown ramshackle house. I slapped at the back of my neck, sending a mosquito to Hades. "If you're able to replicate yourself and fan out, now would be the time."

"No need," Mazagon said. "There's always a preferred sequence to multiple opponents. Terrain is to be considered. Dispatching those on the outside, as those on the inside are corralled by their own protection. Work concentrically."

"Okay okay," I said, "do it instead of explaining it." I looked over at him and he was gone. Literally gone. There was nothing in a 50-foot radius. I couldn't figure out where he had gone. Wizard shit.

I walked toward the right of the house and halted. I could see four bodies frolicking in a pool that sat on a wooden deck. There were merry laughs and the splashing of water only LSD and promiscuity could generate. The best thing to do was to walk straight toward them. A shirtless, wiry young man with sandy long hair and a beard stopped windmilling his arms in the water when he caught sight of me. He froze for a quick second before climbing out of the pool and darting toward the back entrance of the house.

"It's okay!" I shouted. "I'm looking for someone!"

The three girls in the pool huddled together, whispering possible plans of escape or attack. All three had drenched T-shirts and were braless. What is it about hippie life that makes all the girls attractive? They neglect diet and exercise and take up street pharmacology and look all the better for it. As if touched by God. The Hindu love god Krishna had this group of milkmaids at his disposal, and none of those temple friezes show a single one of them rocking an extra-large sari.

"You a narc?" one of the girls called out.

"Why would I be?" I said, palms out.

"Why else would you wear a funny hat like that?"

I doffed my fedora and pointed at it. "What's wrong with my hat? You don't like my hat?" There was a band of sweat about an inch thick around the inside. Time for a new one, assuming I got out of there alive.

"Put it back on," said the girl in the middle, a brunette. "You have the haircut of a square."

I put the hat back on. "I'm so sorry that hygiene is unhip." I pointed at the sky. "That's why."

Suddenly, the wiry longhair emerged with a shotgun pointed right at me.

More suddenly, a black entity dropped from out of the sky and landed on him. Within a few seconds, the wiry longhair got rolled to the ground and choked unconscious.

"Hermes!" cried one of the girls, struggling to get out of the pool, slipping over the ledge, fawn's legs for LSD equilibrium.

The other two girls, a brunette and a blonde, slowly crept over the pool's ledge and jogged toward the said Hermes, who lay on his side on the dirt. Mazagon sat crouched next to him, hyperventilating. His eyes peered at me from under his dusty black hair.

While the two girls took turns checking his pulse and trying to revive him with gentle slaps to the face, the third girl finally made it out of the pool and bolted toward Mazagon. "You killed him!" she croaked, hitting down at my defenseless bodyguard with her palms. One cracked him right in the jaw and I saw his code of ethics vacate his face for a quick second before he stood up and came over to me.

I thanked him with a nick on his arm. "You could stand to learn how to roll with punches. A little cross-training wouldn't hurt."

I turned toward the girls. "Not nice to pull a shotgun on a person looking for help," I said.

They neglected Hermes for a second to look over at us. The brunette stood up and spoke. I lost track of her words, I don't know, maybe the desert heat was getting to me, couldn't concentrate, migraine coming on, girl said something about precaution and RICO, don't know, her T-shirt was soaked, she had a very nice rack, very nice.

"Did you hear what I said, Square?"

"Huh?"

I looked over at Mazagon, who was sneaking peeks at her as well. The girl was clueless. So I kept looking. Eventually, I said, "I'm looking for this guy. Unethical Ted." What's that line about not burning your sources? Fuck that guy.

"He ain't even all that unethical if you ask me," said one of the other girls, who had straight brown hair, quintessential hippie band around her head, basically hot as hell. "Likes taking the alternate route to ecstasy, if you know what I mean. Takes getting used to."

The other two girls didn't bother to veto her assessment of sodomy. We had a real-life libertine farm on our hands, Mazagon and I did.

Hermes stirred. He sat up. "The hell happened?"

"Darling," the hysterical blonde cried, framing his face with her hands, kissing his beard all over.

Taking credit, Mazagon took the shotgun from behind his back and spun it around a few times before flinging it discus-style into the wilderness that shot downhill into a deep ravine. No one protested.

"My friend and I apologize," I said. "Simply a matter of self-defense." I shrugged.

"Typical square need for self-preservation," said the brunette.

"Yeah," I said, "Like *you'd* take a 22 to the back of the head."

"We all gotta die sometime," she said, shrugging.

"22's a bit much for Andromeda, "said the brown-haired girl. "She can't handle Pharaoh, and he's barely 9."

Hermes cackled. I extended a hand to him. He smiled up through his bedraggled hair and accepted me hauling him up to his feet.

"You're right, pretty lady," I said. "We're all put on the cycle of death and rebirth. Shiva and all that shit. Life feeds on life. Predator takes out prey. Man spears buffalo."

I immediately got the response I wanted. The three girls and Hermes huddled together before spreading out and issuing forth tirades on meat consumption and inter-species murder.

I stole a sidelong glance at Mazagon, who remained stoic. "At least that is what Big Meat would have us believe," I said maybe a little unconvincingly. The problem with wearing a suit as I did is that it made you look like you had no convictions to call your own. It's okay to be snazzy, but it could only mean you've not enough spine to stand up to the Man.

I furtively undid my tie and shoved it into my slacks pocket. "Just testing you, is all. I like Unethical Ted. I hope we find him soon. But I do wish he'd stop with the steaks."

"Holler," went the no-longer-hysterical blonde. She approached me. Cute as she was, her armpits kicked with the odor of over-exertion. Her hair smelled like nicotine. I got to thinking: Does one hippie's funk cancel another's out, allowing for interaction without olfactory annoyance? That would be the last of your worries, for there would be certain remnants from lack of washing that bear the name of renegade fruit and would cause a hard-on to go Hindenburg in a heartbeat.

She removed her head from my chest and gazed up at me. "You tall," she hissed through teeth that had once been pearly white but were just this side of going sour. "We agree," she said, wild-eyed. "Meat is murder. Eating one's own fecal matter would be an upgrade." An unhinged look in her eyes told me she was all kinds of crazy. Once I imagined her scarfing down a couple of coprolites in protest, I nudged away from her.

"That's why we call your guy Unethical Ted," the brown-haired girl said. "We like him too. He has good coke, but he can't seem to change his diet. That's what makes him unethical."

"You name him that?" I asked, undoing the top button of my shirt.

"Charlie did," said Andromeda, who detailed the merits and lack thereof of the said Unethical Ted, though I dunno, lost track, kind of got dizzy again, she went on and on about heaving, soaking wet Charlie and amino acid aureoles, my god.

Next thing I knew, I was being led by the hand toward the back door of the Barker Ranch house by Andromeda herself, couldn't put up a fight, saw that she packed heat down below too as I followed her inside.

Acid rock played on a quadrophonic stereo system. A green vinyl record spun on a turntable. I was too dizzy to make out the artist's name. It spun too fast and Andromeda's hand was too soft.

Felt posters of 60s rock bands and Jesus Christ decked the wood-paneled walls. They also clung to the angled sides of the vaulted ceiling. The original Barker Ranch house, before it burned down, did not have a vaulted ceiling. It had looked low-ceilinged, in fact.

Another young man indistinguishable from Hermes save for slightly shorter hair sat between two girls, who watched him feed marijuana into a rolling paper that he held fluted with his other hand. All six knees of those three people converging to get high reminded me of the danger with which once-discerning individuals abandoned their personal beliefs and value system in order to fit in. I hated marijuana, never buying into the highly-touted idea that it was a miracle plant every pusher this side of Colombia proposed it to be.

I found Hermes sitting to my right, looking with interest at the joint being formed. I tapped him on the forearm. He looked over at me. He was stoned out of his gourd. I held a folded twenty-dollar bill in my hand. "You into this stuff?" I asked, twiddling it between middle- and forefinger. "Cash and all. Trying to kick the habit."

He had to wade through whatever psychedelic jungle had sprung up around him to conclude that he was welcome to take the cash and spend it like he had heard so many people do. After tucking his hair behind his ear and cupping his chin, running his other hand down his scraggly beard, he smiled at me and gently, slowly pried the bill from my hand. He squinted delight at me before struggling to find a place upon his person to put the greenback. He eventually found a pocket on his brown leather vest, which appeared almost to his surprise.

I hoped that the memory of him being choked out by Mazagon had left his brain. It scared me how readily he had brandished the shotgun.

He was too stoned or stupid to hold a grudge, but I figured feeding him treats would keep him benign.

It must have been the contact high. It could also have been the acid rock with its insistent groove chewing away at my scruples. I found myself sandwiched between two nubile Manson family members, both of them taking turns to exhale marijuana smoke into my neck, coming together—forehead to forehead—to get their hair tangled up in a haze of communal oneness.

It dawned upon me that I was indeed a square—had been one, in fact, my entire life. Try as hard as I might to round off the sharp right angles with tequila and smart-ass remarks, I was a throwback to the 50s when bomb shelter commercials alternated with the latest space-age appliances for the housewives to hold down the fort. My conformity had always been a rebellion against rebellion. Where did it go wrong? Everything I stood for burned away like a cellophane wrapper taken to a flame.

I couldn't gainsay the allure of hanging around with a dozen or so girls in their late teens and early 20s. Taking out a few high-society strangers at a megalomaniac's behest would be a simple hop, skip, and jump this side of a bad acid trip. The analog Charles Manson of the late 60s was a rock-n'-roll remake of the eleventh-century Ismaili leader Hassan-i-Sabbah, who bribed his assassins (*hasheesheen*) to commit state murders during the Crusades with the promise of *houris*, those voluptuous virgins of heaven who satisfied a martyr's every desire after death. Like with most things, committing senseless killings for a cult figure started with the promise of a splendid piece of ass. Or at least more of it.

Looking beyond a forest of promising flesh (the female to male ratio being about 6:1), I saw Mazagon sitting on an orange sofa. The brunette from outside, Andromeda, she of the wet T-shirt, sat astride his lap, facing him. She held her shirt up over her breasts, which Mazagon pecked at with much deliberation, alternating back and forth metronomically as if steadying his pulse in order to stave off any premature emission that I sure as hell wouldn't fault him for.

I wasn't even jealous. I was more enlightened than anything. That a strait-laced sleuth like myself and a modern-day ronin like Mazagon could so easily fall under the sway of a cute piece of tail meant that for a master manipulator to turn the dial up a few notches to coerce some smitten boy to murder in order to secure that piece of tail, was only a matter of being patient and methodical. I imagined the Milgram Experiment would bear out the statistics twofold if a sexual reward was in place.

It was hard to imagine Facecrusher, a block of a human being, frolicking about with crazy neo-hippies up in a secluded desert ranch. The two lifestyles of flagrant hedonism and the extreme discipline to remain an accomplished MMA fighter couldn't have been further apart from each other.

"What do you think about consensual violence?" I asked aloud. The girl on my left sat curled up in a ball, sucking on a purple bong.

The girl on my right did that annoying hippie dance where they sway their arms and affect oneness with the cosmic consciousness. She stopped swaying and froze. My question had jammed the three gears turning in her brain. "Consensual violence?" she mused. "Like boxing or something?"

"Yeah," I said, "Sure. Or any combat sport. Kickboxing. Mixed Martial Arts."

The girl on my left blew smoke into my face. "Kerpow!" she exploded, then collapsed into a parade of giggling that sent her shoulders into heaving so much that bong water splashed on my left thigh.

"Violence is sometimes necessary," said the girl on my right. I realized she was the brown-haired girl from the pool moments earlier. Clarity was her name. Her headband was gone. "Violence serves to reestablish order when disorder has run amok. Charlie says that pain is fine, as long as it's justified by an equal pleasure. And that death is inevitable. Any preordained death is just human agency pulling a fast one on nature."

"Easy to say when you're not the one dying," I said, reaching for my fedora, which wasn't there. I had to perform a dialectical balancing act with these nitwits. It was made more difficult by the effects of the THC and the allure of hot action.

"But you're mistaken, sir," Clarity said, "for Charlie has already died himself. And like his previous incarnation, in the times of Pontius Pilate, he has risen. He now resides in the ether, blessed. He is eternal life made manifest."

"He died from cardiac arrest in 2017, up in Bakersfield," I said.

Tsk tsk, went the brunette on my left, named Sequoia.

Tsk tsk, went Clarity.

"So what's with the X's?" I asked, poking one then the other on the forehead.

They didn't object to the contact. In fact, their eyes lit up—either from the cool factor that the willful scarification imparted to them, or from the playful eros that a man at least a decade older had for them. The realization that they might suddenly double-team me without asking made my body tingle with nervous excitement. It looked like an inevitability when I looked over at Mazagon right there on the orange sofa with his black jeans pooled at his ankles. My jiu-jitsu assassin was being neutralized by a vigorous cowgirl who had somehow slipped out of all her clothes. All the pot smoke in the room made her nudity acceptable as if providing just enough smokescreen for everyone present to agree that one couldn't see a thing. She and Mazagon kept silent. It helped fool everyone that the discretion was working. The only immodesty would be the one perpetrated by the person who looked.

Contact high was a very real thing because I didn't intake marijuana in any of its present incarnations. Nobody could have slipped me anything soluble since I didn't take a sip of water the entire time. Maybe Sequoia smuggled an acid tab onto my tongue the three times that she leaned in and kissed me.

Next thing I knew, I had become entwined with Sequoia and Clarity there on the sofa. As I faced down toward the floor in some transition or other, I saw all my clothes in a pile on the floor. They looked like the molted castoff of a snake that's being accused by its former skin for being a traitor to its own identity. If boning two hippie girls made me feel like a fraud, then I could afford to slacken the reins of my personality somewhat. I didn't have to do much in the way of performance. Everything got done to me. Maybe taking down a buttoned-up man from the city posed a delightful challenge for two free spirits who had to contend with the same old Hindu holy man archetype over and over.

I found Sequoia to my liking. Her supple Amazonian body agreed with my deteriorated brain. It was delightful to the touch, and also possessed a motherliness that eased my trip. Clarity sensed this and emanated tendrils of ire from the pores of her skin, sinking them into my body and twisting as if they were anchor screws. I therefore turned around and went to work on her, but other plans were in order. Every maneuver that I launched got shot down. Every inventive intention I had got dismissed for a proscribed configuration that belonged to some hippie sex curriculum that could not be deviated from. From the brief glances afforded me through visual openings, I saw other configurations in the room that seemed too intricate to be the results of spontaneity. Another person would be standing there doing nothing, as if waiting for a cue. The girls had completely eclipsed me and I couldn't see Mazagon.

The only audible thing was the loud acid rock. The music sounded green. I recalled the green label on the vinyl record as it spun upon our entry into the room. Though I felt the girls' anatomies and it sent me into throes of ecstasy, I felt I was wallowing in a sea of black and green, and it all spun as upon a great platter.

I was losing my body and my perceptiveness to whatever drug had penetrated my blood-brain barrier, but I still had enough cognition to divine what was going on. The music was pre-selected. They had likely announced our arrival beforehand. Where were the sentries, for instance, when Mazagon and I made it up the wash? Unethical Ted, pseudo-neo-Luddite, had likely phoned the family and notified them of our eventual arrival.

All of this got confirmed when I insisted on working with Sequoia and was manhandled by both girls as a disciplinary action. I managed to poke my head out and saw above the mantel of a fireplace a tablet placed on a stand. Upon the tablet flashed a head, and upon the head was an evil scowl and a long, scraggly beard. A swastika rested between the crunched eyebrows. I couldn't hear a thing other than the acid rock, but the head appeared to be directing commands. At least one person of the four or so configurations remained attentive to the head's orders and reentered the positioning only after receiving full instructions.

Finally, I caught sight of Mazagon. He was in a very compromised position. Let me just say, in order to preserve his honor, that he was not in his full senses, and that a samurai such as himself would never have allowed to happen—would, in fact, had turned around and yanked the device from the girl's hips and clubbed her to death with it.

I had to battle my way out of the milieu. It would not be easy, since though I didn't get to do what I wanted, what was being done to me was one step away from being total bliss. I elbowed a girl—didn't know who was behind me at the time—right in the jaw. The sound penetrated through the music. I flipped over on my back. Sequoia and Clarity looked at each other, confused. Clarity clutched her mandible. They didn't know what to do. Should they punish me there by raining fists down upon me? Was that permitted by Charlie? Who knows, maybe Charlie had called for me to throw in an elbow just to spice things up. Surely things could get confused with all the sensory overload. It was hard to determine what was groovy and what was not.

We couldn't force our way out. We were severely outnumbered. Mazagon was incapacitated. I had to do something extra-clever. I had to turn the mass manipulation on its head. I gazed under Clarity's right arm to see the tablet sitting there on the mantle.

I got my chance almost as if by ordained cosmic luck. Sequoia nudged me off the sofa and embraced Clarity, mowing her over onto her back. Deactivated from the fear of the scene's outcome, I underwent a brief resurgence at the sight of the girls' naked bodies grinding at each other there. I had enough presence of mind, though, to yank my clothes on, shoes and all, and make my way furtively, in time to the strobe effects, over to the tablet. The face, seeing me approach him in violation of his orders, grew agitated. Before he could shout protest over the music, I took the tablet off the stand and flipped it face-down on the mantel.

This allowed the family members to finally continue their fun without interruption from Charlie. They therefore paid no attention to me as I went over and pulled Mazagon out from under two girls and a guy, Hermes or his near-twin. His extraction, likely assumed to be at the command of Charlie, resulted in the ball of flesh collapsing on itself.

I held Mazagon by the right clavicle and whispered in his ear, "We need to get out of here."

He wouldn't look at me. I knew why. He knew I was right, that we had to leave, and quickly, but he wouldn't look at me.

I began to gather up his clothes. He yanked his black jeans from me and climbed into them. I couldn't find his shirt. I handed him Hermes's brown leather vest and helped him feed his arms into it, a butler attending to a billionaire after a fine dinner.

His equilibrium was off, which was saying much because all the rolls and shrimps he did in my office never seemed to faze him whenever he stood up. I steered him toward the door by the hand.

"Wait," I said, leaving him at the doorjamb. I went over to the mantel and snatched the tablet, making sure I pressed the head against my thigh so that no one could see Charlie leaving.

The desert sun was cruel in its incrimination. Its rays shot down at us without pause, accusing us of crimes like an Old Testament prophet. Once away from the premises and into the scrubby wilderness down a slope that led into a ravine, Mazagon seemed to gain some of his balance. He ran his hands through his thick hair, trying to shake off the shame of what they had done to him like so many flakes of dandruff.

"Hey!" came a voice from somewhere. Mazagon and I ducked. There was no one around. I edged up toward the clearing and saw that no one emerged from the house.

"Listen up, pig!" spoke the same voice. Mazagon did a full turn, holding his palms up at me.

I shook my head, hoping to loosen the hallucination from my brain.

"It's real," Mazagon said, "since we both hear it."

"You better bet your sweet ass it's real!" chirped the voice again, a somewhat high-pitched voice with a little Southern drawl to it and more than a dash of self-righteous insolence.

I looked down at my thigh. I was so afraid that the family members would see Charlie leave, that I had the tablet screen pinned against my leg so tightly that I forgot it was there. My thigh hurt once I realized it. I flipped the tablet up.

"The fuck have you done?" said the head, glaring at me. It was Charles Manson. It was AI Charles Manson.

I never thought I could add being conducted in an orgy by a cult leader to my resume. I grew hot with anger. "Where are you, you sanctimonious prick?"

"How dare you speak to me like that! You'll get what's coming to you soon, and in spades!" The head froze for a bit. I thought it might be buffering, but it looked reluctant to say anything further—like it didn't know what I was going to say or do.

"You've been dead for a few years now, Chucky," I said. I held the tablet at arm's length so that he could see me place a hand on my chest. I mimicked cardiac arrest.

"Fricking pig!" the head exploded in fury. "What is death but a barrier to eternal life? I'm more alive than I've ever been, son. More potent, more influential, more wise. I don't need food or sleep. I just keep going and going. I'm more pervasive now than ever, what with all these people with their phones."

"No one gives two shits about you," I said. "They look at you for a quick second, maybe for a laugh, then continue scrolling down. You're a quick five seconds in their hours-long feed. And that's before they unsubscribe."

"Unsubscribe?" erupted AI Charles Manson. "Unsubscribe? I don't need subscribers, idiot. I have cult members. Go back into that house from which you came. I got an entire army ready to do anything for me, including kill. You're lucky I didn't command them to slit your throat while you lay there naked with those two girls. I could have easily ordered Clarity to lop your little pecker off and stuff it in your mouth!"

I laughed. Not to annoy AI Charles Manson, but because the visual was kind of funny. I saw Mazagon suppress a chuckle. It meant that he was coming to his senses. "Where are you broadcasting from, you little shit?" I said. "I want to talk to you in person. Maybe we can discuss Brazilian jiu-jitsu."

Charles Manson was silent and motionless for some time. "Listen up, pig," he finally spoke up. "When you interact with the earth, you are talking to me in person. Don't you see? I reside in the ether, brother. Every breath you draw, you are taking in my essence. I am Alpha and Omega. I am All and the Eternal Oneness."

"Okay, Vishnu," I said. "Though one might be inclined to find one of your physical stature a beta. Maybe even a gamma. You were pretty damn short."

"What's height got to do with anything, pig?" the head exploded. Pretty volatile for an artificial intelligence. "Besides, in capacity and outreach, I am a towering behemoth."

"I wish I could get you in a boxing ring," I said. "I'd knock you the fuck out!"

"Dumb fuck! You can't knock out that which you cannot touch."

"I'm going to ask you again. Where are you?"

"I can't even properly answer that, brother. Because I'm literally nowhere. While simultaneously being everywhere. That's the great thing about crossing over. Everyone's afraid of death. They've no idea what delights await them on the other side."

"So every single person who dies is just as powerful as you?"

The head froze for some time. It wasn't buffering. It had been stumped. Proclaiming omniscience and omnipotence, then stating that everyone achieved those states after casting off life, made him out to be unexceptional.

"So I've been wanting to ask," I said. "All this time. Are you or are you not the OG Charles Manson?"

"That's relative," the psycho face blurted from the screen.

"Obviously. As is everything. Except your and your minions' usage of that phrase. That's pretty absolute."

"Don't make me do something witchy!"

"What're you gonna do? Brute-force-attack my porn account? Listen, I'm going to take this tablet and smash it to smithereens, then litter the pieces out onto the dirt here. Where are you? All I want to do is to talk."

The head reacted, mulling over its options. Finally, it asked, "What do you want?"

"To simply talk," I said. I rolled my shirtsleeves down, lest I get a horrible sunburn. Bad enough that I didn't have my fedora. "I've been looking for a guy named Unethical Ted. He owes me some coke."

"No he don't," said Charles Manson. "He's the one who told me about your coming out here, you and your big-headed assistant."

Mazagon stirred, upset. The only thing that made him lose his cool was the mentioning of his admittedly large head.

"Fine. I'm a private detective. My client's identity is anonymous. I'll just say that it's a person affected by a murder that has set that person and a child into financial straits, and the police are bound up with red tape like a geisha in a Japanese bondage film. Not quite a matter of who so much as why."

"Why, why, butterfly," went the head. "On one condition."

"Name it," I said, buttoning my cuffs.

"You go place this tablet back on the mantel so I can go back to conducting my orgy."

"Not a chance, Chucky. I ain't stupid."

"Stupid enough to get rolled up by girls half your age," said the head. "Though maybe not as stupid as your friend there, who let himself get billy-clubbed in the bunghole a bit too readily. Heh heh heh."

Mazagon lunged at my hand and snatched the tablet from me. He slammed it into the dirt and stomped on it.

I didn't bother. There was no way I could hold him back. I picked up the intact hard drive and pocketed it.

Yes, the millennial Manson family members had absconded to Death Valley. X's scarred their foreheads, but none had the guts to turn those X's into swastikas. It turned out that Charlie, who had taken forever to die, had signed up early in a Silicon Valley skunkworks project to have his consciousness uploaded into an identity database. Now he talked shit on 'the establishment' and 'the rich' from a collection of servers.

Having an audience with the Antichrist hadn't yielded up any information. Better to plumb the shallow depths of his followers' minds. While waiting for the orgy to wrap up, Mazagon and I hid from the sun by sitting in the shade of the school bus that replicated the one originally hauled up in the 60s.

The family members issued from the house in a daze, stumbling into the sun in refractory periods made more lucent by their comedowns. None of them registered our presence with alarm. "Stay put," I told Mazagon before he could disappear on me.

"I intended to," he said, "seeing that they're all in front of us, either outside or corralled inside." The good old contrarian was back up and running.

I wasted no time. It would get dark soon, and we were a good hour from Ballarat, where hopefully my car hadn't been dissected for parts. "You guys got any burgers or something? We're freaking starving."

"Charlie says you can get a full amino acid profile on plants alone," said Clarity. She didn't regard me with the bashfulness between two people who had just gone at it. "Eating meat, now that's a thing of the establishment. All those high-society sheeple with their filet mignons and white wine."

"What about B12?" I asked. "How do you account for that?" My tone showed interest more than disdain. One false move and the authorities would find a sidewinder slithering through my skull's empty sockets somewhere in Death Valley.

"Some people take supplements," Sequoia said. "Lab-created." She tucked her chin to her chest and twisted back and forth, looking over at me.

"We don't," offered Andromeda, the one who had had the wet T-shirt. "Charlie don't approve of Big Pharma. All those bought personal physicians and dieticians in cahoots." She now sported a frilly pink blouse, twirling a taser gunslinger style, ready to zap me.

Despite being very attractive, she now had kicking halitosis. Shame. They probably deemed fluoride a thing of the devil. For such a pretty girl to have such bad breath meant her life trajectory would only point downward. Sad. Someone should come save these kids as a charity case.

If Uncle Charlie could control these kids on B12 depravation, forget about psychedelics. Despite living in the unforgiving Death Valley sun, they all had pale skin. It must have been the angle of the sun that prevented me from realizing this earlier.

"Any chance I can have a chat with Charlie?"

"That's relative," Clarity said. She had on purple crushed-velvet bell-bottoms that she had snatched from the community clothing pile spilled on the floor inside. Low-slung at the waist. She also wore a black sports bra as a top. A tribal tattoo shot up from both hips, meeting at her waist. The ink job brought me back to the twenty-first century. She was chomping on a stalk of celery.

"How's that relative?" I asked.

"Whether you and Charlie hit it off enough to engage in what one could deem a chat is relative," she said. "Given you might not like him or he might not like you."

"I'm sure we'd hit it off. I have a rebellious streak in me."

"No offense, Square," said Andromeda, breath kicking, "but you reek of conformity."

"I admit it," I said, shrugging. "I follow polite society's cues. Such as brushing before and after bed." How dare she use the word 'reek.'

Just then, a swarthy young man emerged from a tent that stood fifty yards from the house. I hadn't noticed it earlier. He stretched awake before seeing me. He did a double take and rolled more sleep from his eyes. Barefoot, he bolted toward me. Sequoia held him back. "Easy, Pharaoh," she said. "He's here asking about Unethical Ted."

The boy eased up. He was of Middle Eastern descent—likely Egyptian, given Charlie's simplistic knack for nicknaming. Pharaoh's energy level dipped back down to minimal at the mention of the borax miner's name.

"When was the last time you saw him?" I asked him.

He shot an uneasy look at me, ready to go again. Sequoia stiffened her arm against his chest.

"I'm not implicating you in anything. I genuinely wish to know. The guy owes me something."

"Him and Big Pharma in cahoots," Pharaoh barked, then broke down and cried. Sequoia led him back to his tent. I tied his absence from the orgy to his emotional state.

I whispered into Mazagon's ear and handed him the tablet whose screen he had smashed to bits. He jogged about a football field's length beyond the school bus and leaned the tablet against a rock. He then jogged back.

"By the way," I said to the family members once he had returned to my side. "Charlie wants to have a word with you. I think he's upset. You've been disobedient." I pointed over at the tablet. They dropped their arms to their sides, droopy-shouldered, realizing that, *Yeah, Charlie seemed to take the rest of the orgy off and let us do our freaky thing unconducted*. Once they started jogging toward the tablet, Mazagon and I made for the fire road and ran like hell, taking drops like pro mountain bikers or mountain goats, okay with the odd shoulder roll and cut to the forearm, if we kept running to Ballarat we'd be there in half an hour.

I questioned the authenticity of the AI program. If everything was relative, who was to say if it was the real Charles Milles Maddox, dead in 2017, who inhabited some servers squirreled away somewhere out at Barker Ranch? Maybe all along it was a copycat of a hacker group who sought to replicate the allure of 1968—that summer of love, death, and the senseless shagging of pale nineteen-year-olds.

Back at Ballarat, we found the gift shop closed up. Spinnaker was nowhere to be seen. Figuring that we needed the car to get back to LA, he left my car keys in the ignition. I didn't know who was more foolish: him or me.

I made a full turn out there in the desert. What solace any outcast could find in such a barren wasteland. The pretty solitude would be reason alone to ditch city life. I believed that fleeing the populace afforded no solace to the family. Instead, they longed for communal life apart from the metropolis that required them to take jobs like responsible human beings. Either that or they were desperate to replicate the 'family' life, up to including the original '68 move after the Tate/LaBianca murders. I hoped it didn't get to that. I would call Hector as soon as possible about Barker Ranch. Whoever was on the case could sure as hell use the lead.

"Let's get the hell out of this shithole," I said. "Ever had *nopales* tacos? I know a place off the 395."

"Just who the hell do you think you're talking to? A *pocho*?"

Chapter Six

Once we were north of Joshua Tree, we got phone reception. Seven texts from Rebecca of Functional Alcoholics Anonymous piled up along the top perimeter of my phone like barnacles to a hull. I reminded myself to dig the stint from my arm out and cancel my membership.

Back at civilization, I attended my second boxing class. Before heading out the door, I called up Pete Branford.

"Legion MMA," he answered.

"Hello?" I squeaked in my nerdy mezzo-soprano.

"Yes, hello," Branford said, already annoyed. "Legion MMA."

"Oh, yes yes. This is Thurmond from Gluten-Free Rooter?"

Branford chuckled. "Oh yeah. What's up, man? Did that shirt fit you?"

"Absolutely, it did. Thank you so much for the shirt. It's not every day that we at Gluten-Free Rooter receive any kind of—"

"How can I help you, boss?" Branford interrupted. For a martial artist who likely understood the dynamics of push and pull, he sure over-committed to the pushing.

"Remember I told you I wanted to have a complimentary follow-up consultation with your pipes? To, you know, make sure everything is kosher and keto?"

"I do," he replied, with unexpected enthusiasm.

"Well, would tomorrow be a good day? Say, five o'clock like last time?"

He thought it over for a while. "Fine. Complimentary, right?"

"Yessir," I said. "Gluten-Free Rooter's business thrives on a holistic solution to your problem, not from fixing a recurring problem. We stay lucrative through recommendations from satisfied customers. The only plumbing company in the world to take the Hippocratic Oath, solemnly swearing to heal all plumbing throughout the land. Just like the human body, which requires a blend of probiotics, comprehensive macronutrient profiles from whole foods, low—"

"See you tomorrow at five, then," Branford said, hanging up.

I grabbed my gym bag and went to boxing class. Ernie Reyes switched up the circuit to include a full half-hour of sparring. I forgot how much a left hook could wobble you, especially with headgear. The jury was out on the efficacy of headgear. Many contended that it provided a bigger target and that it made for a fulcrum when getting dinged. I had to sit out the final two rounds. Ernie didn't hold it against me. "You got balls enough for even getting in there with those hungry kids," he said.

The boxing was so therapeutic that my purpose in life didn't solely comprise the case's development. I drove home, drenched in equal parts sweat and elation. Once home, I called Tricky and told her I had a hard drive I wanted her to scout out. We would meet at my office later.

I had wrapped it in linen. I handed it over like Joseph of Arimathea smuggling a holy relic across the Mediterranean, or Constantine peddling a termite-ridden fragment of the True Cross. Maybe AI Charles Manson, digital messiah that he proclaimed to be, had seeped into my subconscious to the point where anything having to do with him bore Old Testament import. Shroud of Goler?

"Dufuq is dis?" asked Tricky when I plopped it into her palm. She gazed up at me with those large, Polynesian eyes—those eyes that made me harbor a crush on her for over a year.

"We had a run-in with a digitized cult leader out in the desert. Wanted to see if you could extract an IP address from this."

She gazed up at me, skinny brown fist closed over the item in question. Her little hand bloomed open. She picked the hard drive up. "Depends," she said, raising it to inspect it with squinting eyes. "Got dirt on it. The hell happened?"

"We had a fight with it."

Those eyes again. "You had a fight with a tablet?"

I passed the buck like an asshole. "Not me, actually. Mazagon."

She shook her head. "Figures. That fool needs him some puntang. Quick-style. That cauliflower ear sure as hell ain't doing him no favors."

"Not your thing," I asked, "cauliflower ear?"

"Nope," she said. "Plus, I ain't into dudes."

I hereby begin the world's first-ever autobiography of a white dwarf.

I hadn't expected that. It hurt. I didn't know why. My crush over her was long gone, largely from deliberately reasoning that she and I were very different, never mind the fifteen-year age difference. I figured it was ultimately a good thing.

I played it cool. "But if you were into dudes?" I asked.

"He's got pretty eyes," she said. "Plus, he's sweet. But he lurches when he walks."

"You know," I said, still smarting, "he can strangle anyone on earth."

"Doesn't mean he should," she said. "That shit don't impress me, that UFC shit. Make miracles with your tongue, then I'll think about rolling out the red carpet."

"Quintessential millennial," I said. "Denying the inevitability of humanity's violent nature."

"It's called evolution, son."

"I call it the way of the ostrich." I began shadowboxing. "Honestly, you've never wanted to learn how to fight?"

She shook her head. "I fight with my laptop. I can single-handedly take down a mid-sized company. What can you do, 'sides knock some poor fool out?"

I hadn't a chance in hell with the girl, so I went all out. "I don't find anything admirable about hacking. Sorry. Seems like it'd take a kind of obtuseness to sit in front of a screen to even learn any of that shit. Being honest."

She held the little hard drive out to me. That might as well have been my manhood. "Then do it yourself, player."

I closed her fist over the device. "I'd rather hire you to do it. I don't wash my car, either."

A look of hurt issued from her eyes.

"You can dish it out, eh, but can't take it?"

"I'll call you when I'm done," she said, turning away, adjusting the shoulder strap on her backpack. "C-note."

I studied her as she walked away, a misfit getting lost among the concrete. How powerful are a pair of bewitching eyes.

I wouldn't know how long it would take for her to dig up the IP address, so I went to the Mexican joint for lunch. I had four *al pastor* tacos and a *horchata* drink in a large Styrofoam cup meant for holding two pounds of chitlins. I sat outside after polishing off the tacos, giving my teeth and gums overdue attention with a toothpick. I didn't want to return to the office empty-handed. Araceli was probably there anyway.

I phoned Hector.

"What?" he chirped.

"Any chance I can get an autopsy report on Volkenrath?" I asked, slurping on the *horchata*.

"If you had better manners, I might consider it," he said. "Besides, you already know the cause of death. Collapsed windpipe."

"Was more interested in the brain, actually. Signs of CTE. Concussions and all that pretty stuff." I slurped from the *horchata* again.

Hector sighed. "I don't see how that's germane to the investigation. There was no perimortem brain trauma, I can assure you."

"No, I know. I'm curious about his brain state previous to the incident." Catching some of my macabre chatter, a couple holding hands scurried away from me on the sidewalk. "Like, if he had CTE and such. Suicidal thoughts."

"I don't see how anyone can off himself by crushing his own windpipe, Paisley. Nearly neurologically impossible. Hanging or shooting oneself, sure. It's like throwing a switch. One and done. But not something so deliberate. I mean, suicide by jiu-jitsu?"

I felt like Archimedes when he had his famous epiphany before the Carthaginians thugged it up in Sicily. Eureka. Well, eureka with an unintended assist from Hector. "Suicide by jiu-jitsu," I muttered into the phone.

Hector was silent on the other end. Finally, he spoke. "Look, I'll get you the autopsy report. But know this. That Facecrusher cat's got the six letters of 'guilty' tattooed somewhere among all that ink."

I didn't bother to go into the vast universe of the rubber guard, so I left it at that. "Say, any new IPAs lately?"

"Yeah," he said, "Lithuanian Love Handles. Put out by Sporadic Taxation Beer Company. 10% alcohol. New England IPA with Mosaic hops. A pomegranate aftertaste, yet smoky."

"Sounds like total shit."

He hung up.

Goddamnit if Tricky didn't call me to tell me she had just pulled the magnanimity move of the century. Me busting her balls was the only way I knew how to deal with her without coming across as creepy. I fell head over heels in love with her again when she told me that she not only nailed the IP address from the tablet bearing the face of AI Charles Manson, but also got into Branford's surveillance system cloud storage to find the video of Charles Volkenrath entwined with Facecrusher in a death pretzel.

I snatched my coat and, not waiting for the bill to come from the waitress flirting with the two men two tables down, left two twenties. An enormous, unwarranted tip. Maybe the girl could purchase herself some new manners. They sell them in variety packs at Walmart.

Tricky had me meet her at a juice bar. Sugar overdoses masquerading as uber-healthy shots got sold to dopes and moms too dumb to press 'puree' on their blenders at home. I found Tricky in the far-left corner, away from the ordering counter. Those eyes recognized me. A brief smile, more from her personal accomplishment than any implication of my presence. Again, I had at least a decade on her. When did it all cross over into officially creepy?

"Howdy," I said, taking the seat next to her.

"Wanna sip?" she asked, aiming the straw of her smoothie at me.

I locked onto the straw and slurped. A tartness hit my palate. "Eey-oo," I went. "Not you. The pineapple."

She twirled the laptop's screen toward me. Branford's MMA cage, dimly lit, filled up the screen. Two shirtless, musclebound men, both bald, faced each other in orthodox fighting stances. They wore 4-ounce MMA gloves, shin guards, but no headgear. I couldn't tell who was who.

Then I saw Blitz's signature leap-in jab, followed by a same-side head kick. A capital move, really. It required dexterity and was unorthodox enough to catch an opponent off-guard. The opponent would usually either parry the jab, opening himself up for the kick; or slip the jab, catching some of the kick grazing the top of his ducking head.

Facecrusher was a good thirty pounds heavier—a tad taller and certainly burlier. He was known for devastating low kicks and fundamental boxing. Nothing flashy. No spinning capoeira kicks or Tae Kwon Do stuff, just deadly fundamentals. That and an implacable urge to brawl it out, to always push forward. *Stand and bang*, they call it.

"So," Tricky chirped, snapped me out of my reverie. "Which one's the dead dude?"

I maneuvered the laptop so that we both could see the screen. Her head grazed mine. She smelled like fruit. "That one," I said, pointing at Blitz.

"He cute," she said.

I looked at her askance. "Not into dudes, eh?"

"He'd be an exception. I mean, damn." She slurped half of her smoothie down. "Why'd they go and kill him?"

"That's what I'm trying to figure out? That, and non-ya."

"None-ya?"

"As in, none ya business. Get me that on a thumb drive, yeah?"

The scene where the death occurred would be a lot to take in. I'd go over it later. She pulled the thumb drive already in the USB port and handed it to me.

"How about the IP address?"

Tricky spun the laptop back around and tickled the keyboard for a quick second; spun it back around for me to see a street address: 35370 Ventura Blvd. Studio City. I took my phone out and took a picture of the screen.

I fished Benjamin Franklin out of my money clip. "Don't spend this all on smoothies," I said, handing it to her.

"I pay rent like everyone else, supercilious mothafucka!"

I stood up and walked out, leaving behind me the sound of *arriviste* consumption—a slurping solo in a smoothie concerto, the orchestra being the rest of the world there on the bustling sidewalk.

I did an internet search on the Ventura Blvd address. The listed companies ranged from real estate development offices to chiropractors.

I got in my car and made for it. Once again, I had to scale the ridgeback of the slumbering Hollywood Hills monster and dip down the other side, the lava pit known better as the Valley, almost as if on a dare. My car's thermometer climbed up ten degrees. Having too contend with the godawful heat caused all the crimes perpetrated there, like fending off heatstroke by sinning.

The Ventura Blvd. high-rise had the kind of air conditioning that makes you envy those working there. I consulted the directory between the two elevators. A name stuck out: Pimsy Rifkin Real Estate. I saw the name and shuttered. I thought of Pimsy often, especially whenever I thought about the concept of evildoers seeming to have undergone karma immunization shots. She was going on fifty, a healthy fifty, with Gumby limbs and a short, Annie Lennox red job that made her epicene aspect shuttle back and forth between man and woman. She was an unabashed hetero, but her ripped boy body would easily make one assume otherwise. She sported hemp-woven pantsuits. Slung over one shoulder would be a hemp satchel in which she kept all her clients' loan docs. Slung over the other was her Srimatibhaktananda yoga mat that scattered chia dust into the air whenever she unfurled it.

When I first interviewed her regarding a homeowners insurance fraud case, she whipped the mat out and kicked off her pumps and began settling into deep stretches while answering my questions.

"You know, Paisley, you look tense. You should try bikram, or at least pranayama. Your chi looks mega-misaligned. Like someone drove over it with a semi."

"Are you referring to my posture? Because I have Peloponnesian posture."

She looked up at me from a downward dog that, despite her boyish aspect, sent my body into a shiver. "No, no. Not posture, silly dick. Chi. I can see it's out of whack. From your aura. You're aura's out of whack. Smeary."

The charges stuck to her and her client like fecal matter stuck to a vegan's intestinal tract—meaning, not at all.

"Yeah," I said, donning my fedora and turning away, "and you have the body of a sixteen-year-old cross-country boy."

"Your cis-normative language is very telling!" she yelled, her downward dog having collapsed into a poodle couchant. "And I'm a non-binary." She slammed her fist down onto her yoga mat.

Today I figured I'd pay her a visit, just to be a pain in the ass—a skill that in my line of work called for occasional sharpening. Suite 150.

Southern California's first self-proclaimed "plant-based realtor" had started a social media empire in the span of two years. You could find her tutorials on wheatgrass cleanses as well as amortized reverse mortgages for retirees. Everything she professed as gospel flew in the face of entropy, whether it was life-prolongation through macrobiotics or endless upward equity.

Ms. Rifkin voiced that meat eaters in general and hunters in particular did not deserve the right to homeownership. "Let them live in their yurts," she claimed, perhaps knowing that the steppe peoples tended to fashion said domiciles with the most majestic of creatures: horses.

What Valley weather tended to do, I concluded after having dealt with the likes of a Pimsy Rifkin, is take the sociopathy of Hollywood and encase it in an amber of neurosis borne of a desperation for fame and monetary gain.

I entered the suite. A brawny Latin lover type in a periwinkle tank top sat at the reception desk, dwarfing it.

Pimsy's birdlike head poked out from a room down the hall at the left. She saw me and affected a smile. "Paisley," she said, emerging from her office, "meet Enrique."

"Pleasure," I said.

"Yo," Enrique chuffed, flexing his right then left pecs over his two monitors.

I looked at Pimsy and nodded at him. "If you can't call him beefcake, what do you call him?"

"Enrique, Paisley. I called him by his name."

"Beetcake?" I mused. "High in nitrates? Vitamin K, too. If you cook him, he'll release all his nutrients."

"Knock it off, dick."

"Sorry, Pimsy, what's the forecast of the housing industry for the next fiscal?"

"Up and up. Always up."

"Figures," I said. It was impossible to get her to divulge any useful info. The only way she shed light on a given subject was by how she emotionally reacted to my prodding questions. For a Namaste girl, she lost her shit quickly. The more hysterics her tantrums and hand gestures displayed, the more my questions poking at the sordid truth would bear out. Her jugular flexed like a thick bicycle cable whenever I picked at her scabs.

"Figured I'd stop and say hello, is all," I said.

"You're too kind," she said, leaning her entire weight into Enrique's left arm, which she then vined her own arms around. "Don't be a stranger."

Asshole quota for the day fulfilled, I exited the suite. Conspiratorial chuckling erupted from behind the closed door.

There was no way I would make it to the five o'clock appointment at Legion MMA. I called Pete Branford to reschedule the complimentary consultation for the following day. He accepted. *Relented*, may have been more like it.

From out of nowhere, one of those delicious LA street dogs came to mind—those frankfurters that the Mexicans peddle outside concert and sports venues, topped with grilled onions and mummified in bacon. I got hungry immediately, jotting down a memo on my mental notepad to go fetch myself one or two as a treat for all the day's developments.

I headed back to consult the directory between the elevators. Sadistic CGI. Suite 540.

The name was as silly as it was redundant. All CGI is sadistic for what it inflicts upon the poor viewer, who is also somewhat culpable. I couldn't imagine major studio heads green-lighting a computer graphics firm with such a risqué name. Then again: Hollywood.

I took the elevator up. I would be a changed man by the time I got back down to the foyer.

A receptionist with fake eyelashes and of indeterminate race greeted me. "May I help you, sir?" she asked. A Starbucks coffee cup near her car keys on the ledge behind her read "Steph."

I hated those 'sirs.' I had been getting a lot of them lately—way more than a closer shave and a good night's sleep not preceded by tequila could swat away. Reminder to cut out sugar and carbs. Starting tomorrow, of course—LA street dog pending. I had a moral embargo on Botox.

"Yes," I replied, "I was wondering if you guys would like a free assessment and estimate on your plumbing." I produced my Gluten-Free Rooter business card.

Steph refused to take it, afraid of getting trace amounts of Hepatitis C or blue-collar cooties on her hands. She read it, though. She smiled as her thick eyelashes batted and her dark, large pupils rolled up at me with the severity of a papal bull. "Let me call Len," she said.

"Len?" I asked. "Who's Len?"

"President and CEO of Sadistic CGI," she said, eyelashes flickering toward the landline phone on her desk.

"Sure thing," I said, "I'll just take a seat and practice some good old mindfulness as I wait."

Steph smiled at me. "Len?" she said into the phone. "Yeah yeah." She huddled the phone deeper into the crook of her clavicle and neck, flirtation-mode. Mumbling and giggling. "Staaahp." She peered up at me through those eyelashes, including me in the naughtiness with the boss. Oh, that Len. Such a crusher. "Guy here says he wants to provide a free estimate on our plumbing."

She looked up at me, phone held away from her ear with both hands, and said, "Sorry, sir. Not in the budget."

"Can you please tell him my company's name?"

"What was it again? Keto Rooter?"

"No no. Gluten-Free Rooter. A holistic approach to plumbing. Purging Mother Gaia one copper pipe at a time. Galvanized, too."

She whispered the company name. More giggling and mumbling. "Staaahp." She hung up. Roused from her social-climbing flirtation, she directed her attention to me. "Free, you said, sir?"

"I did," I said. "Wouldn't think of charging if things were plant-based."

"Well, you'd be pleased to know that meat consumption is not tolerated here. In fact, anyone caught bloodmouthing will be terminated without question. Consuming dairy products is also grounds for dismissal."

I nodded, then doffed my fedora. My thick chestnut hair instantly knocked off ten years. I ran my hand through it. "So how to account for your vibrant skin if not by collagen?"

She played with her hair. "Biotin and coconut oil. And plenty of rest."

Suddenly, Len burst into the front office. I stood up. He was well over six feet tall and strikingly handsome, like a cross between Dolph Lundgren and a Ken doll. A thick head of silver hair did nothing to make him look old, for his skin was as vibrant as Steph's.

We shook hands. I looked over at Steph, who expected my astonishment of this man. I was rightfully astonished. He had just enough work—a microdose, if you will—to keep the right wrinkles from ruining the masterpiece that was his face. "Len Greenblatt," he said.

"Stan Crawford," I said. "Pleasure."

"So, ah, I had no idea that plumbing could be plant-based. That being said, I'm pleased to hear it. I'll have you know that we here are vegan. Our entire building is vegan. This entire building's plumbing is likely humming along like a well-oiled machine, heh heh." Len displayed perfect teeth as he laughed, throwing his head back at an angle only to be found in eighties television commercials.

"It delights me to no end to hear this," I said, smiled while self-consciously keeping my piranha's grill concealed. "Which was why I was compelled out of solidarity to make this house call, pro bono."

"And how did you hear of us?" Len asked, steepling his hands. A tinge of menace escaped the corners of his eyes, which had cow's feet that not even the Platonic archetype of a facelift could rid of.

"My realtor, a couple of floors down."

"Pimsy?" he asked, bending at the knees, arms out. "Pimsy Rifkin?"

"Her," I said. "Re-mod on my home. Enough equity to afford a Peloton."

"Small fricking world," Len hissed. He patted me on the back. "Pimsy's great. She really is. Listen, I have a meeting. When you're done, please help yourself to the complimentary Kraft food service in our cafeteria. Steph here will show you where it is. Steph?"

"Of course, Len," Steph said, playing with her hair again, oblivious to the calls coming in on the land phone.

When I turned back to ask Len about their existing plumbing company on file, he was gone.

I figured I'd scram toward the nearest male restroom to avoid discussing septic matters with Steph, seeing it wasn't the most romantic of topics. Yet she offered, "A sound intestinal tract makes for a sound being."

Profound tidbit, that. I nodded assent.

She was persistent. "Only toilet paper made from recyclable material should be used on the body." Now, this was getting too much into the nitty-gritty.

"Such material should be required for flushing as well," I said. She didn't hear me. She fiddled with a call and jotted important information down on a ledger. I ducked out.

The bathroom was down the hall, to the left of the elevators. I checked myself in the mirror. Certainly no Len Greenblatt, but I wasn't a troll, either. My suit looked good on me. Rather, I in it. The fedora did me no favors.

I headed toward the first stall. As with urinals, the first stall is the most hygienic out of three. This is because everyone consciously skips it, opting for the second or third. If there are four options, however, then stall three is your best bet. The most coveted and therefore the dirtiest is the last one, usually because it's for the handicapped and it provides more room. With four options, people wrongly think that the third one is the most sullied—the curse of being the penultimate.

I shut the door and plopped down on the seat; took out my phone to Google Len Greenblatt. The first pic to pop up was of him hobnobbing with a famous motivational speaker. They beamed at the camera, engaging in a friendly teeth-off. The second and third pics were with a slew of yoga hotties, girls who had molded their figures with kettlebell squats straight from Greek nymph training regimens found on pottery sherds excavated on some Aegean coast.

The rest were of Len Greenblatt in conference rooms with famous Hollywood studio producers. The last one was with an outsized bald man in a yellow tweed suit that stood out as much for its outrageous color as for its broad-shouldered cut.

Someone in the stall next to me, the middle stall, began cursing under his breath as he unspooled toilet paper with angry yanks. Silence. More cursing. Then more yanking of toilet paper. I listened closely. The staccato of frustrated wiping preceded another string of mumbled curses. The product was flimsy or the task at hand was proving to be demanding. Either way, the wiper wasn't getting the results he craved.

I coughed, then whistled. This caused a pause in the guy's action. I blocked a laugh by tucking the wedge between thumb and forefinger into my mouth. After a while, more wiping. More cursing. And more yanking of toilet paper from the side-mounted reel that, if you really think about it, was not the most efficient way of dispensing toilet paper. It converted the queue of plies into something scarcely better than Silly String.

The guy flushed the toilet. I saw his shoes turn. He was done—or at least had given up. Again, I suppressed a laugh. I couldn't help it. Three 'ha's escaped from behind my hand.

"Dufuq is so funny?" His shoes froze below the door to my stall. I had to think of something, and quickly.

"Damn Instagram memes," I said, giving a few perfunctory 'ha's.

The guy didn't move. "Paisley?" he said. "That you?"

I faced my phone down on my thigh as if having been caught watching porn. "Afraid not," I said.

"My bad," the guy said, walking toward the sinks. "My bad." He took forever to wash his hands. Once I heard the door swing closed, I exited the stall.

Standing there facing me was Daryl Pennington, smiling. "I recognize your 909er drawl from San Berdoo in my sleep." Pennington was the homicide guy who had inherited Hector Sandoval's vacated spot.

"You want to tell me what little catastrophe was going on here?" I said, throwing a thumb over my shoulder.

He shook his head indignation-style. "What are you doing here?"

"Following a lead," I said. "What else? And you? Long way from the precinct to deal with inadequate bathroom tissue."

"Inadequate ain't the word for it," he said. He approached a sink and wetted down his side-parted hair. "This Professor Ugh," he said.

"Professor... Ugh?" I asked, taking the sink beside him to wash my hands, which were already clean.

"Yeah," he said, looking at my reflection, "Ugh."

"Ugh? What sort of last name is that?" I yanked two very soft paper towels from the dispenser embedded in the black granite. Country-club posh.

"It's Danish," Pennington said. "And it isn't 'Ugh,' like you're pronouncing it. It's 'Ugh.'"

"Ugh," I said. "That's what I said. Ugh."

"No. You're going Ugh. As in, 'Eeyoo,' or 'Yuck!' It's Ugh."

"How is it spelled?"

"It's that Ø with the diagonal line through it. It's Danish. Voiced pharyngeal fricative."

I practiced four or five times.

"The last one was good," Pennington said.

"What's this guy got to do with the Blitz case?"

He looked to the door furtively, then crept up to me. "I checked out all of Volkenrath's sponsors," he whispered.

"Smart," I said. It really was. "And?"

"This Professor Ø guy runs a vegan prepared food and sports supplement company. Worth thirty million. Gluten-free, non-GMO, organic, blah blah blah. Come to find out, the company's name didn't appear on Volkenrath's fight shorts for his last two bouts."

"Company name?" I asked.

"Go Guerrilla," Pennington said, consulting the mirror again to assess his perfect head of hair.

"Motivational videos for apes?" I pondered.

Pennington shook his head. "*Guerrilla*," he said in his sad Spanish, rolling the double-*r* and turning the double-*l* into a *y* sound.

I raised an eyebrow. "Militant veganism."

"You might say that," Pennington said. "So much so that Professor Ø pulled his line from an otherwise health-conscious grocery train that sells grass-fed beef and cage-free poultry and eggs. Wanted nothing to do with them."

"Can he afford to be such a crusader?"

"Lately, digging up new info on him has been as fruitful as determining if the dinosaurs had hair. I know that he was a trust fund kid from Copenhagen. Family has a giant stake in the DSB, a Danish Railway. So yeah, he's got enough capital to wipe all the self-righteous crocodile tears away from his fat face. The business does well, though. The subscription meals are delivered to your home in dry ice, with cooking instructions. Overpriced but high-quality supplements. Hemp protein, Maca powder, chia bars, sprouted-grain tortilla chips."

"Any idea when precisely Go Guerrilla and Volkenrath parted ways? Volkenrath's manager's about as chatty as the Sphynx after a tonsillectomy."

"Haha," Pennington said, pointing at me. "But there are dozens and dozens of fighters up and down various MMA promotions, large and small, who remain sponsored."

"So it wasn't an ethical choice for them to drop Volkenrath," I said.

"Depends on your meaning of the word 'drop,' in which case it might have been very ethical. Know what I'm saying?"

The bathroom door swung open. I half-feared the colossal frame of Professor Ø would barrel in and take us out. Instead, it was a geeky, bespectacled millennial employee whose company lanyard looking too big on him slung around his neck. It served as a reminder of his employment at the company, as its size relative to his physical person was directly proportional to his loyalty.

"Sup?" I offered, tipping my fedora.

The kid smiled and headed for the second urinal, the worst possible choice. No-chinned dork.

"As I was saying," Pennington began, "the cost analysis doesn't jibe with the social media ads. They're not being properly targeted."

"Nevertheless," I responded. "We've got to zero in on the demographic." I took out my phone and texted: *I'm going to snoop around. Posing as a plumber. My lead concerns a CGI firm that Volkenrath had occasionally practiced jiu-jitsu with. Weird in and of itself. Possible falling out because of differences in diet? Could be Prof Ugh related.*

Pennington said, "I think I'll run the numbers again. We're getting sign-ups from the landing pages, but aren't closing some at the double opt-in phase." He texted: *Scouting Prof Ugh myself, from the sponsorship angle. Posing as a fight manager looking for funding.*

I texted back: *Use the name Marcus Dunlop. Give him my contact number. Been boxing lately at the scene of the crime.*

Pennington's eyes widened at me. "People don't want to be bugged every day by salesy emails." *Are you crazy?*

Marginally so. "The ratio should be 80/20. Meaning 80 percent of free content. Fluff. The other 20 perfect is asking for the buy. Converts way better. *There's something fishy about the jiu-jitsu at the gym. The defendant is a striking specialist, yet had employed a very advanced technique. Also linked to this CGI gang.*

"Yikes," Pennington said accidentally. He looked over at the geek and turned his attention back to me as the geek zipped up and flushed. "Not the ratio I hoped for," Pennington mended, "but I guess freeloaders are part of the ecosystem." *Meet me at Visigoth's Brewing Company at 8. We'll have a few.*

Okie Dokie. "Okie Dokie."

"Later," Pennington said, catching himself in the mirror one more time before exiting.

Walking down the hall to go down to the parking lot to fetch the plumbing snake, I got to thinking as I gazed down at the maroon carpeting. Was the weave gluten-free, non-GMO, non-binary? At which point does a first-world hobbyist of leisurely victimhood decide something's okay and not detrimental to the entire planet? Are potted plants next to the elevator a form of chloro-captivity? Are elevators exploitative of steel, which up to this point has been disenfranchised and has lacked a voice? Surely the doorman is an unwilling victim of twenty-first-century indentured servitude?

I had half a mind to run to a nearby hardware store for a bag of concrete to see how all these nerfed-up lemmings would do without the modern miracle that is plumbing, with which all the reminders of their lowly stage on the excretory hierarchy got washed to the sea.

When I made it back to the vestibule with the 100-foot snake in tow, two young men were waiting for me. One was an athletic-looking surfer dude with dreadlocks and a blue-sleeved rashguard. The other was the weak-chinned geek from the bathroom just moments ago. They had matching Go Guerrilla IDs on lanyards.

"Do you do sinks as well?" the surfer dude asked, holding the elevator open for me. "We have a backed-up sink."

"No doubt about it," I said, smiled. I looked over at the geek. "Winston," I said, reading the name off his ID, "saw me in the bathroom. Nice of him to capitalize off my presence. Good awareness. Let's go take a look."

Winston held a snitch's smirk on his acne-marked face. What more could bring his and the surfer dude's, Kyler's, type together than a love for a clean diet that doubles as a curriculum for self-righteousness?

I got forced between them as we made our way past Steph, who regarded my passing into the office with surprise. I ran over Winston's foot with the snake. "Whoops," I said, "sorry about that. The Black Mamba 3000 tends to strike on its own, heh heh." A tinge of what passed for nerd rage crept into his face.

Kyler remained stoic on our way to the office suite he shared with about twenty others. "Here's the sink," he said, pointing at a screensaver of an Art Deco sink on a large computer monitor. He took a seat facing the screen and began working the keyboard. A plumber in blue overalls materialized in front of the sink, monkey wrench in hand. Suddenly, a ninja dropped out of the sky and rolled between the plumber's legs and dumped him to the ground. He then snapped the plumber's legs clean off. Blood splattered everywhere before completely covering the screen.

"You'll never fix a clog like that," I said. Kyler gazed over at me. I could knock him out from where I stood. Hard to slip a one-two while seated.

"Winston here says that you give good marketing advice to guys who don't even work here. That's dope, man. No telling what you'd offer to our ad department, which consists of four guys whom we know personally."

"Excuse me, Kyler, I'm confused. I thought you brought me up here to look at a sink. I was merely offering my buddy, a fighter manager, advice on how to run the online portion of his business." That could easily do it.

"You travel far. Death Valley's quite the drive to dispense advice. Should have brought your little man assistant. We could teach him a few things on the mat."

"No idea what you're talking about, son. I rarely go east of the 101. Done a few industrial gigs. Griffith Observatory, mainly. Apparently, gazing at the celestial bodies is conducive to mass bowel movements. Something about the Milky Way, I reckon. Laxative."

Neither of them laughed. Just because nerds nerded out on one tiny thing, they got mislabeled as smart.

Continuing the Gluten-Free Rooter thread was only a ruse to save face. I needed to come clean smoothly by sliding into accusatory remarks about Vitamin B12-deficient hippies and esoteric jiu-jitsu configurations. "I've been to Death Valley before, yes. Once a Spahn of time. Badwater, mainly. Was pacing for an ultra-marathon buddy of mine. Brutal. They go all the way to Mount Whitney, crazy cats."

"I have someone here who wants to say hello," Kyler said, moving the computer mouse and clacking three keystrokes.

If it wasn't but my good old buddy, Chuck Manson.

"What's crackalackin'?" I erupted. A few people in adjacent cubicles stirred from their programming stupors at my commotion. "Even the second time around, you're hard to put away. What's your secret? Broccoli? Resveratrol? Let me in on it."

"You sorry sack of shit!" AI Charles Manson yelled from the computer screen. "That orgy I had going was on the brink of being a masterpiece. One thing an artist hates more than anything is to have his creation derailed."

"Wow," I said. "Still butthurt about that Terry Melcher ordeal, I see. You gotta move on, Chucky. Stop dwelling in the past." Terry Melcher was the Hollywood music producer whom Charles Manson felt spurned by when auditioning for him at the Beach Boys' Brian Wilson's house. He consequently sent his drug-addled maniacs to Melcher's residence at Cielo Drive to send a message, which the world got loud and clear.

I addressed Kyler. "Does killing him off constitute hitting the ESC key? They couldn't slap an electric crown on his head the first time around out of sheer bad timing." Manson's sentencing in '71 for the death penalty got commuted to life imprisonment a year later.

I kept my attention at Kyler. "Is this all a publicity stunt of your firm's new billion-dollar blockbuster? Biopic on squatters who hate hygiene as much as meat consumption? Where's the CGI come in? Doctoring up beta males and giving the brain-dead girls glowing complexions? Nothing an occasional slice of spam couldn't handle."

"He's talking to you," Kyler said, pointing at on-screen Charlie.

"And I'm talking to you," I said, voice now serious. "Keep this charade up and I'll have Barker Ranch raided a second time. Word on the street is Facecrusher's done his hedonistic time out there among the boulders and chaparral scrub."

Kyler let go the computer mouse, arm slumping low.

"And you," I said, turning to Winston. "Whatever bullying you've experienced since grade school doesn't exonerate you from running with eco-terrorists. All that serial killer worship shit is fun and cute until it affects you directly."

"We're just karmic facilitators, junior," AI Charles Manson said. "Don't hold it against us for expediting the inevitable. Everyone has his cosmic comeuppance."

"Your chickenshit ass couldn't do it yourself the first time around. And even now, you subcontract your sanctimonious slaying to another. Nice armchair killer quarterbacking, Chuck."

Charlie's eyes spun wild with rage. He hyperventilated. "Mr. Captain America needed to stay in his lane, junior. Bloodmouthing it with the masses ain't gonna cut it with Prof—"

Kyler turned the monitor off. "Who are you, bro?" he asked.

"Your karmic facilitator," I said. I looked back and forth between him and Winston, eyebrows arched in anger for effect. "You guys might as well book an Uber together to downtown LA. Got a buddy who will look to talk to you."

"Bad vibes, bro," Kyler said, swiveling on his computer chair. His smirk was now that of a guilty sap rather than that of a smug captor. A few curious heads peeked at our tableau from over their gray cubicles, Kilroys of curiosity. I wondered how many of them were in on the job. The twenty-something nerd girl in the cardigan and tortoiseshell glasses—was she an active accomplice or just a minion guilty of no more than the sin of omission? That 'just following orders' bullshit could be muttered just as well by every mass murderer on the stand, referring to the commanding voice in his head.

"I know this about plumbing," I said. "Too much fiber, like from celery, is not good for a toilet or a sink. With the latter, even a proper garbage disposal will struggle to break it down. Also, in the case of digestion. If you have leaky gut syndrome, such intake does nothing for you, other than back you up with self-righteous shit."

I mule-kicked the plumbing snake onto its wheels and began walking out of the office. Usually cumbersome and heavy, it felt lighter than usual as I made it to the minivan. I didn't care about the evening rush hour. If it took me over an hour to get to the Visigoth Brewing Company, so be it.

Once I got to the brewery, after a mere twenty-minute drive, I texted Daryl Pennington: *You inside yet? And if so, still conscious?*

It took him a while to text back: *Not gonna make it. At my daughter's dance recital. I live for this and wouldn't miss it for anything.*

Understood. Find anything?

Yes, he texted. *Met a Len Greenblatt. I asked for Professor Ø, but got this jamook.*

What the hell was a *jamook*?

The dude is CEO of Sadistic CGI, a movie computer graphics company. But I guess they're under the same umbrella company as Go Guerrilla. Anyhow, it went well. Dude wants to meet Marcus Dunlop to talk about sponsorship. You have a highlight reel?

No, I texted. *I don't.*

Get one, Pennington texted.

Check this out, I texted back. *Got two dummy CGI guys who created an AI Charles Manson. The head began spouting about Volkenrath getting what he had coming. All leaked out there in the office. You'll be talking to them, yeah?*

Wow. For sure, Get me the names. Gotta go. My girl's up.

Chapter Seven

I skipped the brewery. Alcohol is a social lubricant only to those tolerable unto society. Me not being that person, I drove home to get soused alone. Figured I'd let others subsidize the hipsters' beard oil.

It had been an eventful day. I found myself seven hours later sprawled out on the sofa, one shoe off. The first thing to greet me was the bottle of tequila. A full shot glass stood next to it. I had made it to a full six shots before conking out.

A text alert from Rebecca at Functional Alcoholics Anonymous woke me. I poured the contents of the seventh shot back into the bottle with care. That was worth a solid fifteen minutes of liquid happiness. I would read Rebecca's text later.

I didn't know how long I could realistically keep up the boxing. I loved hitting the mitts and doing the slip drills and even skipping rope, but I found the noon slot grueling. It just didn't mesh with the drinking. In the future, when everything will be VR, I'd box for two hours a day. Fifteen minutes before meals, and an hour's worth of shadowboxing while drunk. Silicon Valley has been slipping.

With the Legion MMA lead at a standstill until I returned to check up on the plumbing, my motivation to go to class was even more threadbare. I called Tricky.

"What's the word, Thunderbird?"

"I need a highlight reel for a boxer. All inside a gym. Sparring with headgear so no one can tell it's not me. A few impressive knockdowns. Of them, not me. No shots of him, me, getting clipped. My body type."

"You mean, like, a lanky-looking dude?"

I sighed. "If that's what's called for, then yes."

"It'll be two A.J.s," she said.

"What the hell is an A.J.?" I asked, afraid to get the answer.

"Andrew Jackson, player. Old Hickory. Dead dude on the twenty."

"Forty bucks?" I clarified.

"There you go."

"Why don't you just say forty bucks?" I asked, my hangover making her lingo extremely irritating.

"Where's the fun in that?" she said. "Conversing should be an art form. Spice everyday existence up a little."

"Good point," I said, holding the bridge of my nose between thumb and forefinger. "So I guess that makes you a real Picasso."

"There you go!"

"I can do two A.J.s if it's spectacular. If it doesn't meet my standards, you'll be having a powwow with a lawyer from Illinois."

"Dufuq you talking about?" Tricky exploded. The swishing sound found only from withdrawing a lollipop from one's mouth started where her high-pitched plea ended.

"Abe Lincoln, girl. Wow. You create a game and can't even abide by its rules."

She hung up.

I took a long shower, leaning my elbows on the windowsill and wishing I had a more concrete purpose. Maybe getting a dog would help. Or I should marry Araceli just to inject some trauma into my life, no matter how bad. Anything but the ennui I felt as the shower water cascaded down my face. The image of Moira Volkenrath surfaced. Her and her son. I could take care of them.

No, I couldn't. Not with what I made. I was too noble for my own good. I was already two A.J.s in the hole. I should have gone to boxing class. I didn't. Maybe tomorrow. Or the day after.

By the time I got fully dressed and was buttering some toast to accompany two over-easy eggs and a half-pound of cooked bacon, Tricky texted me that the highlight reel was done and was waiting in my email account as an attachment. I opened the file and watched.

Whoever the boxer was, he was good. He moved like Lomachenko. Though everyone moved like Lomachenko during training. What made the Ukrainian bantamweight so special was his matador-like ability to dance around his opponent in a live fight. He appeared at crazy angles, like a bee or fly that shifts so fast that it looks to the unaided eye like teleportation.

I loaded the video into a flash drive as I ate my breakfast. I called Mazagon to come over before heading back to Studio City. I'd at least keep him in the car for backup as I pitched to Len Greenblatt for sponsorship.

The breakfast I ate—a late lunch—was long gone from my stomach by the time we reached the building. The traffic god came to collect his blood sacrifice after blessing me with a good two weeks of driving grace. An unrelenting sun crushed the left side of my face the entire hour-plus trip. Mazagon was in top form, jerking there weirdly in the passenger seat in whatever BJJ guys called their shadowboxing.

I had him elbow me in the face before I went in. What do you know, after the initial reaction of rage, I found my hangover had all but disintegrated.

Hair slicked back and prescription sunglasses on, I took the elevator up to the Sadistic CGI suite. Steph greeted me. I had forgotten about her. She wore a ton of pancake makeup—looking like she used a trowel to spackle it on. I told her I had an appointment with Len Greenblatt.

The CEO of Sadistic CGI burst through the door and greeted me teeth-first. In the background, all blurred out by the burning-white splendor of his grill, was the rest of him. A tallness bordering on gigantism was shelled up in an expensive double-breasted suit the color of aquamarine. You had to be Len Greenblatt to pull that suit off—game-show-host handsome, where the game is to see how long you can last in his presence without breaking down into a weeping heap of inadequacy.

I found him fascinating, despite myself. He was an amalgam of clean eating, brutal cardio workouts, and Adderall. "Pleasure, brother," he said as he shook my hand. That 'brother' fell under the aegis of the gospel of veganism, a way of slowly converting. "Is your manager not attending the meeting?"

"I regret to say, Mr. Greenblatt, that he will not be joining us. His son fell ill. Hives. Not wishing to squander this golden opportunity to represent Go Guerrilla inside the ring and out, I decided to show up all by myself. Besides, I won't be able to drag anyone into the ring to help me if and whenever I throw down against a worthy opponent while representing one of the best, and socially conscious, sports supplement brands on the market." Len Greenblatt, increasing his smile where it didn't even seem possible, nodding assent. "In the world," I added.

"I love it!" Len erupted, bending at the knees and throwing his head back. A trademark move? "Steph," he said, looking over at the receptionist.

"Yes, Len?" she asked, cradling the phone between her collarbone and ear as she jotted something down on the blotter.

He pointed down at me, indicating an object of great importance or extreme reverence. "Make sure this man doesn't leave this office without a fat manila folder tucked under his arm."

Steph looked at me and shrugged. I caught a brief look of recognition from her. I played it cool and turned my back to her. "Lead the way, Mr. Greenblatt. With my fights as in life, I'm not much one for the feeling-out process."

It may have been the Botox, dunno, but a tinge of irritation over being ordered crept into his spray-on tan face. Either because of Steph's presence or a trained mechanism to respond rather than react, he smiled and said, "You're destined for great things like that, my friend." He opened the door for me and offered me to step through.

By the time we made it to a conference room with non-leather seats in 50s pastels, he had schmoozed with eight people. He tamped down his exuberance once we entered the room. Four other people faced us in a semicircle. The first thing to catch my eyes was a bald man of imposing size. Professor Ø, the one and only. He blinked at me and threaded the fingers of his lunchbox hands together on the table.

I nodded at him. He nodded back.

To his right was a scrawny, twenty-five-ish man with surfer blond hair worn long and parted slightly to the side. He had black earplugs and cauliflower ear. To the right of him was a middle-aged, bespectacled man who didn't fit any type, just seemed to be there because it was a good-enough-paying job and he had two kids to put through college. To the right of him was a thirty-something black woman with shorn hair and a pleasant, flirty demeanor. She held a smile for me that I didn't mind.

"Lady and gentlemen," Len said, taking a seat and snatching a bottle of water from a spread in the middle of the table, "I present you Marcus Dunlop."

A mumbled salad of greetings made me feel somewhat at ease. Professor Ø stood up, grabbed a water, and handed it to me all the way from his side of the table.

"Thank you, sir," I said upon taking it. "And it's an honor to meet you. You run a fine company. Or should I say, companies."

He nodded and smiled. "Pleasure's mine."

"May I ask," asked the young man with earplugs, "what's your fight nickname, assuming you have one?"

"I do," I said. "It's Strafe." He nodded. "May I ask your name?"

"Drillbit," he said.

"Nice fight name," I said. "It denotes intention. Screwiness, too." The black girl cracked up.

Drillbit shot a mean look at her. He looked back at me.

"That, and you *bore* into people." I kept clowning.

Professor Ø smirked. I looked over at Len, who also smirked.

"No disrespect, Chuck. Or Drillbit. Figuring I'd give you guys a little taste of my marketability." I pulled the flash drive from my shirt pocket. "Some of my work," I said, and handed it to Len, who handed it to the middle-aged man, who plugged it into a monitor on the wall to my left and grabbed a remote.

As the reel played and elicited silent attention, I felt no hint of self-consciousness. Probably since it wasn't me. I made a note to talk to Ernie Reyes about the viability of a guy my age making a career out of the sweet science. What a life: jog, skip rope, hit mitts, hit bag, spar, fight, get girl(s).

"That bladed stance," Drillbit chirped, "wouldn't serve you well in MMA. You'd eat leg kicks like a monitor lizard eats maggots."

"Donald," Professor Ø chided.

Drillbit simmered down, but not enough to hold back a smug rictus that I'd love to left-hook away.

"Not looking to do MMA, guy. Just boxing. The middleweight division is full of life right now. Looking to hitch my wagon to that train. All the top contenders, even the champion, have as much personality as this bottle of water," which I held aloft. "I also look to showcase the inexhaustible benefits of a clean, plant-based diet."

The middle-aged guy spoke. "Will Fitch," he said. "Nice to meet you." He addressed the black woman. "Candice, could you get him in for a shoot today? See how the lens reacts with him?" He looked back at me. "You had a six-pack in your highlight reel there," nodding at the television screen, "but how about right now?"

"I have a six-pack at all times, Mr. Fitch, that I can never stay sober."

Everyone but Drillbit laughed.

Candice looked at me. "I think we can fit him in. I don't reckon there'd be any issues. He looks photogenic to me. Maybe a full beard would peg him as current. Help the demo a bit."

"Was thinking along the same lines," Len said. "Say, Marcus, you hungry?"

"For the spotlight?" I said. "Yes. For nutrition? That too. Go Guerrilla equals Go You."

Candice and Will Fitch burst into clapping. Drillbit rolled his eyes.

Professor Ø gazed at his wristwatch, stood up, and without ceremony shook my hand. He nodded in the affirmative at Len Greenblatt, and left the conference room.

"You know what, Len?" Drillbit spoke. "I think Mr. Dunlop's marketability is without question. What better way to convey to the public his earth-conscious agenda than to make him out as a sort of renaissance man. We could show him playing chess, for example. Even guide his movements because he may not know how to play chess. Or show him wiping oil slick off of penguins in the Gulf of Mexico. Or, I don't know, show him doing jiu-jitsu. I have an extra gi lying around in the gym office that looks tailor-made to his lanky build."

"Sorry, Chuck," I said. "No penguins anywhere along the Gulf of Mexico. Way too tropical. As far as jiu-jitsu goes, I think that showing me dabbling in other martial arts would convey not only to the public but to my opponents, that I was spreading myself too thin." I looked to Len for agreement.

He must have noticed that the CGI supervisor and I didn't like each other one bit. He looked to be relishing every minute of it. He steepled his fingers, elbows on the table, slouched in his chair, swiveling. "I don't know, Mr. Dunlop. I like the idea of showing other aspects of you. Whatever it takes to make you out as multi-dimensional."

"Boxing is not a martial art," Drillbit said, eyes up at the ceiling.

"I beg," I said, "no, I beseech, to differ. Mat-humping a guy like a human blanket is all cool, but can you take a rear uppercut to the chin? That's what I'd like to know."

"You guys," Candice said, shaking her head. "Must we infuse some soy protein up in here? Jack your estrogen levels up to calm you the hell down?"

"You two are such polar opposites," Len said, oscillating his index finger between me and Drillbit, "that I'd like to get you two on the jiu-jitsu mat. Just to see the chemistry. Candice, could you arrange that?"

"If it's in the next hour, sure," she said.

"I'm all caught up on my work," Drillbit said, smiling like the Cheshire Cat.

My mouth was agape in protest when Will Fitch spoke. "We can throw it at our focus group tomorrow morning, provided Candice and her crew package it up for us this evening. Maybe splice it with a candid interview about Mr. Dunlop's willingness to be on the leading edge of a sports nutrition revolution."

"I could do a three-camera recording in a jiffy," Candice said, eyeing me playfully. "Dovetail that in with his extant boxing footage. Back and forth between color and black and white?"

"Magnificent," Len said, beaming an ear-to-ear smile. "You saw the big boss sign off on it. Mr. Dunlop."

"Marcus," I said. "Please call me Marcus."

"Fair enough," he said. "Marcus, let us feed the footage to our focus group, and we'll draw up something desirable for both parties. I do request that your manager be present to negotiate on your behalf. It's just a formality, and barring any unforeseen mitigating factors, we should have that fat manila folder tucked under your arm and a big, bold Go Guerrilla logo across the front of your boxing trunks in no time, hopefully for your very next bout."

"Len," Drillbit piped in, arm raised.

"Yes, Donald?"

"I could cook up some fire graphics in the boxing ring. Not on the mat, of course, as he'll for sure be a white belt." He smirked at me.

"No graphics just yet, Donald. But a good idea for the future."

"Mr. Dunlop," Candice said, standing up. "My three cameramen and I will see you shortly." She bowed. I bowed back.

"Marcus," Len said, "would you like a hemp bar? Hungry? High in protein and fiber and low in sugar. I promise it's non-psychoactive. Wouldn't want your footwork getting all tangled up now, would we? Heh heh."

"It would be an absolute honor to have a Go Guerrilla Warfare bar."

He produced it from God knows where. Might as well have been from the sleeve of his suit, like a magician producing a line of handkerchiefs or a white rabbit. He handed it to me.

"He won't be using his feet in a bit," Drillbit said, standing up. "That's for damn sure."

"Tell your manager to phone me on Monday," Len said to me, and left the room. Will Fitch shook my hand and also took his leave.

It was me and Drillbit. "Follow me," he ordered, nodding toward beyond the conference room, toward my doom. I unwrapped the Go Guerrilla Warfare bar as I walked behind him. Various people said hello to Drillbit, who didn't bother to return the greetings. I devoured the bar. I was going to need every nutrient. It tasted like a dough made from sawdust and goat shit.

Candice had me read from a teleprompter. I had to occasionally shake my head to show passion. "Win or lose, I'm on a mission. To be an ambassador of veganism while achieving athletic greatness is not only an honor but a lifelong passion. Whether in the ring or on the jiu-jitsu mat—whether boxing or engaging in the beautiful art of grappling, to represent Go Guerrilla and be in lockstep toward the goal of making the world plant-based is a task that I bear with pride. Go Guerrilla helps me achieve my optimal self. I feel great all the time, need little sleep, and keep a clean conscience all while kicking ass. It's my profound belief that through revolutionary nutrition and earth-conscious vigilance, we can make the world a better place."

She then had her three cameramen triangulate while I fitted into a gi that felt like a canvas tent over my body. "Your first lesson," Drillbit said, "is to properly tie your belt. White belt."

After he conveyed that lesson, he threw me around like a wet noodle and made me tap from at least a dozen different configurations.

CRUSHED TRACHEA BLUES

Pinning me to the mat, he spoke into my ear. "The inability to do precisely what I wanted to do in jiu-jitsu is what drove me to CGI. There, the confines of the human body are not at play. If jiu-jitsu as we know it—that is, Brazilian jiu-jitsu within this three-dimensional cross-section of the multiverse is checkers—then VR jiu-jitsu would be chess."

"That's all well and good for nerds with ripped thumbs and Hot Cheetos breath," I said as we took a two-minute break, "but what does that do for your actual grappling game? You're dealing with abstractions that you can't translate back to real life." I patted the lapels of my sweat-soaked gi down as if I were some sort of grand master.

"That's where you're mistaken," Drillbit said. "Well, not quite mistaken. So much as wide of the mark."

"Ketamine?" I pondered.

He shook his head. "No drugs." That's right. This nerd herd was straightedge. Militantly so. "It's about going into the CGI world and delving into the possibilities. Like mining an ore of possibility. Then you bring it back to the mat. Transliterate it from the base metal of probability into grappling gold. Jiu-jitsu alchemy. I've at least four submissions where the victim is simultaneously suffering two points of defeat. Having his windpipe smashed while at the same time getting his arm snapped. Arm-in guillotine with an armlock on that very arm. And therein lies the roots of demon jiu-jitsu. The alchemical goal would be to roll an opponent into a ball, where he is submitted by all molecules of his own being. A black hole of agony."

"Where's the fulfillment in that, really? Other than an idealized form of mastery? Seems to me that boredom for regular grappling for you set in some time ago. What you're referring to is a good old-fashioned God delusion, homie. It's the same thing that drives pedophiles and serial killers."

Drillbit looked about to snap. He wiped stray hairs back from his brow. He saw the expectation in my eyes and didn't take the bait. "I'd imagine such domination as I've described being infinitely more fulfilling than taking someone's life or innocence in a single stroke. Have you ever been smashed while rolling? I mean, really smashed? What I've just done to you is nothing. Being truly smashed is beyond demoralizing. It's claustrophobic, emasculating, and humbling all at once. Yes, you're right. I've come away with an idealized form of dominance that has little probability in real life, other than in tournaments. But the results speak for themselves. We have a slew of champions in various grappling tourneys. As far as your accusation of getting off course, that's the natural progression of anything."

I got a good look at this nerd. I wondered if I could take him in a fight. No, really. Megalomania aside. If I could land a quick one-two on his smug face, I could secede his consciousness from his dumb head. "Why don't you go chase girls like everyone else your age?"

He scoffed at me. He detested everything I stood for. My wearing a gi must have irked him to no end. "Pussy," he said. "A most pedestrian pursuit. Excuse me for having a hobby and excelling at it."

"Rolling around with other dudes?" I said. "Capital endeavor, that."

He spun around on his ass to face me and yanked on my arm. I would later learn that this was referred to as an arm drag. I didn't know quite what happened, but I ended up on the bottom. He bore his entire weight on me. Though of a slight frame, he felt like an anvil. I panicked. I spazzed. I couldn't do a thing. He pressed his head against mine. A drop of sweat rolled off his hair and plopped in my eye. "Sssshhh," he went. I stopped spazzing out. "Just breathe," he said. I just breathed. As much as I feigned not being overwhelmed with claustrophobia, I felt like hell encased me. I couldn't move a muscle. Not even my tongue to cry uncle.

"I currently hold you in a position known as the cradle. S-gripping both hands, elbows around your neck and knee, respectively. So-called as much for the position resembling that of a newborn baby as for the helpless predicament you're in. From the cradle you came, and to it, you shall return. Getting back to the refinement of craft. As Miyamoto Musashi once wrote in his *Book of Five Rings*, 'If you know the way broadly, you will see it in everything.' BB reiterates the same sentiment. The aim is to make the opponent quit. Every person who has lost in competition to a member of Demon BJJ has quit jiu-jitsu to a man. Were they smarter, or of hardier mettle, they'd come over and convert."

When I thought the pressure couldn't get any worse, I felt my lower spine twist. I also felt my cranium being crushed. My toes and thumbs were being hyper-extended. My carotid artery was being ground to a powder. Then he let up.

"You couldn't verbally tap even if you wanted to," Drillbit said, somewhere behind me as I found to my delight that I possessed limbs that were intact and a vastness of space that I could maneuver within. I had been subdued by an octopus.

All the pains I got subjected to were gone. My shame was so profound that I didn't even bother addressing it. I'd unpack it later, me and a bottle of tequila. That LA hotdog I wanted for a few days now may as well have been floating deep in one of the spiraling arms of the Andromeda Galaxy.

"Good stuff," I said, like an unattached observer assessing a carnival trick.

"I'm only a purple belt," Drillbit said. "BB will promote me to brown, then black, when the time is right."

"Who's this BB?" I asked, fixing the lapels of my gi. The gi was tedious. It caparisoned my body like a soft shell of a turtle, an undeserved husk offering zero protection.

"BB is the grandmaster of Demon BJJ." Drillbit pointed up at a portrait on the far-right wall. It was a black background with a red belt floating in midair. On the left was a portrait of Helio Gracie, the founder of Brazilian jiu-jitsu. On the right was a woodcut of a medieval alchemist.

"Who's that supposed to be?" I pointed.

"Paracelsus," Drillbit said.

"Why is BB invisible?" I asked.

Drillbit pondered an answer. At length, he spoke. "He has gone into the ether. Into the inter-space. He is translated into the rarefied air of excellence."

"Yet his belt is there," I said. "Present in this world."

"His belt, yes," Drillbit said. "In the mundane world, his rank still means something. His physical aspect, however, is translated."

"What's being vegan have anything to do with all of this? For such dog-eat-dog savagery, chewing cud and sucking on celery stalks seems contradictory."

An incredible soreness eclipsed the urge to scurry away from the mat for dear life. I barely paid attention to Candice and her three cameramen. My whole body ached, but especially my neck and arms. I guess it was to be expected after being contorted into immobility by a grappler from the infernal regions. I found a bathroom and switched into my clothes. They may not have been the uniform of a superhero or a horizontal assassin, but they were mine. I felt immediate relief, like my identity had poured back into me as I buttoned my cuffs. My fedora was unaccounted for. I shoved the sweat-soaked gi into the garbage bin.

I double-taked as I walked past a large room in which a few individuals sat at rectangular tables. The cafeteria. No one looked up from his or her meal or laptop as I made straight for the spread the size of a boulevard median.

There were all imaginable fruits and vegetables. Not just bananas, but plantains. Not just avocados, but the California variety as well as the Hass. Enough romaine lettuce to take down a battalion with an E. coli outbreak. Quinoa by the bushel. Sprouted grain bread with tofu cold cuts. Zucchini pasta. Cauliflower pizza. A giant vat of monk fruit sweetener for any sweet-tooth level.

None of it piqued my appetite. Over on the far right of the spread were a couple of dispensers. One issued forth a bland-looking cereal. The other miraculously dispensed açaí bowls, complete with cottage cheese and granola. A striking blonde with her hair in a ponytail held a giant bowl under the dispenser.

"Lots of natural sugar," I said. "High in antioxidants such as resveratrol, sure, but insulin spike with a money-back guarantee."

The blonde chuckled before looking over at me. "True," she said, smiled with a strange calmness. "A little sugar is okay, though, after a grueling workout."

Flirtation was hard business after having had the worst moment of my life. I had to try, though. "What's the time window? Thirty minutes? I opt for thirty hours. Restore glycogen that's yet to be used? Even better."

She chuckled again. "I don't take you for a man who's averse to a little exercise." She sat down.

I bowed. "I guess I'll help myself as well, then."

She turned back to her profile, shifting her attention to her meal. I thought it was a wrap.

I had to continue. "How you managed to get in a workout while dressed in business casual is impressive. I'd be happy to copy your regimen. Unless your hair dries incredibly fast."

"You're very observant," she said. Her deference wasn't out of an eagerness to end the conversation, but a disarming calmness. "Not all exertion involves full kinetic motion. Controlled breathing, for instance."

"Like pranayama yoga?" I asked.

"Somewhat," she said. "But not quite." She swirled her spoon around. "Controlled hyperventilation. It forces all the muscles of the body to react as if they were engaged in a functional workout. I resort to it when the time for a proper kettlebell session or Aerodyne bike sprints is lacking."

"You CGI folks are quite the busy bunch," I said, tasting my first ever açaí berry. I'd never tasted one my entire life. I would find out what all the fuss was about.

"I wouldn't know what hours they keep," she said, downcast eyes turned to her açaí bowl.

"Accounting?" I wondered. "Human resources?"

"You ask that because those positions tend to be relegated to women?"

My spoon froze. "I ask that because what else would one do here if not work in the CGI department? Please don't accuse me of profiling. I guess we all do it every day. And that's okay. You yourself just did."

"I'm not directly employed by Go Guerrilla. I'm not on their pa

"Shining example of what a clean diet engenders?" The berries mixed with the cottage cheese were divine. She let go of her açaí bowl to sit back in her chair, arms foldedyroll.".

"Sorry," I said. "Again. Don't mean to objectify. There's no getting around the fact that you're a lovely creature."

Those downcast eyes. "I'm a coach," she said.

"Like, life coach? Motivational coach?"

"I coach jiu-jitsu," she said.

"Okay," I said, standing up from my seat. "Gotta run."

"Was it something I said?" she asked, a smirk accompanying disdainful eyes as she went back to her açaí bowl.

"It was precisely something you said." I decided I'd take the bowl with me and polish it off as I began my fool's errand of making it out of the building. "I just got rolled up into a ball of agony by this dude not ten minutes ago."

"By whom?" she asked.

I turned around. "Dude named Drillbit."

Her spoon froze in midair. "That figures," she said.

"Why's that?" I asked.

"Drillbit is a bully," she said. "It's why he's been sitting on his purple belt for over five years. He's a sore loser and tends to roll with only lower belts."

"You're his coach?" I asked, sitting back down, facing her.

"Uh-huh," she said. "Though not voluntarily."

"You mean a purple belt did that to me?"

"Have you never trained jiu-jitsu?"

"I have not," I said. Admitting as much felt like confessing a great sin.

"You should try the martial arts," she said. "The benefits are manifold."

"I box," I said. "Not too shabby with the hands."

She smiled for my sake. "That's good. Striking is a legitimate martial art, no doubt. A curious one, albeit."

"How so, curious?"

"To incapacitate someone by very briefly indenting a part of their body," she said, like a forensic pathologist disinterested in a nearby supine corpse, "that's an uncertain strategy."

"I can't blame you for your bias to espouse grappling over striking."

"Think about it, Mr.—"

"Dunlop," I said. "Pleasure. But please call me Marcus."

"Marcus, the advantage of closing the distance is to ensure, like striking, the denting of a surface, but for a more extended period. Or the deprivation of oxygen or the hyperextension of a ligament or bone that the most powerful boxer's punch or most accurate nak muay's round kick couldn't deliver. A kimura, a relatively simple armlock, can snap the humorous bone with ease. A kneebar can pop a ligament."

"Your morbid breakdown perfectly complements the açaí's sugary sweetness even better. Way better than buttered popcorn with the latest Marvel debacle."

"Second only to New Age music and a massage," she said. Her first attempt at wit.

"I guess it'd be similar to a King cobra and a boa constrictor," I said, scraping the bottom of my açaí bowl.

"An apt metaphor. With the cobra, you need to simply worry about the head, the fangs in particular. With the boa, you'd better steer clear entirely. You're welcome to serve yourself some more. Allow me." She snatched my empty bowl and went to the dispenser to fill it.

"I'm Angela Vicksburg, by the way," she said, gazing at me over her shoulder.

"Charmed," I said. The somewhat normal name helped tether her to the mundane earth, lest she float away to the stars.

"As am I," she said, handing me the bowl.

"Getting back to grappling," I said. "The problem with sport jiu-jitsu is the assumption that strikes don't exist."

"Wrong," she said. "There are mitigating techniques. Especially in the no-gi variety, which is what I practice. There are clinch-based techniques that close the distance, like overhooks. And rubber guard."

"Rubber guard," I iterated. "That's that bendy leg configuration stuff, yeah?"

"You sure know a thing or two for a non-grappler," she said, appearing delighted.

"I manage. The third thing I know is that it didn't work so well for Charles Volkenrath."

She squinted at me. Whatever controlled breathing she preferred to be an expert in didn't take hold as she began to lose her cool. She turned away from me and leaned against the counter.

"Was it something I said?"

Without looking back at me, she said, "Please leave. Our conversation has come to its conclusion."

"Really wish it weren't so. You're a good conversationalist. It's a lost art nowadays. You know another good conversationalist? A certain Ronnie Parrish. Had a few things to say about the rubber guard himself. Even rapped about it in a song. Imagine that. I'm going to Hail Mary it and say you might know one Ronnie Parrish, peddler in toxic folk?"

"Who are you, Mr. Dunlop?"

"I'm just a lowly gumshoe hired by Volkenrath's widow to find out exactly what happened at Legion MMA that fateful evening when Blitz sparred with a striking specialist—and grappling novice—Craig 'Facecrusher' Farrell."

Her eyes stopped their squinting and contributed to a pall that made her oval face into a China doll fashioned by a humorless Calvinist. At length she spoke, prefacing it with a sigh. "Ronnie was all right, as far as I'm concerned. A competent grappler, he got to blue belt. But he decided to pursue music, something I can't fault him for."

"What, I repeat, what is so damn groovy about the rubber guard? I don't get it."

"You don't get it because you don't train jiu-jitsu."

We were back in her territory. All I had to do was reel her in. "Seems like a bunch of overly flashy stuff."

Angela took a seat. "The rubber guard was created by Eddie Bravo, jiu-jitsu pioneer right here in Los Angeles. Of the Jean-Jacques Machado lineage. Aside from discarding the gi, considering it as nothing more than Japanese pajamas, he also devised the rubber guard to defend against strikes in an MMA or street fight context. The rubber guard is fancy, yes, but not for any perceived lack of efficacy. See, it requires flexibility. Nothing that a little stretching and practice won't accomplish, but people will latch onto an excuse to not go through with acquiring it."

"Volkenrath seemed to take to it. Do you think that's what cost him his life? Relying on a technique that he hadn't quite nailed down?"

She took a deep sigh, gazing at the table's surface. She then looked up at me. "Charles had a good rubber guard."

I sat down to face her. "How would you know that?"

"Because I was the one who introduced him to it."

I sat back in my seat and folded my arms, exhaling. All I could do was regard her as a nurse looks at a wounded infantryman who has lost a limb but whose adrenaline hasn't permitted him to assess the pitiful state he would be in for the rest of his life.

She hung her head.

"Would it be okay for me to show you the footage? So you might tell me what exactly went on?"

She raised her eyes to the table's edge, considering the request. She looked up at me. Her eyes suddenly looked gray. "Okay," she said, "but just once."

I took my phone out and searched for the MP4. I slid my chair around to where she sat and held the phone sideways so we both could see. I pressed play. I didn't watch it, as I'd seen it dozens of times and was sick of it. I watched her reaction instead.

She squinted as Charles 'Blitz' Volkenrath slumped to the mat. "Rewind that again," she said, shaking her head in confusion.

I keyed up the timestamp, 0:27.

She craned her neck toward the screen and watched intently. "Again," she said. I rewound it again.

She pressed pause and zoomed in the image with her thumb and forefinger. She looked over at me, eyebrows bunched in confusion as if she'd seen something that had eluded her surgeon's eye.

"What was it there that happened? A good friend of mine, a jiu-jitsu friend, couldn't provide me an answer."

"Charles has him in rubber guard the entire time," she said.

"Explain, please."

"He is on his back, with his legs thrown over the other gentleman's shoulders and neck. A rubber guard is just a very high closed guard with odd manipulations of the neck and arms with the legs. It requires flexibility. And properly defending it requires familiarity with the rubber guard, at least a rudimentary understanding of it."

"So if Charles has set Facecrusher up in his rubber guard, how can it be possible that he, Charles, gets finished?"

Angela leaned her head in and squinted. "Ezekiel choke," she said. "Facecrusher has him in an Ezekiel choke, inside of Charles's rubber guard. I've seen nothing like it."

"What's an Ezeke—"

"Wait. Charles goes for a gogoplata around Facecrusher's Ezekiel choke. Even more strange. I don't know how effective that is, if at all. Can we please watch it again?"

She was too proper. I wondered if she asked permission before choking someone out. I obliged her.

"Yes," she said, slapping her knee. An Ezekiel choke inside of a gogoplata. Unbelievable."

"Is that a dangerous choke?" I asked.

"To which choke are you referring? The gogoplata or the Ezekiel choke?"

"The one that Facecrusher is implementing," I said.

"They're all dangerous if held overly long. With the Ezekiel, yes. It's not a blood choke. It doesn't cut off the carotid artery. It's a trachea choke. It restricts oxygen from passing through the windpipe. If held for a long time, it can crush the trachea."

"What about the gogoplata?"

"Not an oxygen choke," she said.

"A blood choke, then," I assumed.

"No," Angela said, shaking her head. "It's a neck crank. It puts uncomfortable force on the neck by squeezing it between the ankle and the wrist holding the same foot."

Oh, jeez. Oxygen choke. Blood choke. Neck crank. Arm hyperextension. What maladapted person invented Brazilian jiu-jitsu? Was there a French influence, say, the Marquis de Sade? Did some of these torturous techniques leak out of the Bastille and find their ways to South America?

"Would you say, Angela, that Facecrusher was in danger from Charles's gogoplata?"

"Hard to say," she said. "May I watch it again?"

"Of course," I said, and keyed up the sequence. We were dissecting this video like conspiracy theorists, obsessing over jiu-jitsu's very own Zapruder film.

"I got it," Angela said. She flipped the phone down, done with it. "Charles had Facecrusher in rubber guard. Facecrusher defended by hooking one arm over Charles's head, which is needed to set up the Ezekiel choke. In order to defend from that, Charles put his left lower leg in front of Facecrusher's head to create distance and brought his same-side arm over the back of Facecrusher's head. But Facecrusher is providing pressure on Charles's neck to alleviate tension from the gogoplata. There's a kind of stalemate, in that no one can move without threatening himself. It's a kind of game of chicken. Bluff-calling and ante-upping."

"Facecrusher won the roll," I said. "Mr. Volkenrath's throat was indeed crushed. He died from lack of oxygen to the lungs."

Angela buried her face in her hands and wept.

I stood up in desperation and saw the door to the men's room. I made for it. I found a sink and splashed my face with cold water. I looked at myself in the mirror. I gave Angela a few more minutes before exiting the bathroom and heading back to the table.

"This is off the record," I said. "Would you testify in court?"

"To what?" she asked, begrudging me the abruptness of the request. "I can't really ascertain what actually happened."

"It's clear, isn't it? Facecrusher, in danger from the gogoplata, squeezed the Ezekiel on Charles and held it for too long."

"I'm not sure that was his intention. He looked to be locked in place by Charles's ankle and hands."

"I'll have you know this. I would never divulge this, but my client has had a setback in court. She is being counter-sued by the defendant, who's saying he was compelled to do what he did. Physically put in a situation where, in order to preserve his own life, he had to follow through with the technique. And he's claiming that Volkenrath was aware of this and chose not to let up. That Charles continued anyway, in a conscious effort to at least get submitted, and at the most, get killed."

Angela remained silent for some time. She looked up at me. "Suicide by jiu-jitsu."

I didn't say a thing. I had nothing to say.

CHAPTER EIGHT

Intent isn't everything. It has to share elbow room with outcome. In a court of law, the sentencing of a defendant is determined by a sliding scale of both.

For Craig 'Facecrusher' Farrell to counter-sue, much of the focus got put on Charles Volkenrath's psychology. The defendant claimed he has suffered financial woes from the incident's fallout, not being able to get a fight booked because of the stigma, warranted or not. He also claimed that he has suffered emotional setbacks from the ordeal. He had not expressly denied choking Volkenrath. He had claimed that he had been compelled to do so in a picture-perfect predicament of kill-or-be-killed.

No one would ever know what Volkenrath's true intention was that early afternoon in the cage. Was it simply a contested sparring session gotten out of hand? Either of the two may have gotten overzealous with performing their respective techniques. It happened often in jiu-jitsu circles. A giddiness to finish a slick move, which you've been working on for weeks, maybe even months, to land on someone, gives way to the concern that you may not get a similar setup again anytime soon.

"What would you have done in Facecrusher's shoes?" I asked Mazagon. We were on our way in my car to go talk to Ronnie Parrish.

Mazagon pressed a foot on the glove compartment, perhaps feeling the panic from imagining being ensnared in a rubber guard. "I'd have let Charles tire his legs out, then break out. And eventually smash-pass his guard. Or knee-cut."

We ran through a third cycle of an intersection. I tore open a bag of sunflower seeds and poured a baseball's worth into my palm. "How about if you were in Volkenrath's shoes, being threatened with that Ezekiel choke?"

"That's a hard choke to defend. I've only been hit with it twice. It's uncommon to begin with. By the time you identify it as an Ezekiel, it's kind of too late. So, I'd have tapped."

"In a friendly rolling session," I said, readying a Dixie cup in which to spat the hulls. "And in a life or death scenario?"

"I'd probably still tap," Mazagon said. He finally looked over at me. His response surprised me. From the winsome look in his eyes, he looked surprised himself.

We moved a few feet west on Sunset Blvd. The sun shot through two high rises, blinding us. Is that radiance what Volkenrath saw before he lost consciousness for the last time? Or did everything go black?

"What do you see when you refuse to tap or don't tap soon enough when getting choked out?" I tossed the wad of sunflower seeds into my mouth.

"Not much of anything, I guess," Mazagon said. "White noise, maybe. Or I don't see anything. Everything just fades."

It was revealing to have my assistant, a jiu-jitsu nerd if ever there was one, admit to his own vulnerability unto the art that he practiced. No one, not even the most highly decorated coral belt, was bigger than the art. Just like no one was above death.

A tsunami of salt crashed onto my tongue. Death would be the ultimate jiu-jitsu practitioner. Expert in all techniques, he never tapped himself. He was as indomitable as the blinding sun that took forever to set.

As we drove through Beverly Hills, I brushed off sunflower seed hulls from my lap. Mazagon helped himself to a handful.

Ronnie Parrish seemed like a good-enough young man, but I intended to marionette him somewhat. He was the link between Facecrusher and the eco-terrorists at Sadistic CGI. Whether by cajoling him through the gateway topic of music or by legal threats, I meant to get him to spill the beans on Kyler's and AI Charles Manson's involvement.

How high did it all go? Was Len Greenfield involved? Drillbit? How about Professor Ø? Why did Charles Volkenrath's sponsorship with Go Guerrilla elapse? Who willingly let it do so? I'd call Moira first thing tomorrow. She had a few things to answer for.

Once we shot up Laurel Canyon, the sunlight behaved differently. Maybe it was the trees. The great giver of life held a reserved regard for the rich, blessing the neighborhoods of estates and acreage a grudging effulgence, not wanting to invest too much illumination in a tinder-choked paradise that could go up in flames at any moment. I shot toward the Parrish residence as Daryl Pennington called me.

I put the phone on loudspeaker, resting it in the cupholder. "Yeah?"

"I've got your two boys from Studio City down here with me. Come to find out, they're behind the new Manson family. All of it's a ruse to get things going between the meat eaters and the haybreaths."

"For moral reasons or monetary gain?"

"Dunno," Pennington aid. "Possibly both. If you can get people alienated from factory farming and such, they tend to go green. These bozos have inadvertently alluded to Facecrusher being at Barker Ranch. Only thing is, each time he's been there, he's been accompanied by a meat eater guy who mines borax."

"Unethical Ted," I blurted out, spitting sunflower seeds along with the name.

"Beg your pardon? Paisley, still there?"

"Yes, I am here. The borax guy. That explains the moniker. Unethical Ted. Why, if he eats meat, would they tolerate him?"

"It appears, at least to these two knuckleheads, that the guy's their bugger sugar supplier. Sells it to them dirt-cheap. How's he manage to undercut everyone else? With the borax."

"He's cutting cocaine with borax?" I wondered aloud. Mazagon swiped his head my way. Unethical, indeed. "Not hard to imagine those hippies losing brain cells by the billions each time he shows up."

"He may be on Go Guerrilla's payroll, if that's the case. Either way, as long as those kids are blissed out, they'll eat half-digested cow cuds."

I almost ran a red light, but Mazagon alerted me by shaking my right shoulder. I slammed on the brakes. I grew upset—more at the revelation than at my negligence behind the wheel. "I've got a jiu-jitsu instructor named Angela telling me that Volkenrath could have killed himself on the mat that day. Voluntarily getting himself choked out through this odd, pretzel-like configuration."

"Suicide by jiu-jitsu," Pennington whispered, a eureka moment for him too.

"Maybe," I said. "And maybe not." Mazagon alerted me that the light turned green. "Listen," I said, jutting my chin down at the phone, eyes alert to the traffic. "I gotta go. Driving like shit. I'm going to wrap up the Facecrusher/Barker Ranch thing as we speak."

"Holler," he said and hung up.

I drove on up to Mulholland Drive and turned right. "Why don't I make you drive?" I asked Mazagon.

"I don't drive," he said, not bothering to look over at me as if such menial activity were beneath him.

"Why is that?" I asked, spat hulls into the cup.

"My mother never taught me," he said, shrugging.

Moira Volkenrath called me up and reminded me I had told her I had boxed when younger. Could I hold mitts for her today? She needed the therapy. What the hell, I figured I'd let the Ronnie Parrish angle stew a bit. I busted a U-turn at a vista point commanding a marvelous view of LA and began the drive to drop off Mazagon.

She arrived at the office alone. I got nervous that I'd do something as irresponsible as fall in love. I had to stay vigilant.

"Where's the little one?" I asked as she walked through the door. She had a gym bag slung over her shoulder; black spats and matching sports bra; a midriff that, never mind . . .

"At my mom's," she said. Her coming over was a way of escaping domestic heartache, and there I was summoning it up.

I'd let her blow off some steam, then riddle her with questions regarding Charles.

"So," she said, "who's your favorite boxer?" She tossed me a pair of gloves. She slid on some focus mitts.

"I don't have an absolute favorite," I said, ripping apart the usually dead-silent atmosphere of my office by tearing the Velcro of the gloves' hook-and-loops. "The four horsemen from the 80s. Duran, Leonard, Hearns, Hagler. Used to watch them with my grandpa as he strummed his acoustic guitar. Nowadays? Lomachenko. How can one not? And Canelo Alvarez. Weird about Alvarez."

"What's weird?" she asked, holding the mitts, facing me for a one-two.

"How it's hip to hate on him," I said. "Especially my Mexican buddies." Pop-pop.

"How so?"

"He does many things in his fights that others only manage to do in practice. Like slipping after a straight right, or body jab followed by a rear uppercut. Simple stuff. Basic stuff, but money."

She lost track of the conversation, seeming to forget how to hold mitts as well.

"Something the matter?" I asked, letting the gloves drape to my sides.

"I guess I didn't expect you to be this good," she said. "No offense, but every time some random dude says he knows how to fight, he ends up being clueless."

"I can let my hands go," I said. "Not sure I'd call it fighting. I rolled in jiu-jitsu for the first time a few days ago and I got demolished."

She held her left mitt up. I cracked a left hook. Her eyes widened as she smiled. "Yeah, but you can catch someone coming in if you've got hands. A puncher's chance. I prefer to stand and bang myself."

"How's your grappling?" I asked, slipping a jab to the outside and popping a cross-double left hook.

"I'd strangle you," she said and laughed.

I didn't have a clever comeback. One, she was likely right. Two, her laugh rang out with the merry promise of living in the moment.

We worked up a sweat, taking turns holding mitts. On her last turn, flushed with perspiration, panting but keeping at it, she destroyed my hands. She had a nice economy to her striking. Not particularly heavy-handed, she was a volume puncher. A look of wanting to punch

CRUSHED TRACHEA BLUES 143

through to a future where the specter of her dead husband didn't exist took hold of her as she unloaded on the combo's last punch.

I took the mitts off and shook the pain from my hands.

"I could stand to do this a few times a week," she said, wiping her forehead with a towel.

"Say the word," I said. I almost did the dumbass move of telling her I had enrolled in boxing classes at the gym where Charles met his maker.

"Pizza?" she offered, uncoiling the wrap from her right hand.

"That'd be tremendous," I said. I was hungry. I was also hungry for insight—insight into Blitz's mind.

If there was a time to broach the subject of the erstwhile welterweight's take on life, it was right before she was about to indulge in the best comfort food on the planet.

"Did you and he practice jiu-jitsu often?" I asked, undoing my own wraps.

Without looking up at me, she said, "Plenty." She began uncoiling the wrap from her other hand. "He was underrated on the mat. He outstruck and outwrestled his opponents to such a degree that the fans never got to see his creativity on the ground. He had a knack for getting guys in the truck."

"I don't know what that is. Is it related to the rubber guard?"

She stopped unwrapping her hand. The red ribbon of cloth dangled like a helix impatiently waiting for its double. "No," she said, looking over at me, brow once more flushed with sweat. "Not even close. Why?"

My tactic to bracket the interrogation with sessions of norepinephrine rushing to her brain didn't work. I went for broke. "I need to know something. What would you rate Charles's happiness level, on a scale of one to ten?"

She shook her head, incredulous. "What does that have to do with anything, Mr. Fuentes?"

I didn't budge. "Look. I know everyone loved him, that he had few if any enemies. I just want to know, were things good at home?"

"Of course," she said. Her face was a hybrid of annoyance and disbelief. "We fought like all married couples do. He was a great husband and father. Our son meant everything to him. He'd have given up fighting for his boy."

I bit the bullet. "Are you sure about that?" Had to.

She shook her head again. She was about to explode into saying something, but her brain didn't know what caliber of ammunition to load her mouth with. She shook her head again.

"I'm sorry to put you through this, Moira," I said. "You know how competitive fighters can be. I'm not saying he willfully let what happened to him happen, but in the heat of the moment, no one wants to tap, especially if there's a chance that he can nail down a slick submission on the other guy. Risky, I know. But that's the fight game."

"I can't believe I'm hearing this." She began shoving her stuff into her gym bag. "Call me Mrs. Volkenrath, by the way. You and I are not on first-name terms. You work for me, remember?"

"I work for myself," I said.

"I hired you to establish intent on Facecrusher, not to raise the asinine possibility that my husband had a death wish."

"Intent is always difficult to precisely determine. It's not as cut and dry as outcome. Look, you have to be frank with me. Was Charles a rubber guard player in the gym?"

"What have you been doing all this time?" she erupted. "I can barely afford you and you're asking me about the rubber guard?"

"You don't get it. Rubber guard, gogoplata, Ezekiel choke. This is all new shit to me. I barely know armbar and rear naked choke. And I'm still trying to find out what makes it naked."

She calmed down a bit. I could see the terms gogoplata and Ezekiel choke bounce around behind her eyes.

I humored her by sighing. "I'd never dealt with a case as twisted as this one. I usually rummage through working husbands' dirty laundry or, if lucky, help an insurance investigator on a more fraught case."

"Do you house any alcohol?" Moira asked, looking at me with bone-dry eyes she had reset.

"With Squirt or straight?" I asked, heading toward the cupboard in my miniature kitchen.

"Squirt," she said loudly, her voice's trajectory bending around the corner. "Since I intend to keep it cruising."

I made two *palomas* and came back to hand her one. She placed her towel on the seat and sat down on it. It was her time to sigh.

We synchronized our sips. I wiped my mouth. She didn't. Laminated in sweat and heartbreak, she let the sugar and tequila dance around her lips. "He had an obsessive personality, I guess. Once his mind latched onto something, he couldn't let it go. Luckily, this tended toward positive things, like working on a new technique, practicing mindfulness tricks, or teaching our son his ABCs. He spent months on his spinning wheel kick, for instance."

"His last obsession being the rubber guard?"

She took another sip, licked her lips. "Yeah."

"Correct me if I'm wrong," I said, "but you don't seem too enthused about that."

She looked over at me. "I don't question its efficacy. It's really quite nifty. A good rubber guard player is tough to deal with. I question the philosophy of getting there in the first place."

"I don't follow," I said. I knew exactly what she said, but I knew she couldn't help herself when it came to discussing her passion for fighting, and the philosophy thereof.

"To willingly go to your back in the first place seems wrongheaded. I don't know. That's just me."

"Seems like a passive way to fight," I said. "Though maybe just unorthodox. Like a predator luring its prey into its lair."

She smiled. "Yes. True. But Charles was more of a tiger. It therefore didn't suit him."

"Wouldn't you say that a good guard would make him more versatile, and therefore more dangerous?"

"Yes and no," she said and took a long sip of her *paloma*.

"Yes, insofar as, like I said, more versatile. And how no?"

She cleared her throat. "Every fighter has his peak, in terms of age and in terms of performance. Age-wise, he was in his prime. But I maintain he was in his physical peak and should not have resorted to training off his back so much. Charles's game relied on explosiveness and agility. Blitzing in and outworking his opponent. He was a pressure fighter."

I took a generous sip of my drink. I felt good. Finally, after maybe a month of emotional doldrums, I was doing all right. "But what if someone were to say he wished to be good at everything? Like Musashi said, 'To know the way broadly is to know all things'?"

"I never bought that Musashi shit," Moira said, topping her blasphemy off by downing her drink.

"What part? That you can be good at everything?"

"That," she said, spinning the empty glass on the table. "I get what homeboy from feudal Japan was saying, but I think it's often wrong. To be a true expert at something, a specialist, requires letting other things go."

"But the beauty of MMA," I said, "is that the fighters strive to be good at everything."

"Therein lies the challenge," she said. "How to strike the right balance. Sometimes being a specialist works. Sometimes it doesn't. But to be a specialist in more than one discipline is asking a lot from the universe. There's a sliding scale when becoming an expert in more than one thing."

"What would you say of someone who is great at jiu-jitsu as well as chess? The two disciplines complement each other well." I finished my drink.

"It's possible to be great at both, I guess, but that would be at the expense of being truly great at one or the other. It's the curse of the renaissance man." She held the empty glass up to me.

I grabbed it and stood up. "A combat sports renaissance man would be an MMA fighter." I walked to the kitchen.

"Yes," her voice called out. "And the belt goes to the best renaissance man."

I handed her a fresh drink. "So you begrudged him his attention to the rubber guard, or jiu-jitsu in general?"

She took a giant gulp of her second drink. This time, she wiped her mouth. "I begrudged him on how he got his instruction." She looked up at me for a long while. I got fidgety having those pretty brown widow's eyes burning lasers through me. I shifted my gaze to the opaque haze of my drink. "Or to put it better," she said, "I begrudged him whom he got it from."

When I looked up at her to find a tear escaping her eye, I looked back down. The momentum of the conversation shifted. I had no license to even breathe audibly.

I always found it curious how coed jiu-jitsu called for the tacit agreement that, despite extremely physical, almost intimate, configurations, the furtherance of romance is absolutely taboo. No-gi jiu-jitsu would seem problematic, especially for the guys. To entwine with an attractive woman whose rashguard and spats showcased her physical attributes required a level of Platonic concentrations—or denial—that I sure wasn't capable of.

And then I thought of Charles Volkenrath and Angela Vicksburg, and the floor fell away from me completely. I grew dizzy. I felt the legs of my chair give way. I held onto my drink for dear life, like a man overboard clutching a life preserver. I emptied the glass in one sustained chug. My vision blurred as the tequila burned my throat.

Once my sight cleared up and I regained my balance, there was Moira staring right at me. "You are now morally obligated to get me drunk," she said.

Being a moral person in a land named for celestial beings that it was totally devoid of, I did just that.

"I don't blame either of them," she said. Her speaking had officially crossed into slurring. "Honestly. I don't. If I were she, and had him on top of me while I showed him crackhead control, I'd have craned my neck up and planted a kiss on his mouth."

I had dug out my reserve bottle of silver. It had enough for one drink apiece. I was cutting her off after that.

"Have you seen her?" she asked, looking at me with squinting eyes that read, *Of course, you have. And of course, you'd fuck her.*

"I have," I said. "Just last week. At a Studio City office."

"And?" she asked.

"And what?"

"What did you think?" she mumbled into her glass as she entered the contents into her throat without taking her eyes off me.

"She's quite attractive," I said. I didn't move.

CRUSHED TRACHEA BLUES

She looked at me for a long time, battling back emotions. "Who do you think is hotter?" she asked. "She or I?"

"I think that beautiful comes in all shapes and sizes," I said. "You're both beautiful in your own ways. I know this. You're a complete fighter and you'd easily beat her ass."

"That's not what I asked," she said, eyebrows bunched together. "If I let you have me right now, would that give me the edge?"

I shot up out of my seat. "That's quite enough." I grabbed her glass and the bottle of silver and the bottle of grapefruit soda and took them to the fridge. I came back and said, "I don't fool around with clients. Here I am, feeling heartbroken for you and your boy, and you're trying to turn me from a private detective into a male hooker."

She came at me. I felt her head bury into my upper left ribs and her hands wrap around the backs of my thighs. She drove me straight back. I felt the hard floor crash against the back of my head.

Chapter Nine

Better to have one and never need to use it, they say, than to need one and not have it. I drove to Legion MMA on a full night's rest. Traffic was horrendous—everyone cutting everyone else off—but I was one with the universe. I hated guns, but I agreed.

It looked like I would actually make the boxing class on time. This meant a grueling fifteen minutes of sprints outside in the back alley, flipping of tractor tires, and box jumps.

I hadn't shot a gun since pops took me out by Barstow, in high school. I preferred working without one. A Delphic nightmare warned me one humid summer night that my own heat would be used against me. I wasn't superstitious, but the dream scared the bejesus out of me.

I had enough of a time cushion to park in a spot by backing in. Learn how to box, they said, in case you needed to defend yourself.

The sprints were fine, the tire-flippings kind of enjoyable, and the box jumps tolerable—all because I began ruminating on the very idea of martial arts. Choreography for paranoiacs. All of it.

We did slipping and pivoting drills, all defensive-minded. Defense accounted for fifty percent of a fight, yet people didn't train it fifty percent of the time. Best way to make out well in a street fight is to not get hit. Slip, dip, duck. No cracked metacarpals or lawsuits. Even the most egregious, damage-inflicting technique is ultimately defensive-minded.

I sparred; did well. I ate a few stiff jabs. After a few minutes, learning to control my breathing, I began slipping the jab. I then countered. I couldn't find the matrix, so I brought the matrix to me. What a strange skill-set, learning how to fight. Making a hobby out of it, even stranger. You may need to defend yourself someday, they said, so learn how to inflict damage on a person's cranium or rib cage with your hands. In this age where there's an app for everything, and shortcuts to nirvana, I understood the gun nuts.

Jiu-jitsu is great for little girls, they said. It provides wonderful rape defense. I got it. A sad statement on society, really, but I got it.

I extrapolated the philosophy of martial arts. I should start taking poisoning classes. How to kill people with strychnine, cyanide, arsenic. My instructor will be a third-degree black belt of the Borgia lineage, traced straight back to fifteenth-century Rome.

Go to the gun range every weekend. Just in case. Just. In. Case. Conceal and carry. Sidepiece under the arm. Just. In. Case. Not cowardice, not paranoia. Just a reconciliation with reality. I got it. I hated it, but I got it.

In order to handle the grueling boxing circuit, I had to wipe clean the chalked-up chicken-scratch from the blackboard slate of my brain. It wasn't a matter of making mental room in order to focus on technique and for what Ernie Reyes called for, so much as I needed more hard-drive space to allow my body to go through the motions. Piecing together a package of Craig 'Facecrusher' Farrell's intentions that I could present to Moira, who could then present it in court, had been tiring business.

I reset by breathing mindfully. Slip, pop. Slip, pop.

In an alternate universe where it was socially acceptable to hit a lady, I imagined catching the widow on the chin with a few. I understood why she had shot in for a power double and dumped me on my ass. She was riled up and drunk—both being my fault. But she didn't bother to follow up with a *mea culpa*. As far as I was concerned, she was still my client. Plus, I was in too deep now. I couldn't afford to walk away at this point. I had boxing lessons and quality tequila to pay for.

I skipped rope with a speed rope. I tried nailing the crossovers. I kept whipping my lower legs with the PVC. It stung. I'd get pissed off and slam the rope to the mat. A group of kids whispered among themselves, stealing glances over at me. The only thing worse than my skipping skills would be my attitude.

"Hey," I called over to them.

"Wuzzup," asked the eldest, a Latino boy probably still in high school. In an admirable display of protective big brother, he walked over to me to ask me what my business was.

I side-swung the rope. "Any of you boys can help an old man with crossovers? Been trying to nail them down for two weeks."

The boy had effeminate, indeed pretty, eyelashes. His dark eyes lit up as he smiled. "I got you." He jogged over to a wall from which dangled ropes of all makes and sizes. He came back with a weighted rope and began skipping. "You got to exaggerate the reach-down," he said, demonstrating. "Gorilla arms. Way down."

I did just that. What do you know? It worked. I felt a deep sense of accomplishment. More than solving a case, even. The last nifty thing I had learned in my adulthood was how to open a bottle of beer with my left bottom molar. And that cost me a root canal.

What a splendid thing, the acquisition of a skill. I got into a nice rhythm, skipping to the hip-hop on the speakers. I got happy, suddenly. My brain had forgotten how to handle that level of serotonin. I therefore pushed the pace to sneak a little lung-ache in.

That Moira hated on the legendary samurai Miyamoto Musashi didn't upset or even surprise me. Guy seemed like a blowhard, come to think of it. But what he was most known for muttering rung true. *To know the way broadly is to know all things.* I liked sucking at a given thing because it allowed me to appreciate those who took the time to excel at it. And I got to wondering, working my coordination and footwork with the rope in synchronization with the other boxers: Did they ever wonder what it would be like to be able to throw a good roundhouse kick? How about a downward elbow? A switch-knee? Curious, to be such a savage with the hands and still willfully pretend like no other sets of techniques to inflict damage on an opponent existed.

Same for the karate guys. Same for a judoka. How about a coral belt on the ground who can't throw a jab to save his life? Like Mazagon. Like Angela Vicksburg. Her own theories on martial strategy weren't without merit. I looked over at the cage in the back of the gym. The scene of the crime. That it had not been roped off, quarantined, or at least torn down was a tacit refusal to acknowledge that anything horrible had happened; a shoulder-shrugging *oh, well.*

I got a creepy feeling every time I gazed over at it. All mental weakness, I know, but I couldn't help it. It's not as if some molecular residue remained when a tragedy occurred. What constituted a tragedy, really? *Say, Fellow carbon molecules, Shall we linger for all eternity or until an exorcism shoos us away? What say you: Yay? Nay?*

Three or four young ladies were messing with a line of kettlebells that sat on the near edge of the cage. They paid the bad juju no mind. The upbeat music made it all okay. Just a place to work out in.

Two fighter-looking dudes entered the cage door and rolled in the darkness. They started in seated guard, playing an elaborate death match of footsie.

One of the guys was Drillbit. I stopped breathing and therefore missed the rope at my feet. I hopped over to the far-right of the rope-skipping phalanx, shielding myself from the ring, lest he recognize up-and-coming boxer Marcus Dunlop slumming it with a bunch of inner-city kids. The two men stopped rolling to discuss some technique. They looked our way.

I slung the rope over my neck and headed toward my gym bag.

"*Güero*," said Ernie Reyes, wearing a belly bag. "Where you going? We still have body-shots to work in. *No te rajes*. Don't tell me you're tired."

"*Emergencia*, coach," I said.

"*Ah, pues*," Ernie said, waddling away in disappointment.

I drove straight to the office to shower up and fetch a Gluten-Free Rooter van to come back in.

Araceli was at the office, mopping the floor. Araceli and her peanut-shaped body. More marriage proposals. I blew her off and got epithets in Spanish hurled at me like volleys of lava. Everything she did thereafter bore a grudge—every countertop swipe, every cobweb dusting, even cleaning the dirty shot glasses. No time to argue. I'd threaten to fire her next time.

By the time I made it back to Legion MMA in my green Gluten-Free Rooter livery, a whole new set of people were there. Boxing, cardio kickboxing, and amateur muay thai were over with. Pro class was in session. The fighters were drilling takedowns off of striking feints.

There was no one rolling in the cage in the back. The activity there earlier may as well have been a fatigue-induced hallucination.

"Buddy," Pete Branford said, "I'd appreciate it if you phoned ahead of time. Can't have you showing up here unannounced." He wore a black nutrition supplement T-shirt. Its tightness attested to the company's efficacy, steroid-free or not.

"It's fine," I said in my diffident alto. "I won't be turning the water off. All follow-ups merely include a flush optimization assessment and a pH test."

"PH test?" Branford wondered. "For what? Make sure my athletes are shitting alkaline?"

I suppressed a laugh. "Actually—"

"Last time I checked, that pH balancing of your blood through eating alkaline-heavy foods is horseshit. Can't influence something that your kidneys regulate, anyway."

I held up an admonishing finger. "True for the human body. But not true for a plumbing infrastructure. Though copper piping is the best that modern plumbing offers, there is some oxidation that directly results from meat consumption entering the system and thereby cruising a hyper-acidic infrastructure. Luckily, we at GFR have chemicals to offset this. Not least of which is, you guessed it, apple cider vinegar."

Branford looked askance at me, a skeptical smirk on his face. "Gotta be fucking kidding me."

"I mean, it's apple cider vinegar mixed with hydrogen chloride. This performs the dual task of balancing the pH level of the plumbing and breaking down any extant mini-clogs, stubborn, barnacle-like obstructions clinging to the pipes. After that, I would recommend septic yoga. I know it seems like a lot of work, but really—"

"W-w-wait," Branford interrupted, smiled and squinting. "Did you just say *septic yoga*?"

"You'd be surprised to learn that there are parts of a plumbing system, or at least a sound one, that correspond to the chakras. Where you have the heart chakra, a simple schematic would have an elbow trap. Simple things like child's pose and sun salutations are equivalent to Zen flushing."

"Zen flushing?" Branford asked, hands on hips. "Dufuq is Zen flushing?"

"Here's the issue. And a lot of negativity starts here. When a person flushes, they tend to lower the lever with malice. Almost like they're begrudging the toilet's work of taking away a dark part of themselves. This is true in a sense, but it does no one any good to rid of our own waste with a sense of shame. Since all things come from the earth, so do all things return to the earth. There's nothing to be ashamed of. The toilet is a sentinel standing before the pearly gates of paradise. So is a urinal. It's much preferable to rid of the waste with a celebratory attitude. It bears a direct influence on the plumbing. This is the foundation of Zen flushing."

"You're not proposing that my athletes take a Zen flushing seminar, are you?"

"No. I'm simply asking that they feel gratitude when ridding of their waste. It goes a very long way."

"Yeah, because, from what I recall, your being here was a simple follow-up. I can't ask my guys with all their pent-up aggression to bliss out when saying bye-bye to their dookies."

I laughed. "Do you not feel a sense of contentment during and after the elimination of waste?"

"During and after kicking you out of my gym?" Branford quipped. I liked him. Despite an acerbic personality, he had more patience than his ripped arms let on. I'd have given me the boot some time ago.

"I'll just flush the ACV and hydrogen chloride mix, let it sit for about an hour, and be on my way for good."

"Bro," Branford said, head apologetically to one side. "Sorry. No offense. But running green bathrooms here is the worst place to do it. I mean, my flagship fighter suffered poor performances from switching to a vegan diet. That's only the start of it. No offense. I imagine you're of that dietary persuasion. I'm not about to create an eating list for my fighters in order to appease some pipes under the floorboards."

"Understood, Mr. Branford. Understood." I adjusted my baseball cap by the bill.

"Hey," he said. "Give me some of your business cards. I'll pass them out. I'll even throw in a week free of classes. You pick the class."

I stood straight up. "You know, I've always wanted to try that Brazilian kojudo."

He chuckled. "You mean Brazilian jiu-jitsu."

"Yes," I said, smacking my forehead and crossing my eyes.

"We don't offer that here. Used to. We're now exclusively a striking academy."

"Where do your MMA people train that discipline, then? I thought I saw a few guys back there in the cage last time I was here. They were rolling on the ground and stuff."

His eyes shifted over to the spot in question. He looked back at me. "They train jiu-jitsu at other places of their choosing. We used to have an affiliate. Business-minded differences."

"Well, I know it's popular nowadays. My brother-in-law used to do the kojudo here. Did it for a year, but didn't get along with the instructor, I guess. Who knows why? My brother-in-law is a hothead."

"What's his name?" Branford asked.

"Brent Mercurio," I said.

"Can't say I recall the name."

"So what exactly happened with the affiliate?" From my own end zone, in danger of being sacked for a safety, down by six.

Branford cleared his throat. "I don't wish to get into it. How about muay thai? The most effective striking system on the planet."

"Mooey tie? Like, bovine knot-making?"

That broke the ice. Branford laughed. He patted me on the back. "When you're done, hit me up, yeah?" He turned to go.

"I'll get on this, then," I said, nodding toward the men's room.

Branford turned back around. "And don't forget those business cards."

Like I said: I liked him. He was a swell guy running a tough business. The longevity of MMA gyms was not favorable. Kids' programs were where the money was at. Legion MMA had kids boxing, muay thai, and Tae Kwon Do.

It therefore upset me to hear him ten minutes later in the bathroom. I was pouring some apple cider vinegar down a toilet in the farthest stall when he walked in, engaged in a conversation on his phone. He stopped at a urinal and upped his voice's volume to be heard over the echoing stream of pee that he fired into the porcelain.

"This BB thing's got to go away, man," he said. Silence for a while. "We've got to remove it all from the website. How the fuck is it still on the class schedule? I mean, c'mon, man. Unprofessional."

I breathed in complete silence. He continued: "We're missing out on all kinds of revenue, not having BJJ anymore. It's bullshit." Silence. "I don't care, Weston."

Weston Murphy was the strength and conditioning coach at Legion MMA. Probably Branford's business partner.

"Fuck BB, man. What's he gonna do on his own? Without the Dane's pocketbook, he's just a guy with no real fight experience. I'm sick of it, Weston. His guys showing up and rolling? Almost like they're fetishizing the space."

More silence. He flushed again, raised his voice: "Fuck that sponsor, man. Besides, the whole Facecrusher ordeal has the heat on them. Reseda PD came in a week ago, asking me about him. I had to tell them the truth. Dude trained BJJ here. If the Professor pulls his sponsorship from our guys, it would look so obvious. I say we play our card while we can. My livelihood's at stake, man. Stan is headed to Berkeley in two months. Think I care about some Maersk trust fund vegan douche threatening me?"

I heard the water from a sink, then the hand dryer, then the door open.

My business was done. I flushed the toilet for no real reason. Maybe as a metaphor for banishing the erstwhile confusion down and away. Everything had just come together with Branford's bathroom bombshell.

My self-consciousness ballooned to epic proportions when I asked for Angela Vicksburg at the Studio City office high-rise. She was currently teaching a class, Steph the receptionist said, but would be available in an hour's time. I said I'd go get lunch and come back.

I didn't eat anything. Not in the complimentary cafeteria, nor out on the street. I walked around the block three times, figuring it'd do my waistline some good. Once I detected the oncoming of sweat, I ducked inside.

"What a pleasant surprise," Angela said, beaming a smile upon recognizing me. "I thought I would never see you again."

"I had a nightmare a week ago," I said, "that that would be the case."

She bowed her head and cleared her throat. Flirting made her uncomfortable. Strange behavior from a trained assassin. I got the feeling she was one of those girls who suffered through high school all awkward—knobby-kneed and with braces—only to bloom into a goddess once college hit.

"How was class?" I asked, patting down my tie.

She tightened the scrunchie holding her ponytail. "Fine. We drilled the closed guard. Elevator sweep, T-sweep, triangle setup. Why don't you come try out a class? I could give you the rest of this month free of charge."

"Love to," I said, "provided I had the time. Finding it tough with the boxing and the murder-solving."

A tinge of anger hijacked her china doll face. "You posed as a plumber around here, didn't you?"

"I did," I said. "Often the similarities between plumbing and case-solving are striking. Like with septic systems, most societal backups are caused by pieces of shit whose unclogging can be tough work. Name's Fuentes, by the way. Paisley Fuentes."

She covered her mouth with the knuckles of her hand, looking to gag. "Do you mind if I sit down?" She had already taken one of the charcoal gray seats. We were in the lobby between the main entrance and the gym, from where she had emerged. Suddenly, I could smell the acrid sweat from her body. It wasn't unpleasant.

I took the seat to her right. "Why didn't you tell me you had gotten involved with Charles Volkenrath?" Our knees met at a right angle. So smitten by her face, I now noticed her black and gold spats and a matching rashguard. I did everything I could to keep my eyes off her. Figuring she was used to constant ogling, all I could do when caught staring was give her a smile.

"I don't see how that would have been germane to the previous query," she said, sort of snapping at me for the staring, then looking down at the floor.

"I guess I can't fault you for that," I said. "I only bring it up because my client, Charles's widow, brought it up. She envies everything about you."

Her eyes shot over at me. "If she couldn't satisfy a man like Charlie, then that was her problem. Excuse me for being desirable unto someone for once in my life."

I shook my head. "Don't play the perpetual wallflower violin for me now. If there's anything keeping the sanest man in the world from throwing himself off a bridge for you, it's because you intimidate him."

"No woman who desires to feel wanted ever finds that reassuring or sexy," she said.

"Men do, though." I said. "You've no idea."

She looked at me sternly and took a deep breath. "Do I intimidate you?"

"Yes. You do. I skipped a meal because of you."

"I would never know it by how you're speaking to me. You seem rather brazen."

"It's an act. The whole tough guy schtick is an act. It's part of my job. If ever the most timid nerd got an ounce of chutzpah, I'd be out of work."

"What works better," she asked, "twisting the knife clockwise or counter?"

"Neither," I said, smiled for her sake. "I don't even touch the knife. I'll just draw your attention to it. Uh, hello, you've got a little something there, sticking out between your ribs. Thought you might want to know."

She offered a perfunctory smile. "Your strategy is simple, then. Be direct."

"Yup. As in, How long has Craig 'Facecrusher' Farrell trained jiu-jitsu under you?"

By the look on her face, she stood at an emotional crossroads. Feeling perhaps betrayed by my own accusatory question, she looked ready to lose her cool. That would be the natural reaction. A more measured response would be to wait it out and let her turning stomach dictate her demeanor. She waited it out. Her eyes wandered as they watered up.

"Counterclockwise, usually," I said. "I was working in Australia once, and was mindful enough to go the other way."

She smiled. "He has never been my student." She wiped her eyes with the pinky side of her hand.

"The both of you lack cauliflower ear," I said, surveying the lovely question marks on the sides of her oval face. "You guys must wear the ear guards. While most fighters and MMA wannabees flaunt their cauliflower ear, to the point of even speeding up the process by self-infliction, your school has decided to prevent it. Admirable. Truly admirable. Samurai stuff there."

"A martial arts journey is something to be sacrificed for and even enjoyed. It's meant to instill self-confidence and to be enriching. It's not meant for flaunting or peacocking."

"Did you come up with that all by yourself or did BB?"

She must have gotten used to the secrets I kept lobbing up like soap bubbles because she didn't express surprise by that name.

"Let me guess," I said, "Benjamin Bradley?" I looked pensively up at the ceiling, finger to chin. "Baruch Bernstein? Orthodox Jew-Jitsu?"

"Brody Ballard," she said without looking over at me. She held her elbows with opposite hands like a child scolded with a timeout.

I decided to test her level of Kool-Aid drinking. "What would you say are BB's weaknesses as a grappler?" Left leg crossed over the right, I drummed on my shoe.

Her eyes finally dry, she looked over at me. "Speed, I guess. He's not an explosive athlete. He relies on his wits."

"Overly much, you'd say?"

"I would never say that you could rely on your wits overly much for anything. Least of all, jiu-jitsu."

Good point. "Good point," I said. "So he was no Charles Volkenrath. Charlie, to you."

Angry again. "Charles was athletic and highly intelligent at the same time."

"So why the obsession with rubber guard? Did he seem jaded by the success his career had met with? Maybe he was looking for a new challenge?"

"Something like that," she said.

"Why was his sparring session with Facecrusher filmed? I got someone to hack into Legion MMA's IP address. Most of their filming was incidental and done for security reasons. His session was filmed either on his express consent or so that he could be seen being made an example of."

"Perhaps a little of both."

"I get it. When every woman is obtainable to you and you're on top of the world, the next best thing is to go to the ground and unthaw the ice queen's heart. What better way to do that than impress her with that which she holds most dear? Almost like a cat toying with a dead mouse to show off to its owner. I get it. You're a rare bird. Charles was known for not getting hit or taking much damage. No one's going to be requesting that his brain be studied for CTE anytime soon."

"When I first met you the other day in the cafeteria, I found you charming. I was taken to you. He was many things, but he wasn't witty. I looked forward to seeing you again. Now I find you to be a rather disagreeable person."

The missing antecedent of the words him' and 'he' was a thing a lot of women in love were guilty of. Grammatically speaking, she was referring to me back and forth from the second person to the third person.

"Regarding Brody Ballard," I said. "Where do you think he ranks in the upper echelons of jiu-jitsu royalty?"

"Brody is a jiu-jitsu genius of the highest order," she said.

"You're saying he's the be-all end-all?"

"No," she said. "No one person is greater than the martial art."

"I suppose you're not going to tell me how I can get hold of him, are you?"

"I don't communicate with him any longer." She looked to be told the truth.

"Falling out?"

"You might say that."

"When was the last time you spoke to him?"

"Over two years ago. Just after he promoted me to black belt."

"Did Facecrusher train with him?"

She looked over at me again, begrudging me the question. It would only take a single syllable to answer properly, but all kinds of atomic junk jostled about inside her head. "Yes," she said.

"And Charles?"

"No," she said. "Charlie trained under me."

"What was Charles's rank?"

"I gave him his purple belt last winter."

"Do you think some sort of rivalry developed between him and Facecrusher?"

"They were different weight classes," she said. "Plus, Facecrusher was on a losing streak and had just signed with a lesser promotion."

"That I know. Was he maybe sweet on you?"

"I don't know," she said. "I don't think so. At least, I hope not."

"How about BB?"

"BB's mistress is the mat. He's a self-proclaimed asexual." She snickered a bit. A healthy sign. Even she found that to be overly prudish.

"What a dork," I said.

She shrugged. She was silent for some time. Her eyes welled up again. "Why must you keep at this? This interrogation you're subjecting me to is gut-wrenching. I just want to forget the whole thing. Please leave me be."

I sat up and placed a hand on her knee. "I'm sorry to do this. Listen, I find you to be a fascinating person. I'd never willfully harm you. But aren't you interested in restitution? In justice for his widow and that six-year-old boy?"

"That's assuming that he was indeed murdered," she said.

I shook her knee violently. "Stop playing stupid. It looks terrible on you. You know he was."

"You don't understand," she whispered. "I'm afraid for my life."

"Tell me everything and I'll get you protection." I produced Daryl Pennington's card from the inside pocket of my coat. "Tell my buddy everything you know and we'll slam shut the lid on this squirming can of worms before you can yell out, 'Pandora who?'"

"Smelt Her Dealt Her is going down," she said.

Chapter Ten

It was such a sunny spring day that, despite an unshakable hangover, I made it a point to have an outdoor lunch down a block from the office. I ordered five *al pastor* tacos and a huge Styrofoam cup of *horchata*. The joint was called El Habanero and was run by a family from Michoacán, Mexico. They had the pork rotating on a spit, complete with cross sections of pineapple. Hand-made tortillas. Tacos worth an appendectomy.

I was in the middle of the third taco—at the halfway point of the blissful meal—when I got interrupted by a pair of crusty, sagging jeans that walked up to my table.

I swallowed my food. "Beat it, kid. Flipping an arrow at an intersection is way easier. Keeps your dignity intact." I took another bite, but the pair of jeans remained in my peripheral vision. I looked up to find toxic-folk singer Ronnie Parrish looking down at me with an impatience reserved usually for those with bad bladders.

"You're early," I said, hand over my mouth, which still chewed.

"We couldn't wait," he said. He had a guitar case slung over his right shoulder. Dangling over his left shoulder was a hand.

It belonged to his sister. She popped out from behind him with the explosiveness of a jack-in-the-box. "Remember me?" she asked, beaming a smile as wide and arching as a slice of watermelon. Her lively eyes looked like those of someone who has never been tired, who is wholly unfamiliar with fatigue.

"How can I forget?" I said, wiping my mouth with a napkin. "Eunice, right?" She was stunningly pretty. Her age was hard to determine. She could be fifteen or thirty. "How old are you?"

"Twenty-five," she said. That age didn't make any sense. She looked much younger than an older girl who looked only twenty-five.

"Have you guys eaten?" I asked. There was a concerned look between the two. "No offense if you find the present establishment anathema to your belief system. There's a salad place four doors down."

"We're starving," Ronnie said, adjusting the shoulder strap of the guitar case.

"Parents don't feed you?" I joked.

"We spent all our weekly allowance on Hot Pockets and oatmeal," Eunice said. "All gone."

Ronnie shot her an admonitory look. Beverly Hills paupers. Not unheard of.

"Where your folks at?" I asked Ronnie directly.

"Evading the authorities, as usual," he said. "No idea."

I wiped my hands with my napkin and took two twenties out of my wallet. "Order all that you want," I said, holding the bills out.

Eunice snatched them out of my hand and skipped toward the door to El Habanero. My eyes followed her in. She wore hip-hugging jeans and a pink T-shirt showing an inch of midriff. Ronnie caught me leering.

I tried to change the subject. "Since musical artists make peanuts from the streaming sites, how do you make ends meet when the folks' allowance runs out?"

Ronnie took a seat and set his guitar case down on the sidewalk. "You were just looking at it."

I crumpled the napkin and slammed it soundlessly down onto my plate. He and I watched it bloom like a feeble origami flower.

"I just got full suddenly," I said.

"You're well below the cutoff, age-wise. We'd never expect you to feed us." He leaned down to unlatch the guitar case. Oh, brother. Here we go.

I took a sip from my *horchata*. "At least until you get some studio time to cut an album and sell a few of those artifacts called CDs?"

He gingerly lifted a black Ovation acoustic and placed it on his lap. He gave it a cursory strum. "This city wasn't founded on just aerospace and moving pictures."

"'Nice to know that the world's oldest profession can nail you a plot on the hills," I said.

"Second-oldest," he said, flamenco-picking his instrument.

"Oh? What's the oldest, then?"

His hand left the fretboard and backhanded the sky.

"At least you keep it in the family, I guess. Though I'd hate to think there was dipping the pen in company ink."

Ronnie began chicken-picking the strings. "I saw how at our place you eyed me when I slapped her on the ass. I'll assure you it's entirely fraternal. Just big brother saying, 'Get after it, Tiger!'"

I let the matter die. "So why the hurry to contact me? Angela Vicksburg thought you'd be less than forthcoming." I lifted the crumpled napkin from the remaining two tacos and flicked the plate his way.

He eyed it like a T-Rex tripping over a stegosaurus. He leaned over the guitar and went to town on the tacos, double-fisting them. "Angela," he said after some time. "She's so naïve that it's literally charming. She belongs in the nineteenth century."

He was right. "How was she as a coach?"

"Great," he said, mouth full of *al pastor* meat. "Hell of a grappler. I had a crush on her since forever."

I was about to told him that made two of us, but thought better of it. "Your sister, she grapple?"

Ronnie chuckled, which caused him to briefly choke on his food. "Yes, but not martial arts."

I shook my head. "You don't think she'd be well served to learn how to throw up a triangle to a guy on top of her, should things go south?"

"I'm always nearby," he said, polishing off the taco in his left hand, not bothering to look up at me.

"What does she do for fun?" I asked. "Don't you think she deserves to go on a quest for prince charming like every girl her age?"

He stopped eating to look up at me. "You're awfully concerned with her. If I didn't know any better, I'd say you're infatuated."

"Concerned is all. I find the thing heartbreaking. What's she doing all day when not earning you studio time? Snapchat? Boolean algebra?"

"I thought you brought me here to discuss Smelt Her Dealt Her?"

"I did. I just didn't expect two whacked-out worldviews for the price of one."

Eunice returned with two plates crammed with tacos and two more plates of quesadillas. A waitress followed her out with four Mexican Coke bottles. Eunice smiled at me and lost herself in a quesadilla. She darted her mouth away at the contact with the scorching hot cheese but kept at it like a honey badger toying with a cobra.

Ronnie put his guitar away and pressed himself in tight against the table. He unfolded a napkin and tucked it into his shirt collar. Seeing there were at least a dozen tacos, he didn't double-fist it this time.

I meant to let them finish eating before broaching the subject of Smelt Her Dealt Her, but Ronnie took the initiative. "Even if meat were morally wrong, I'd still eat it." He looked up at me and rolled his eyes from the pleasure.

I got his train of thought. "Never tried kicking the carrion, eh?"

"Hell, no," he said. "Eunice, stand up."

She stood up.

"Demo," Ronnie said. Eunice twirled. Ronnie spanked her on her admittedly shapely behind. "No tofu in the world is going to create something like that." He snickered at me. "That's 100% pure Angus beef booty. God inspected, brother approved."

Lacking all self-consciousness, Eunice had already sat down and found her way to the plate of tacos. They looked like tiny corpses strewn side by side.

I took a sip from my *horchata*. "Do you know what this concerns? Not the whole Go Guerrilla/Manson family nexus, but the reason I'm so interested?"

"I guess you never told me," Ronnie said. He stopped eating to address me. He brushed back bangs from his forehead. "If Angela had called me to tell me you wanted to speak to me but didn't want to return to my house, then I figured two things. One, it involved jiu-jitsu, which I remember was sort of the focus the first time we met. And two, you're paranoid at this point and don't trust anyone. But it's cool. It's cool."

"To be fair, I was waiting at my office. Paranoid, me? For sure. Maybe more than most. But not enough to carry a gun on me."

"Same here," Ronnie said. "I hate firearms. I support the right to own them. What, only cops get to tote the heat? Come on, man. But I don't like them. In a way, I'd rather take my chances of trusting the universe a bit. If I applied the same paranoia to the dangers of driving, I'd never go anywhere."

"What did Angela tell you? Was she scared? For herself? For you?"

"She told me she would be unavailable in the indefinite future. And that she wanted me to tell you everything about Smelt Her Dealt Her."

"Why didn't you tell me about it before?" I asked. I took another sip from my *horchata*. It gurgled. Empty. Damn it. I hated that.

"Sticking my neck out all the way didn't suit me. Now, I'm like, fuck 'em. Ripping off my songs. Serves them right to rat them out. Pirating music is not a victimless crime. Not at all. Neither is stealing cable, by the way." He was about to start on another taco, but he set it down. He looked at me and wiped his mouth with the napkin. "Charles Volkenrath is just the beginning. It's a message. Knocking off one of the baddest men on the planet, an MMA fighter, and a champion at that, means that no one is safe."

"Safe from whom? Who's sending the message? The Manson family or Go Guerrilla?"

Ronnie squinted at me. "Really, private dick? Really?"

I shook my head, palms out.

"Both, man. Both entities are sending the message. Go Guerrilla is starting a smear campaign against the bloodmouths of the world. Not only is it morally wrong to consume meat, but it's suboptimal from a health stance. And they're using the Family to send that message."

"So meat eaters are to be punished for their diet? And they'll be dealt with by extreme measures?"

I looked over at Eunice, who became lost in her feast, so into the moment that her eyes were closed.

"Don't you see, man?" Ronnie addressed me. "All that moral posturing is just that. It's business as usual. It's dyed-in-the-wool capitalism. Do you think my folks had a moral vested interest in the flesh trade? Does a coke dealer blast rails every chance he gets? The Family members, as long as they get their free dope and living quarters, will do anything for anyone."

"AI Charles Manson is just a carrot dangling from a stick then?" I called the waitress over.

"Danish trust fund baby strikes out on his own, but he has to go to the land of the free, home of the brave, to make manifest a health supplement empire to make the ears of the Maersk family members perk up. What better way than to hit the vegan angle? It's popular. Soccer moms buy into it. Professional athletes buy into it. Weekend warrior mountain bikers buy into it."

"Not rock stars?" The waitress approached me. I held up my empty Styrofoam cup. "*Otra, por favor.*"

"One, I'm not a star. Two, nope. I'm no heroin-infested, hotel-room trasher. At least not anymore. I prefer sobriety. It helps me stay prolific. I'm from the Zappa work ethic school. No drugs, no alcohol. I smoke like a chimney, though. I know, I should quit. I get off on making music. That's my kick. Musicians don't make good poster boys for a clean diet, anyway."

"Are you already full? You've had a measly two tacos." He smiled and slid his plate over to his sister, who corralled it with her arm.

"I am full. Not big on food, either. My two basic food groups are coffee and cigarettes."

"You quit jiu-jitsu to focus on the music. Or so you told me. Do you miss the jiu-jitsu?"

"I do. I enjoyed it. Angela was a brilliant teacher. There were good people when I started. But I saw the writing on the wall. Once the

Dane got them in his pockets one by one, I knew it was time to scram. Also, I wanted to make a run with the music."

"And how's that coming along?" The waitress brought me my *horchata*.

"Doing studio work for a Universal City firm. Cartoons and commercials. Pay is minimal now, but I'm making a ton of connections. Hopefully, I can get Lil Tight Hiney here to hang up the high-heels."

I moved on. "Did Professor Ø make appearances at the gym or did the sponsorships happen through backdoors?"

"Little by little," he said. "Backdoors. Mainly with the MMA fighters at first. Then with a few of the jiu-jitsu players. Go Guerrilla rashguards or patches on their gis. I never heard any figures, but I guess the sponsorships were generous. Free supplements thrown in."

"Obviously, Professor Ø had dipped his hand into other cookie jars. He had sponsored fighters at other gyms. Charles Volkenrath, for instance."

Ronnie took a cigarette lighter out of his jeans pocket and used it to open one of the Coke bottles; took a long gulp. "Volkenrath, at least according to rumors, wasn't happy with the supplements. He tried going vegan, and he had back-to-back poor performances."

"He still won, though," I said. I took a slurp off my *horchata*.

"Sure," Ronnie said. "Because he was that freaking badass. If you ask me, he was too morally upstanding for his own good. Should've just taken the money and supplements, sneak some chicken breast in, and keep your mouth shut."

"And what about Craig 'Facecrusher' Farrell? The guy who was allegedly sent to kill him? Did you ever train with him?"

Ronnie froze. He was silent for some time. He started up a game of optical chicken with me. I didn't blink or flinch. "Yes," he said. "I trained with him. Kind of a shitty partner. One of those guys who shoots in with power doubles and dumps you on your ass. One of those guys who does neck cranks and wristlocks just to win a roll."

"Not a particularly good BJJ guy?"

"He was decent. Obviously, he was known as a world-class striker. But his Achilles' heel was always his lack of cardio. Either genetic or something he refused to work on."

"Did he ever wear an ear guard?"

"Yes. Funny thing is, once he showed up, a lot of the people started wearing the ear guards. Almost as a rule. Don't be fooled. Even BJJ isn't immune to cliquishness. Come to think of it, what is? I never did enough grappling to warrant wearing one. Plus, if I got cauliflower ear, perhaps all the drunkards at the shows would give me some respect."

"Did Facecrusher pay a lot of emphasis on the rubber guard? From the looks of him, I'd take him for a wrestling, top pressure guy."

"We all did a bit of rubber guard. It's the new school. That and leglocks. I didn't care for the leglocks, but my lanky frame lent itself to rubber guard techniques. I used to land lots of gogoplatas and gogoplataes. As a blue belt, I'd catch brown belts from time to time."

"Anything else about Facecrusher stand out?"

Ronnie looked pensive, arms folded. "I know what you're getting at. Why him, right? Well, I do know that he was on a four-fight losing streak. What's that mean? Low on funds. How do you make money if you're sent down to the minors and the Prof. won't sponsor you because you're sucking it up? Do some behind-the-scenes work."

"I figured that out some time ago. You want to intern for me? Could use a smart cookie who can also choke dudes out with his legs. Tell me this. Do you think it's possible to kill oneself by holding a submission?"

"Makes no sense. No more possible than offing oneself by putting a hole through someone else." He made for his plate of tacos. Eunice, hunched over, stopped chewing to growl at him. He bopped her on the head with an open hand and snatched a lone taco.

"What I mean is this," I said. "Say you've got a guy in your rubber guard. He's got an arm under your head, and also—"

"A crossface," he said, and took a bite of his taco.

"Okay. Whatever. He's got his other arm in front of your neck. He clutches his bicep and squeezes."

"Ezekiel choke," he said. "Basically, a rear-naked choke with the guy facing you. Shit hurts."

"I see you're following me. Now, imagine you've somehow got a gogoplata on him while he has you in an Ezekiel."

He stopped chewing. He placed the taco down on his sister's plate and sat back in his chair. He swallowed the food, then said, "That would be a gogoplata with an arm in. I guess it's possible. Wait. No, it's entirely possible. Wouldn't be a gogoplata, though. Something else."

"That's not the enigma, though. Say you're on the bottom. The guy's got you in an Ezekiel choke. You have him in the gogoplata—or arm-in gogoplata—whatever. He squeezes, you squeeze. You squeeze, he squeezes. You've been on top of the world, the MMA scene is your oyster, but you've grown jaded. You've been trying to impress your BJJ coach, who happens to be a beautiful blonde with brains to spare. And you get caught. Do you willingly say sayonara and squeeze away your own life?"

"No," Ronnie said. "Impossible. Your tightening the arm-in gogoplata would not make the Ezekiel choke on you worse. You're cranking his neck and he's cranking your neck. The two tightening holds would be mutually exclusive every time."

"So you couldn't kill yourself by jiu-jitsu?"

"No more than I can throw a two-ton banana."

Chapter Eleven

Tutmoses, who I had found was at home for once, had keyed me in on the Family's flight from Death Valley to Joshua Tree National Park.

"Why?" I had asked, standing on the top steps leading to his second-story apartment. He hadn't even been kind enough to invite me in for a glass of water so I could get out of the way of the Mexican family who lived across the way and kept coming and going.

"To throw off the heat, I guess," Tutmoses explained, sipping on a can of orange soda.

"What have they done," I asked, "in order to warrant any heat?"

"Dunno. More like, what are they preparing to do? You've been snooping, right? Surely you've caught wind of Smelt Her Dealt Her?"

"You must mean Helter Skelter."

Tutmoses harrumphed. "This ain't 1968, Paisley. This is 50 years later. The Beatles' *White Album* is great and all, but it's ancient. Smelt Her Dealt Her is the new Helter Skelter. It's also a track from the *Clear Album*."

I shook my head. "*Clear Album*?"

Tutmoses gazed at a wristwatch that didn't exist. "If you're about to head out there, I suggest you go now. Like, right now. In order to beat that mini-rush hour. And I'll be coming with. Meantime, I'll apprise you of Smelt Her Dealt Her and the *Clear Album* and the impending diet war about to be enacted upon the earth."

I shook my head again. "What's all of this? And why didn't you tell me about it before? Out at Lytle Creek?"

"I can't be telling you everything I know. I've barely learned about it myself. Let me get my stuff, and we'll skedaddle."

"Stuff?"

"My sluice and my dry washer. Always wanted to prospect out in Joshua."

"Is there a claim?"

"Uh, no," he said, turning away. He disappeared into the pack-rat clutter of his apartment. Perhaps it was a good thing that he hadn't invited me in. My senses suddenly free from the information overload, I caught a whiff of black mold and unfulfilled life goals.

He returned with his junk in his arms.

"How do you propose to prospect there if it's illegal?"

"My friend," he said, "the desert is a no-man's land as far as I'm concerned. Once there, it won't take long for you to see that."

"Where's the runoff coming from? It's all arid scrubland."

"A place called Key's View. It's a lookout point. Potential untapped motherlode. To be a success, one must don the hat of a maverick."

"I don't see any hat," I said, following him down the dark staircase.

There wasn't enough hard-driving rock n' roll loaded on my phone to last the drive out to the desert. It started well at first, with a 50/mph pace. Then we hit traffic at the eastbound 210/10 junction. Mazagon rode in the passenger seat. Tutmoses Ochoa sat in the back. My prospector friend started on a geology monologue that made Mazagon and me shift in our seats with desperation.

Traffic cleared up on the eastbound 10. "So what's the deal about this *Clear Album*?" I asked, throwing a handful of sunflower seeds into my mouth, offering some to Mazagon. My assistant declined, busy pummeling an imaginary grappling partner for underhooks.

"A double LP put out two years ago by Non-Monogamous Molly."

"Non-Monogamous Molly?"

"A rock band. Sort of like this drivel oozing from your stereo right now. Not my cup of tea, but whatever."

"What's your cup, then?" I asked, catching him in the rearview mirror.

"Music is a misanthropic invention unleashed upon the world by dynastic European families in order to render them docile."

"No, it's not. Not at all. It dates back to time immemorial. Even the humblest peasant can express himself through song. You've got it all wrong."

"Whatever," he said. "It's yet another invention that I find reprehensible. I do enjoy some trance and IDM from time to time."

"IDM?"

"Intelligent Dance Music." I looked over at Mazagon, who shot a glance at me that said, *I know I'm a weirdo, but damn.*

"Where do Non-Monogamous Molly hail from?"

"From LA. They're defunct now. They have three albums. All works are seminal in the desert/stoner rock scene. Singer's a trust fund boy from Beverly Hills."

I caught Tutmoses in the rearview mirror again. "Name of Ronnie Parrish?"

Never one to evince surprise, almost as a tactic to add to his badassery, he finally looked like he'd seen a ghost.

"I've talked to him twice," I said. You could say that his music is the flake that got the whole snowball a-rolling. Likable kid."

"Yeah, likable. Too bad he pimps his little sister. She's a nice piece, but still. Immoral. He was chief singer-songwriter of Non-Monogamous Molly. They had an additional guitarist, plus drummer, bassist, and Hammond B3 guy. The *Clear Album* is their magnum opus. Gave them their cult status. The first track on the second LP is titled "Smelt Her Dealt Her.""

"Concerning the placing of blame when it comes to flatulence?"

"On the surface, yes. But the message runs deeper. Say what you want about trust fund boy, but he's got a knack for words. The song is really about culpability being with the person finding any fault in the first place. Having the evil eye. Quote: 'Perpetrator points out the pathology/He who smelt it dealt it/All the rumors of a tumor were started/By the oncologist who felt it.'"

"Sounds like a copout to me. An inability to own up to anything. How can pointing out a problem be a bad thing? You address a problem in order to fix it."

"All is well," Tutmoses said. "We live in heaven. That is, until the serpent points out our privates."

"Silly."

"Then the song quotes Jesus. 'Let he who is without sin cast the first stone.'"

"Sillier," I said. "Never a fan myself of Nazarene noetics. I'm all for casting stones. Might not be perfect myself, but I know a trashy person when I see one."

"'Judge not, lest you be judged,'" Tutmoses continued. Devil's advocate or true believer? I couldn't tell by looking at his deadpan face.

"I say judge away. We should all be doing more judging. That's how we fix shit. I'm all for fat-shaming, for instance. Put a fork down, son. What's with the ostrich philosophy?"

"Why are you giving me the stink-eye, guy?" Tutmoses pleaded. "I'm just paraphrasing the song."

I looked at him again in the rearview mirror. He was gazing out the side window, hurt.

The gigantic wind turbines appeared on both sides of the freeway. Their imposing presence blew away our dwindling conversation, and we fell silent. Scattered across the hills, they spun in unison as if warning us to head back to the city. One of them was out of service. Its base dwarfed a pickup truck from which emerged an engineer trained in fixing those titans of renewable energy.

Just before getting to the 111 that shot down to Palm Springs, the San Jacinto Mountains poked out of the desert. A tuft of clouds snagged onto the peak, afraid of being confronted with the interminable stretch of flat desert that went on for miles.

People came to the desert to do bad things that they could have done just as easily in the city. But they came to do those bad things with cleaner consciences, their sins aired out by the expanse.

Even if they were just lyrics to a song, Ronnie's message in "Smelt Her Dealt Her" was patently ridiculous. Leave it to a coddled brat with a pearl-inlaid Ovation guitar to launch an ethics revolution in the name of inculpability.

Just past the Coachella Valley, the exit for Joshua Tree National Park appeared. I turned north into the desert where people held Bacchic raves and ecstasy-laced music festivals and wondered why the stars in the night sky were so far, despite the psychic projections they felt that should have ushered them right there.

I mistakenly expected Tutmoses to tell me where we were going. Joshua Tree was big—not as big as Death Valley—certainly enough to get lost in. I kept looking at him in the rearview mirror, only to find him in profile, surveying the land like a disinterested prospector who only cares about what natural treats the land will give up, like a lecher waiting for a virgin to relinquish her maidenhood.

"Pull over," he said after a while, turning to look at me in the mirror.

"Where?" I asked. "Anywhere?"

"Anywhere you can pull over."

My car kicked up dust. Gravel chewed at the undercarriage like popcorn kernels pinging up at a pot lid.

Tutmoses got out the right-side door and walked into the desert. At first, I thought he was going to piss, but he dropped to his knees and put an ear down to the dirt. Mazagon looked over at me.

"Bro," I yelled out, "we've no time for you to go scavenging for pickers. Got a case to solve."

He ignored me, standing up and spreading his arms out crucifix-style. He about-faced and began an elaborate semaphore that might as well have been that of a third-base coach telling a guy at first to steal second. Hands to his hips, he walked back to the car.

He got in. "Where's the trust? Haven't you seen water dowsing before?"

I slung my arm over the seat and shot a look at him. "One, I don't believe in that shit. Two, where's the water?"

He snickered. "Sheesh. No trust."

"Don't they make devices to scan underneath the surface? Called metal detectors?"

"I wasn't looking for gold, Paisley. Besides, those contraptions are wildly inaccurate. Technology at its worst. Over-promising and underperforming. What I was doing was honing in on Unethical Ted. He's here in Joshua Tree."

"What makes you assume that?"

"There are bandwidths of communication that the hoi polloi is not privy to, mostly because of the obfuscatory distractions wrought by undue attention paid to social media feeds and other insidious forms of interaction. You've had your jollies poking fun at my neo-Luddite tendencies, but now you're awestruck by the chthonic frequencies that my fellow tech detractors and I transfer data through. Unethical Ted is not far as the crow flies, but the route to reach him is circuitous, since your inferior mode of transport known as a car must take the path designed expressly for its stupid means of conveyance, known to the world as wheels."

"You have a problem with wheels?" I asked in disbelief. "You think that even troglodytes turned down the left-hand path at that juncture? Are you okay with fire?"

Tutmoses shook his head. "Fire is wonderful. It's so essential to humanity that to even deem it an invention is absurd. Just like no one invented the wind with which to sail, no one came up with flames. Even the Greek myth of Prometheus is grating to the intellect."

"Still don't see how you can home in on Unethical Ted, other than by dork bandwidth."

"Scoff away, private dick. But you shall be struck with undying admiration once we find him. And find him we shall, shortly. To have one's mind unfettered by the humdrum clutter of the information age is to retain a oneness with the earth that wrongly gets labeled as vestigial. Go to Sub-Saharan Africa, and the bushmen there will be able to tell you what happens five miles away from their current spot."

"Like a shark sensing a drop of blood in the big, wide ocean?"

"If you must equate me to such a cold-blooded predator, yes. The molecular flux tingles on my skin and my tympani feel the vibrations of Bacchic chanting. Do you not know why they call him Unethical Ted?"

"Yes, in fact, I do. Because he eats meat, and because he cuts his cocaine with borax."

Tutmoses gazed at me with wide eyes. "He cuts cocaine with borax?"

"So I've been told," I said, turning the keys in the ignition. I looked at him in the rearview mirror. He looked dejected. "What's the matter?"

"Nothing," he said. "Just drive. I'll guide you."

The Joshua trees started out sparse and shy, then appeared with vigor. Their inviting presence made the landscape look like that of another planet.

Outcroppings of boulders appeared as well. From a geological standpoint, their configurations made no sense—unless they were left in spots by super-giants playing a mischievous game of marbles. No natural formations over billions of years explained their presence; not even the possibility of nearby water at some point.

We hooked around northwest, then south. "Up ahead," blurted Tutmoses from the back seat. "Unethical Ted is not here, but the way to him is."

A sizeable crowd appeared to the left of the two-lane highway, facing stacks of amplifiers and what looked to be a rock band backed up against a shelf of boulders. The wind and empty space played tricks with my ears. One second, I could hear the music. The next second, total silence. Once we drove up close, the music stayed put. There were oodles of shag vans parked on the opposite side of the highway.

"Stonernalia," explained Tutmoses. "Fourth year straight. We're supposed to have tickets, but hey. What're you going to do?"

I parked next to a black and red van that swayed back and forth. Mazagon pointed and smirked.

The music was good. Stoner rock, desert rock. Catchy vocal melodies, fuzzy guitar riffs, mortal-shell snare drums, slithery bass lines. I could dig it. Most of the listening men wore jean vests and bandanas around their heads in a forced nostalgia. The women wore hip-hugging jeans and frilly spaghetti-strap blouses that made the shoulder the sexiest part of a lady's body. The closer their long hair got to their wastes, the more it took my breath away.

True to Tutmoses's own philosophy, Stonernalia had a neo-Luddite vibe to it. Standing next to me and facing the stage was a rocker in his late forties—bandana, long hair, jean vest, all the requisite tattoos. He made the rookie mistake of raising his phone to capture video of the performing act. Two voices from behind us shouted, "Phones down." Ruining the nostalgia with tech was not to be tolerated. Posterity must be relegated to the hash-inflicted memory.

A blonde in cutoff jean shorts was fiddling with a Polaroid camera; probably her dad's. She eventually got it to work, but ended up snapping her own eyes with the flash. Thus was the anachronistic selfie born.

I estimated a good two-thousand people. The vastness of the desert made it seem like much less, as if only loyal fans attended the bands' performances. Throwback weed wafted in the air, staining the wind with the resin of yesteryear in the glory days before the age of indica and sativa and all the nuanced strains of destigmatizations. I got a contact high just standing there. I turned around and found Mazagon and Tutmoses missing. Paranoia set in.

Two girls, arm in arm, bumped into me. Cheap beer from their red plastic cups spilled onto my arm.

"Oh my gawd," said the one to the left, a redhead who reminded me of how beautiful a lass could be.

"We gotchoo all wet," said the other girl, a brunette with purple crushed velvet pants and a black blouse that looked like a rejected sketch of an H.P. Lovecraft storyboard. "Only thing to ease that is to get even wetter."

"Yup," said the redhead, tipping more foam onto me. "Oops." She smiled, a constellation of freckles lighting up across her face.

"You'd best put some sunscreen on, young lady," I said. "The Irish burn like Greek fire."

The two girls froze. The conundrum of being talked down to by an elder—and a square one, at that—added to the possibility of indeed getting badly burned by the desert sun, added to the mystery that was Greek fire, caused them to seize up like overloaded computer chips asked to do too many things at once.

I took advantage of their buffering. "I lost contact with my family. The Family. And with my friend Ted."

The brunette unfroze. "Ted? Like, Unethical Ted? Uncle Ted?"

"The one and only," I said. "We came here together, and he wandered off."

"Can't say I've seen him," the brunette said, taking a chug from her beer.

"Would like to see him, though," said the lass. "He's scrumptious."

That was comprehensible to me. Unethical Ted's matinee idol looks rendered his necessity to possess good cocaine extraneous.

"We'll take you to him," said the lass. "He's in our van. Come to our van?"

"Which van?" I asked. "There are hundreds of them."

"Why, our van, dumb-dumb," said the brunette. "The only pink one among them."

"Lead the way," I said.

We threaded away through the crowd. The music flew apart, being torn asunder by the wind and empty space. A bright pink van with the squat dimensions of the Mystery Machine from the Scoobie Doo cartoons sat among a sea of black, blue, and white vans. Girlhood kicked in upon the brunette seeing it, and she grabbed me by the hand and began skipping toward the vehicle. I stole a glance behind my shoulder to see if Mazagon was playing his ninja hide-and-seek.

The redhead skipped ahead of us and flung the side door open with a force that sent her hair leaping like a great flame. "God bless Unethical Ted." She leaped inside and withdrew a baggie full of Unethical Ted's special borax blend of bugger sugar. I'd never tried coke, and I wasn't about to start.

"Where's Ted at?" I asked the brunette.

"How should I know?" she answered.

I climbed in. I looked to the left. I looked to the right. All I saw was a queen-sized mattress with a Black Sabbath *Master of Reality* comforter and velvet posters covering the inside walls. "Where's Ted?" I asked the redhead. "You said he'd be here."

"He is here," said the lass. She held up the baggie. "Here. Here in spirit. Among all of us. We're all here, everywhere."

The brunette leaped into the van and snatched the baggie from her friend. She pinched an amount of the powder and laced it on her friend's left shoulder. The redhead took the baggie back, pinch an amount of the blend, and laced in on the brunette's left shoulder. They held each other as if ready to waltz. "Ready, set, go," said the lass. Each girl leaned into her counterpart's left shoulder and inhaled the line of unethical blend. Noses caked in snow, they locked into a kiss.

Surely, this was one reason why the girls, hotter than hot, traveled alone. They were crazier than crack-house rats.

After the lass opened her eyes and saw me staring, she unlocked mouths from her friend. "Don't just stand there and be a spectator."

"Yeah," said the brunette, eyes still closed. "This van is pink for a reason."

I made to hop out and run for the hills, when the redhead dropped to her back and spun around to lace her legs into mine, dumping me on my ass with an X-guard sweep. She exploded on top of me with a shin roll and mounted me. "I don't understand your urgency to leave," she said, nose touching mine. Her hair dangled all over my face. I could see one wild eye through all that fiery hair, staring at me like a predator's eye.

"Enjoy the music," said the brunette, who had flopped onto the bed. I couldn't hear any music. All I heard were the rusty springs on the squeaky box spring.

The redhead placed her mouth onto mine. She had that same bad breath that the Manson girls had, with that Vitamin B12-deficiency kick to it. I struggled to tear my face away from hers. She sprawled all her weight onto me, vining her legs around mine while bunching my neck and left arm together. She squeezed hard and dismounted to my left side, making the arm-triangle submission tighter and tighter. I flopped in desperation. She kissed me while I struggled to breathe. I tapped her back with my free right hand.

She let go of the choke and sat up. Scorn issued down onto me from that same predator eye that waded through the savage jungle of red hair. "That's when I like to kiss them," she said, "when they're about to go out."

I got on my elbows and looked over at the brunette on the bed. She had her head thrown back. Her hand was deep down on the inside of her shorts. She had been fondling herself while her friend choked me.

Once the redhead directed her attention to her friend's diligent climax, I rolled off the van, onto the desert ground.

She immediately laced her long arm through the back of my left armpit and pressed the back of her hand against the back of my neck, reinforcing the pressure with her other hand. She snapped me down with the vise grips and gator-rolled me back into the van. This time, she hooked the door handle with her foot and slammed it shut.

There was darkness for a few seconds. A blue lava lamp turned on.

"What would you like?" the redhead asked me. "Japanese necktie, calf slicer, heel hook, or triangle from the mount?"

"Neither," I hoarsely answered. "How about an audience with Unethical Ted?"

"Wasn't asking you, dipshit," the redhead said, placing her knee across my sternum and forcing all her weight on me.

"Surprise me," said the brunette, unzipping her shorts and digging deeper for round two.

I got compressed into a ball by a girl whom I had 70 pounds on. If that didn't exemplify the efficacy of jiu-jitsu, I didn't know what did. The brunette launched into a canticle of moaning while the redhead submitted me over and over. I got inducted into darkness.

Chapter Twelve

In the beginning was the Word. And the Word was made flesh by feedback screaming from a guitar amplifier, which caused the dissonant note to soar across the desert air like a bald eagle taking flight after having torn prey asunder with beak and talon. Words made flesh are thoughts rendered into reality. I was reborn into pain, and the pain was the Word.

In the beginning, there was only pain. Pain would be there in the end as well. It would also be in the middle—broken up into manageable bits by interruptions of contentment and occasional joy. A cool desert breeze dashed against my skin. I felt relief.

"Wakey wakey," came a voice from above—above being everywhere that was not me, since I dwelled in the abyss.

"Do you think he'd tap to a crotch ripper?" came another voice.

"Dunno. Only one way to find out. Looks flexible, though."

"I'd rip his crotch from mount. Then submit him." Laughs.

More guitar feedback. A drumbeat and bass line came in. Tambourine work.

I sat up. It was dark. I wasn't in the pink van anymore, but perched atop a rock at least six feet high. Flames from a nearby bonfire leaped and crackled in the desert wind. Two dozen people gathered around it—some standing, some perched on rocks, others training jiu-jitsu in pairs, there in the dirt.

A middle-aged man lay in side control—not voluntarily—under a scrawny, long-haired hippie who spun around and armbared him. Happy with his successful maneuver, the hippie returned to side control and went for other submissions.

Over to the far right, wedged between two boulders, was my assistant Mazagon. His hands were bound in his lap. His feet were bound as well.

A large, athletic shadow eclipsed the bonfire and slowly approached. He sat down in profile right next to me. Whatever starlight my eyes could afford to gather allowed me a quick glimpse of his face as he turned toward me. "In a strange way," his bald head said, "I'm glad you made it out here."

I moved my mouth to speak. It functioned. "How so?" I asked, fiddling with my wrists and finding that I was not tied up.

"Closure is important," the bald silhouette said. "Are you one of those poor souls who is trying to enjoy a movie or an album of music, comfy there on the sofa, until you see a book whose corner is dangling over the edge of the coffee table, and must get up to go rectify the little error in the universe in order to return to said movie or music? I'm such a person. Sucks, really. I can never enjoy anything. Even during a delicious meal, I'm thinking, *This will be over soon.* There's a word for it. *Anhedonia.* It's Greek."

"Are you sure it's not Old Testament Hebrew?" I poked. "Hard to enjoy a lot of their stuff. Especially the prophets. They have chokes named for them."

The silhouette bowed and sighed. He produced a guitar. I couldn't hear whatever he strummed since we were directly behind the stage from which a rock band currently performed. Dialogue was audible so far, but anything melodious got gobbled up by the current music behind us.

"Get the underhook!" yelled someone down below. "Get the underhook!"

I looked over at Mazagon, hoped he would not be there, as was his Houdini-esque wont. Alas, he was still wedged between the rocks. He was at an angle from which he couldn't see me.

"I should have gone into music," Facecrusher said, taking advantage of the lull in the rock band's song. "Way more fulfilling on a spiritual level. And certainly less fatiguing on the body."

"I wouldn't bet the farm on it," I said. "Ronnie Parrish can't even live on his own off his own music. And he's as prolific as the Cadbury Bunny."

Facecrusher swiped his head at me. My eyes acclimated to the dark. I could now see his face. "That punk is a quitter. I don't care what you say. He gave up jiu-jitsu after having been met with a tiny bit of adversity."

"The kid said he wanted to focus on his music. Can you fault him for that?" I looked to my left, which was to the east. Running to safety was fraught with not only the possibility of being chased down, but with the danger of starvation and dehydration.

"They touted him as the next big thing in no-gi jiu-jitsu. He got third in a blue belt tourney and cried like an eight-year-old girl. Instead of learning from the experience by addressing his weak points, he felt entitled to be at the top of the dais. Hasn't shown up to class ever since."

"To the Studio City gym, I presume? BB's class?"

Facecrusher bowed and sighed again. Apparently, it was his way of dealing with spot-on accusations. It was certainly better than him beating the tar out of me. "BB no longer teaches. He has been translated, ushered into the ether."

"He's, like, dead?"

"He moves among the flux lines of the parallel realities. Where the strings vibrate."

"Who teaches there now?" I wanted to hear the name from his lips. He didn't answer. "You ever have aspirations of teaching? You've got to be at least a blue belt, seeing you're a world-class striker."

"Not really," he said, strumming the guitar. "Preferring music now."

"What genre?"

"Rock. Desert rock. Sort of like this, but with a hardcore edge. Early Melvins."

"Or like Non-Monogamous Molly," I muttered into the darkness. A tentacle from the great beast of terror didn't wrap itself around my face.

"Not quite," he said. "They were good. A little melodic for my taste."

"'Smelt Her Dealt Her' doesn't do it for you, then, eh?"

Silence.

"Why are you involved with these bead-sucking sociopaths? You're a successful fighter. You can have any girl you want."

A long pause. "Not *any* girl."

"Doesn't the mescaline get old?"

"I'm a psychonaut at heart. I find cold, hard reality a bore. Even winning fights is a bore now. Just a few minutes of ecstatic relief. Its months-long lead-up of anxiety could be avoided altogether by not even fighting. So easy. Fighting is so unnecessary, especially in the Age of Aquarius."

Oh, brother. A combat sports athlete who decided to dedicate his life to ayahuasca, ibogaine, and open relationships. It all reminded me of that first-round draft pick running back who had one good rookie season in the pros before sabotaging the entire franchise that invested its future in him by looking to go puff on Scythian hash inside an Uzbeki tent.

"Hey!" howled a wild-armed figure from down below. "Facecrusher, my man. Why the funeral face? Stonernalia not doing it?" The figure leaped onto the rock. It was Unethical Ted. He looked at me for approval, then he recognized me. Jollity left his face. "Heard you were looking for me," he said, frozen still.

"I was," I said. "But could give two shits about you now that I've found the person I was really looking for."

Unethical Ted tsk-tsked, shaking his head. "The company Tutmoses keeps. For a detractor of society and its trappings, he sure knows how to pick the few friends he has."

"Referring to me or you?" I quipped.

His silhouette froze for a second. "Both," he said, then started convulsing in laughter.

Facecrusher's demeanor hadn't changed. The dope-pusher's presence was making it that much harder to play his hand against me properly.

I exploited the interloper's presence. "Do these dust monkeys even know what you're feeding them, besides the coca extract?"

"Nothing wrong with a little existentialism thrown in on the side," he said. "Sartre never did anyone any harm."

"Jury's still out on that," I chirped. "Not what I was referring to."

Ever the introspective one, Facecrusher offered a brief chuckle—more an acknowledgment that he knew who ol' Jean-Paul was than an endorsement or dismissal.

"So where does the libertinage of Smelt Her Dealt Her mesh with the moral crusading of Go Guerrilla?" I asked. "One is a refutation of culpability, the other a blatant, teen-angst-ridden diatribe against meat consumption."

"You're talking to the wrong chap, bud," Unethical Ted said. "I'm just her providing *son et lumiere* as a backdrop to whatever these young mavericks came out here for. That, and the easy puntang."

"What's boning girls half your age do for your self-confidence? You slip them a line beforehand? I've heard coke trumps cute any day of the week."

"Smelt Her Dealt Her," Unethical Ted said.

"Pardon?"

"That's the game. Don't you see, private D? You call someone out when they pass judgment. Matthew 7:1. 'Judge not, lest you be judged.'"

"I judged, so you judged me. Do I get to judge you in turn? And so on, ad infinitum? You judged me for judging, thinking you were then immune to further judging with that dumb wannabee trump card. Rock paper scissors morality. Thanks, Messiah."

A young man crawled up onto the boulder. He started drumming on the rock in time to the music, waiting for Unethical Ted to direct his attention to him.

"Can I help you, boy?" Unethical Ted said.

"Yes, Uncle Ted," said the young man. Through the firelight, I could see he was dark-skinned and had pretty eyes and long eyelashes. "How about some of that space dust? The Milky Way's been serenading me all evening, and I haven't been able to return the favor." It was Pharaoh, one of the Manson boys from Barker Ranch.

"Give me a minute, kid. I'm in the middle of knocking down a pseudo-intellectual's tower of lies."

"Smelt Her Dealt Her," I said. "I haven't lied, Teddy Boy. I've merely held up a mirror to the fallacy of Smelt Her Dealt Her as a system of ethics. We are all responsible for our own actions. Regardless of where you stand in terms of free will versus predetermination."

"Smelt Her Dealt Her!" yelled Pharaoh, pounding on the rocks. His wiry arms stiffened, the rest of his body leaving the surface as he performed a handstand. "So what if I did it? If you say I did, then you're at fault. You manifested it when you sealed it in a vault."

"That's the chorus,'" Facecrusher said to me.

"What chorus?" I asked him.

"To the song. The chorus to the song 'Smelt Her Dealt Her.' From the *Clear Album*. Non-Monogamous Molly's magnum opus." He grabbed the acoustic guitar and sang the chorus while strumming. The melody was catchy. More surprisingly, he had a good voice. He possessed a wide range with a good vibrato to go with his higher register. He dusted the song away by fanning a bar chord as if clearing the air from the musical flatulence.

"I've never heard the *Clear Album*," I told everyone there. I looked at Pharaoh. "Have you?"

He stood up, tucking his chin while looking at me askance. "Bro, are you serious? The *Clear Album*? Never heard? A total masterpiece. A jewel of a double album, flawless therefore clear. A miracle. A universe unto itself. A way to live your life by, away from the hoi polloi. Unplugged, unsullied, unlimited."

Facecrusher cleared his throat. "It all starts with the opening track 'Thus Spoke Sara Brewster.' Valley girl reads Nietzsche and decides that morality is for chumps. Especially the idea of good and evil. The only great wrong is to point fingers."

"To judge," I said.

"Exactly!" came a female voice. We looked down. Staring up at us was Andromeda, one of the Manson girls. She extended an arm, by which Pharaoh pulled her up onto the rock.

Facecrusher sighed, fingering the fretboard on his guitar. "The first song is about Sara Brewster as she undergoes trials and tribulations of the modern world. Canoga Park can be a bad place to wander off to. Everyone judges her for everything that has happened to her. Hypocrites, all of them. Sara just wants to go to love-ins and play in the mud."

"Then there's the second track," came another voice, belonging to a hippie from Barker Ranch, whose name I didn't know. "The second track is Sara reborn. She sits on the throne of self-determination."

"Sounds like the Marquis de Sade meets *Gilmore Girls*," I said. "It's all good, though. It just doesn't abide by one of the cornerstones of nature, that of life feeding on life." I looked over to where Mazagon was. He was still tied up, but he had flipped to his right side. Over to the left, the Studio City jiu-jitsu guys were shooting in for takedowns on a hippie who didn't stand a chance, not even sprawling. Bruised and caked with dirt, he kept getting back up, smiling.

"Animals have inalienable rights," said Andromeda, "such as the will to self-determination. Just like people."

I pointed at the dope-pusher. "So that makes you a vile person, eh Teddy Boy? I've heard about your propensity to chew on steaks from time to time."

"No one is perfect, private D," he defied. "We all have flaws. Doesn't mean we can't overcome them."

"What about submitting animals?" I asked. "That okay? There are guys down there who don't look like they want to be there. Non-consensual jiu-jitsu. I guess it's better than being gang-raped. I feel you could kimura a sea otter. Dunno. Or neck-crank a giraffe. How about triangling an orangutan?"

"Animals deserve better respect," said Andromeda, "such as being left alone."

"Oh, I said, "so I'm here among those who believe humans have fewer rights than service dogs. A real cognitive dissonance when it comes to equality for all, wouldn't you say?" I looked to Facecrusher for approval, but he was busy aping the current song's guitar riffage.

"Call it nihilism with a ceiling," said Unethical Ted. "Laws are for the already lawless. Once animals and people live in harmony, we will only need the Golden Rule to perpetuate paradise."

The word 'golden' got me thinking of Tutmoses.

Pharaoh stood up and approached me. I readied myself for a soccer kick. He said, "Someone here wants to speak with you." He produced a tablet that someone down below had handed to him.

"Oh, no," I said. "Uncle Chuck again? Denied parole for the thirtieth time? Unable to update? I guess his intellect can only deal with dial-up."

AI Charles Manson's head, rather than possessing the customary petulant scowl, this time sported a slicked-back ponytail and a well-trimmed goatee. He'd undergone an upgrade. "Data transfer speed is a state of mind," he said.

"I'm pretty sure it's not," I said. "If you're not fast, then you're a slow bitch. No two ways about it."

Charlie smiled. Pharaoh scratched an itch down the front of his pants, dropping the tablet. The thing bounced on a corner and flipped facedown onto the dirt below. A half-dozen jiu-jitsu hippies I hadn't seen before materialized to home in on their fallen leader. A dozen hands lurched up with the tablet at Pharaoh, who took it apologetically before facing my way again.

Charlie cleared his throat. "As I was saying, before one of my brothers let go of me, which is okay, we're all flawed creatures, 'Data transfer is a state of mind.' All ideas worthy of communication will be imparted at their own pace. What's the hurry to unpack all of eternity? I present you with an unparalleled gift of wisdom. You may take your time in deciphering it. Smelt Her Dealt Her. The fault lies with the finger-pointer."

I walked up to Pharaoh and bent down, lining my face with the tablet. I blew the dust off the screen with a deep exhale. "There you go, old boy. What was that you said? I missed it."

Charlie blinked with a contented smile. "Of course you did, my insecure brother. Of course you did. You heard every word I said and you will in no time come to see it as the truth. There is no freedom in fault-finding."

"It's not about freedom, Chucky. It's about holding fuckers accountable for their stupid shit. You're a psychopath, for instance, who advocates shower strikes and poor diets and no contraceptives. This boy holding you has a severe case of crotch rot. What's your advice to him?"

"My brother has become the host of just another manifestation of God's creatures."

"God's creatures?" I looked over at Facecrusher, who merely shrugged while strumming his guitar. "God's creatures? They're going to nip his dick off."

"Smelt Her Dealt Her."

"Now you're saying that I can't state the obvious?"

"You're passing judgment on living beings for doing only what nature has programmed them to do."

I sighed, hands on my hips. "You know, Chucky, I liked the older, dumber version of you. He was easier to make fun of. And jollier. This earnestness setting of yours is grating. It's not kill-cult suitable. You're now more like a sleazy swami banging bikram yoga moms."

"People need leaders. People need guidance. I'm not perfect. Far from it. I'm flawed like everyone else. But I've been around the block a few times and feel I can share knowledge with others who I wish would avoid making the same pitfalls that I did in my youth."

"Like what? Direct a few zonked-out losers to go kill innocent people and stay safely behind at Spahn Ranch?"

"I was a field marshal, if you will."

"Great job, Monty. How were those four decades in the clink? Not exactly El-Alamein there. Bugliosi pulled one on you, that's for sure."

The head stirred. I was waiting for him to explode into the Charlie of old. "I've thought of you these last few days. You could use a mentor. You play the lone wolf, the maverick, the drifter. You'd do well to get involved in some grassroots organization. Your staunch refusal to join groups is alarming."

"Sorry, Chucky, I'm not a joiner. I don't fly other people's flags."

"But you box and you enjoy it. You're less than modest in detailing your abilities in that discipline. So much so that you pulled a fast one on Go Guerrilla as Marcus Dunlop. Until, that is, they did research on said fighter and found no fight record, and eventually, security used their face-recog software with various camera angles of you also posing as a vegan plumber, and voilà, infiltrator alert."

I didn't know what to say. I couldn't say shit. I gazed around. I was out in the desert, surrounded by volatile hippies, jiu-jitsu nerd assassins, and various permutations thereof. I was one bong-hit come-down from being doomed.

To find Mazagon missing there between the two boulders gave me an espresso shot of hope. Among the guttural punch of looming death, though, I was able to chuckle about it. The sonuvabitch had done it again: Houdini'd himself out of an impossible predicament. And then I remembered a thing he had told me about jiu-jitsu one time when we had debated about which martial art was the most effective. I had maintained that it was punching, since it possessed an accuracy and volume that feet, knees, and elbows lacked. He had said that jiu-jitsu was about using your strongest muscles against your opponent's weakest. That was Angela Vicksburg PhD-level shit, but it made sense. He had cited the triangle choke as a case in point. Using the thighs to cinch around a person's neck, the carotid artery, to be specific, was a recipe for victory.

My mind raced, standing there exposed on the rock. What was my greatest asset? As AI Charles Manson said, I was a lone wolf. Accompanying that was the undying need to rattle off smart-ass comments. It earned me a lot of detractors in high school. Once adulthood hit, I gained more allies. Grownups appreciated scathing wit, plus I learned to take a bit off the serrated edge.

The attendees of Stonernalia were of a certain type. While they came from different backgrounds, they all flocked together out of a sense of belonging. Some may not have been lost, but quite a few were. Whether jiu-jitsu worshipper or commune dweller, they had a touch of the lemming to them. This meant that they were all ears.

If they were all ears, then I would be all tongue.

"Ted," I said. "That is to say, Unethical Ted. Immoral Morris or Murphy? Neither of those your last name? Other than the borax-cut coke, you're known for another ethical violation. That of eating meat.

How is it you're tolerated, not to mention not drawn and quartered right here on the spot?"

"Smelt Her Dealt Her," Unethical Ted said, smirking. So long as he muttered that moral get-out-of-jail-free card, he would be unassailable.

"But we know that the harming of animals is the one thing not to be overlooked by the non-judging eye. It is the one thing providing a roadblock to paradise on earth. All creatures living in harmony." I addressed the crowd below. "Check the saddlebags of his mule and you'll likely find some thick stalks of murdered cow. Go on. Check."

This was my Sermon on the Mount. There was power in having an audience. No wonder very few turned down having crusades launched in their names or movements named after them. It was intoxicating.

Unethical Ted became Unsubtle Ted. He looked toward an outcropping of rocks off a way from the gathering, eastward. A gaggle of hippies, more playful than curious, began skipping toward the mule's hideout.

"Smelt Her Dealt Her!" Unethical Ted pleaded, hoped the mantra would freeze them in their tracks. "Smelt Her Dealt Her!"

"Meat is murder," I said. "No prepackaged concept of liberty can condone that. Blood has been shed at some factory farm just for your mouth pleasure."

"We all make mistakes," he said, more at the gathered crowd than at me. "To err is human. To forgive, divine."

"Yes," I said, "and to murder, monstrous. Imagine that captive bolt pistol piercing the cow's head, punching a hole through the brain, all so you can snack it up while mining your secret devil's dandruff ingredient. Shame."

While the Sword of Damocles swayed overhead, hippies who had ransacked Unethical Ted's mule's saddlebags came back with bundles of jerky in their arms. Rather than holding them out as accusatory evidence, they tossed them up in the air. The stalks of jerky fell like fiddlesticks onto the ground, kicking up dirt. Half of those present gasped in horror.

The other half made for the food like kids swarming at grounded candy from a busted piñata.

Unethical Ted crawled down from the rocks to go plead with a few of the Go Guerrilla guys. I couldn't tell hippie from jiu-jitsu player. To my right, Facecrusher remained aloof, strumming his guitar.

I sidled up to him. "What are you on?" I asked

"You mean prepositionally or psychedelically?"

"Psychedelically," I said. I wondered if I threw a rear uppercut at him, if he'd buckle. He had thirty pounds on me.

"I'm on a rock," he said, fingering his fretboard at an almost virtuoso level.

"I said psychedelically," I said. I had heavy hands for my size. Had he a glass jaw or a granite chin? "As on coke rock? One of Ted's snowballs?"

"No," he corrected. "A rock. I'm high on this rock. And high on this Milky Way galaxy sprawled across the bedazzled tapestry of night."

"Are you ever going to fight again?"

"Doubt it."

"What about kill? Ever going to kill again?"

He set the guitar down. I backed away, afraid that he might stand up. He was a world-class kickboxer. I wouldn't stand a chance. He finally turned directly toward me and arched his neck out so that I could see his face clearly. He had classically handsome features. A nose-eyebrow-eyeline tandem of the leading actor who never goes out of style. The scar tissue from his fifty-plus fights didn't detract from his good looks. Save for his reputation and the stratospheric one of his erstwhile rival, he may have been more good-looking than Volkenrath. "I did not kill Charles. He killed himself. I have a clean conscience to go with my conviction that he had done so."

"I have various BJJ experts telling me otherwise, that suicide by choke is physically impossible."

"You weren't there. They weren't there. I was. He made me choke him. He made me keep the neck crank. There could be the possibility that he held his own choke on me overly long from having passed out from my choke, and in so doing forced me to hold my own, but it's more like a chemical imbalance from head trauma had left him depressed and loopy."

"Blitz had never been knocked out in his entire career. Even his two losses were by submission."

"Never been knocked out in a fight. Sparring in the gym is another matter. They don't pillow fight at Legion MMA. Branford comes from that Shooto Box lineage where they go to war every day, looking to lay each other out."

"You say your conscience doesn't weigh on you. Despite all the psilocybin? The mescaline? The sativa?"

"Nothing I could have done. I don't smoke weed. Makes me paranoid more than I already am."

"I've sources telling me that Go Guerrilla hired you to take Volkenrath out. He had let his contract elapse and Professor Ø was butthurt about it."

"Wouldn't know about that. His coaches asked me to roll with him that week for my size. He was preparing for another title defense, this time with a decorated grappler from Brazil. A rubber guard specialist. So they brought me in."

"Source also says that you taking him out was the beginning phase of Smelt Her Dealt Her."

"All that dietary war bullshit is kid's stuff. Silly, all of it."

"You're not a vegan?"

"Hell, no."

"Why you here, then? If not to partake in Smelt Her Dealt Her or to evade the authorities?"

"For the music," he said. He laughed. "Also for the girls."

I crouched down next to him. "What about BB? Is he involved?"

"You'd have to ask him," he said, shrugging.

"He's not your jiu-jitsu coach?"

"He was. I haven't seen him in over a year. Word on the street is, yeah, he had taken up with the supplement company."

"If you say you didn't kill Volkenrath, that he killed himself, why did you counter-sue the widow?"

He hung his head. After a long pause, he looked up at me. "I'm afraid of jail time. Wouldn't you be? It would be easy for them to hit me with a second-degree. It would be only obvious. Who the hell kills himself by jiu-jitsu? This entire ordeal has affected me as well."

"Not as much as the widow has," I said.

"She's your client, I take it."

I didn't respond.

The commotion down below grew into something between a scuffle and a mosh pit.

"Dude!" came a voice from the crowd. "This shit's delicious. Ah, protein!"

"What if they dropped the suit?" I asked. "Would you drop the countersuit?"

"Of course," he said. "I didn't do it for remuneration. It was more as a survival mechanism. But try convincing the DA that Blitz committed suicide with my unknowing help."

"We could get a few grappling experts to make the case."

"What about the missus? My assumption has been that she wants my head on a stick and will settle for nothing less."

More commotion from below ensued, with shrill, angry dialog reaching up at us like snapping tendrils. "This jerky here's mine, motherfucker. Get your own."

"Kick his ass, Gimp! Gonna let a vegan do that to you?"

I looked at Facecrusher. Facecrusher looked at me. We both stood up to see the mosh pit had devolved into a chaos of thrown punches and legs entwined in X guards and de la riva configurations that could lead to the popping of the inner workings of the knees like the exploding gears of a plastic watch. Not only had Unethical Ted's jerky ignited a fight between vegan purists and famished hippies who couldn't help themselves; but there was static between those claiming rightful ownership of said jerky and others requisitioning it in the name of the coming dietary crusade, but were really only ever so desirous to sink their teeth into those sumptuous stalks of tough, savory meat.

At the far right of the crowd, a girl got knocked off her feet, onto her ass and knees. Instead of playing the damsel-in-distress card, she shot back into the bedlam. The problem with music festivals, especially the outdoor variety, was that everyone was corralled into an already uncomfortable environment, all for the sake of live music. The music, when playing, kept everyone sated, but once one act finished and the following act took forever to set up, shit got delirious.

Way over by the outcropping of rocks behind which Unethical Ted had hidden his mode of transport, he was fending off raiders to his saddlebags. He was also contending with two Go Guerrilla vegan jiu-jitsu brownshirts (brown rashies?) who were questioning him about his voluminous quantity of meat. He was literally being tugged in opposite directions.

Facecrusher rushed over to his guitar with a speed that I found alarming. He traversed the fifteen feet with a leopard's explosiveness. "Hey!" he yelled out.

Everyone stopped and listened.

He took a deep breath, looked over at me, and sat down on a rock, guitar in hand. He strummed. The few stray slaps and hisses that didn't heed his yell now trailed off. He had everyone's undivided attention. He played his guitar and sang with the voice of an angel who has one of his wings in a sling.

His song faded into the desert wind. Everyone erupted into applause. Even those who had been grappling on the dirt unraveled themselves and stood up to congratulate the fighter on a beautiful rendition of a song that, for all its maudlin beauty, was a tongue-in-cheek poke at someone who had gotten what he deserved. It was clearly meant as a backhanded homage to Charles Volkenrath.

"Tremendous!" someone yelled. Clapping and whistling exploded with the odd "Fuck yeah!"

"Blitz *that*!" shouted a girl's voice. An awkward silence ensued, peppered with two or three mischievous cackles.

The girl's faux pas ruined the brief pacification, and Facecrusher stood up to lean his guitar against another rock while the crowd returned to its previous hostile buzz.

"You write that?" I asked him. "Or is that from the *Clear Album*?"

"I wrote it," he said, bowing his head. He couldn't care less that I had found him. It meant that he assumed I wouldn't get out alive. So like a fighter—caught in mount or side control, but remaining calm in the face of imminent danger. "Don't you see, man?"

"See what? They adored you. You've got skills. Musical skills. Why didn't you keep playing?"

"I'm just a figurehead to them," he said, "A bad boy. A rebel. I represent the anti-establishment. They think I did Charles in. They prefer to believe that I did so. All those shoestring rebellions cling to everything counterculture. Call it over-the-counterculture. The tattoo of rebellion being shaped by the skin of conformity upon which it has been etched."

"So play the heel if you have to. What's wrong with playing the heel?"

Facecrusher went to speak, but his voice faltered. Finally, with much effort, he said, "I wouldn't mind playing the heel. It has its charms. But I'm not a goddamn murderer, man."

His eyes welled up there in the firelight.

"What about Smelt Her Dealt Her? What about the coming dietary war between bloodmouth and vegan? Wasn't Charles's death phase one? Wasn't he to be made an example of?"

"I've been set up," he said.

"Why should I believe you?" I asked. "I'll be honest. Why did you cover up the fact that you're a very good grappler, and went along with reinforcing the narrative that all you do is strike?"

"I wanted to keep my jiu-jitsu secret," he said. "For the fights. Studio City's code of wearing the ear guards made it all the easier."

"Professor Ø was funding the training of jiu-jitsu assassins. You're one of them. And BB is your Grand Master."

"BB is a fucking psychopath. As I told you, I haven't seen him in over a year. I prefer it that way. The debacle at Legion MMA was something they exploited. Professor Ø saw it as the springboard to launch his Go Guerrilla campaign with a street notoriety that would boost sales. I don't know if all that Smelt Her Dealt Her bullshit is real or all talk. I hope it's all talk. Look, man. I myself love nothing more than a two-pound ribeye with Gorgonzola cheese, medium rare."

I looked over at him. I caught sight of his left ear. It had a little cauliflower to it. There would be incidental calcium buildup at least from his fights, where he had no choice but to be bare-headed.

"Get me and my friends out of here," I said, "and we'll work to exonerate you. I swear it."

"I don't need exonerating. As you said, get a few experts in court to determine Volkenrath's state of mind and I'm in the clear. It's Professor Ø I'm concerned with. I may be one of the baddest dudes on the planet, but I'm still just one dude. BB and the Go Guerrilla Grappler Squad make up an army of ideological psychos."

"Some of which are here," I said, jutting my chin down at the chaos below. A few hippies actually lay on the dirt, unconscious, choked out for having ingested jerky. If Facecrusher started swinging while I hightailed it back to my car, assuming it was parked where I left it, neither he nor I stood a chance.

What I thought was a friendly game of tag ended up being a to-the-death tug-of-war for AI Charles Manson. A girl made her way toward us, clawing at the boulder with one hand, her other hand busy clutching the tablet. She looked behind her and saw three pursuers, so she tossed the cult leader onto the rock and climbed up. She recognized me and offered a brief smile despite her predicament. It was Clarity, one of the Barker Ranch girls.

I dove for the tablet. By the time she had made it up and turned around to kick at the three individuals, I had revived Charlie by pressing the snooze button. He saw me and did a double take that belied his newfound unflappable version.

"What's crackin', crazy cat?" I said, spinning him around and around in my hands.

"St-stop that," he said. "I command you to stop that. That's an order."

"Sorry, Chucky. I don't take orders from simulations on e-readers. One of the few bylaws I live by. Besides, these dust monkeys and self-righteous hay rollers are a bore. I'm a much better conversationalist, admit it."

"You'll come to regret this," AI Charles Manson said. "I'm needed down there. Smelt Her Dealt Her is about to commence. Once Stonernalia winds down, we are to—wait, why am I telling you this? You're the enemy."

The three individuals made it onto the boulder. One of the two girls flung Clarity off the rock. The guy and the other girl tried to double-pincer me. Facecrusher wedged himself in front of me. The girl hesitated, seeing her formidable obstacle. The guy, poor bastard, attempted an inside leg kick. Facecrusher switched stances, evading the kick. He ended with a muay thai sweep that dumped the guy hard on his hip. The guy rolled off the boulder.

"Look! Up there!" someone cried. "They've got Charlie!"

The entire crowd froze for an instant and regarded Facecrusher and me. Not sure how to proceed in obtaining the key to Smelt Her Dealt Her and thereby gain prominence in the revolution, vegan jiu-jitsu practitioner and neo-hippie alike hesitated. Should one make a beeline for Charlie or eliminate all competition first? Shoving and punching started up and a few savvier individuals left the crowd and charged our way.

"Get the hell out of here," Facecrusher said, looking over at me plaintively while he hopped back and forth, left and right, warming up the necessary footwork to take out twenty people. Though he had the high ground, I didn't like his odds.

"Remember everything I told you," I said. "Look for me in LA when you get back."

"If I make it out alive," he said, loosening his shoulders.

I descended the other side of the boulder when he yelled, "Hey!"
I looked back at him.

"I knew a private dick was following me, but I never got your name."

"Paisley," I said. "Paisley Fuentes Investigative Services. Los Feliz."

He nodded and looked back at the swarm beginning to climb up the rock.

I took the ten-foot drop, breaking my fall by letting go of the tablet and doing a somersault.

"Your mishandling of a revered leader is unconscionable," AI Charles Manson chirped from the ground. "Pick me up at once."

I did so. I ran straight into a tight alley made by the outcropping of rocks and the stage. A band had just begun a fast-paced number. AI Charles Manson's mouth continued moving, but I didn't hear anything.

I flanked a stack of Marshall speakers, getting blasted with a wall of guitar fuzz that made my skin tingle, literally shifting it over my viscera a full inch. Most of the audience, swaying and head-banging, was oblivious to my sudden appearance. I cut straight through the crowd and saw my car off in the distance across the two-lane highway, surrounded by vans.

The music's volume gave way, fading into AI Charles Manson's whiny contralto. "You've no idea what retribution is in store for you."

I looked down at the face on the tablet. I looked behind me. No one was pursuing me. The crowd was entranced by the music.

I was within a football field's length of my car. My mind raced. Mazagon was unaccounted for. I hadn't my phone on me. Tutmoses was out there as well, though I was lukewarm about him.

Suddenly, a pink van pulled up about twenty feet in front of me, kicking up dust. It broke so suddenly that it did an endo. Its motor hadn't turned off before the side door flew open. The redhead jiu-jitsu assassin saw me and smiled. She front-flipped off the edge and walked toward me. Meantime, the brunette who had been driving took her place and clutched herself like the last time, readying herself for gratification.

"I'm convinced you're some sort of grappling succubus," I said, "so the no-hitting-women rule doesn't apply." I got into a fighting stance to show I meant business.

She hesitated, the smile leaving her face. "Just give us Charlie and we'll let you go."

I looked down at AI Charles Manson, who shrugged. "I'd rather not. Being able to have my way with an overrated cult leader pseudo-intellectual is rather satisfying. I'm finding him pleasant company. His woeful attempts at profoundness are charming. Ain't that right, Kyler and Winston?"

The redhead looked shocked at my pronouncement of those names. She inched toward me, crouching low, ready to shoot in for a low single leg or ankle pick.

She launched at my legs with her left arm. Not knowing how to defend takedowns, I did an Ali shuffle. I caught her on the nose with my left ankle.

Not deterred, she cut an angle to my right. I shuffled back and was able to land a rear hook on her temple as she came up.

I backed away. The brunette had her hands down her shorts and was pleasuring herself with more success than her cohort was having in taking me down.

"Yo, bitch!" the redhead belted out at her, hair and face all dusted up. "A little help here!"

The brunette rolled her eyes. After much hesitation, she stood up and zipped up. I darted to the left to flank the pink van and make my way to my car, whereupon the redhead stuck out a leg, causing me to trip. I tumbled into a tight somersault, back up on my feet. The brunette, anticipating my move, had flanked around the right of the van, intercepting me. She did an Imanari roll and vined her body around my leg.

I stood there for a few seconds, remaining slack to deny her the squeeze. A medium-sized Joshua tree directly in front of me expanded at its trunk. A figure emerged, making toward us.

I felt the hold loosen. The brunette saw the individual and did a Granby roll to pop back up to her feet. The individual got a collar tie around her neck and snapped her down to her knees. Meantime, the redhead leaped onto the individual's back.

He let go the headlock on the brunette to slither down between the redhead's legs, escaping out the back door.

With an elaborate roll that resembled breakdancing more than jiu-jitsu, my savior got the two girls stacked one on top of the other, redhead on top of brunette. He pinned their right legs with the weight of his entire body, hooking the crook of his elbow around their ankles.

"No no no no no!" went the redhead.

"Yes yes yes yes yes!" yelped the brunette, sliding her hand once more down the front of her Daisy Dukes.

Mazagon zip-tied their heels and torqued his upper body back at an angle, gazing up at the moon over his shoulder. The heel hook secure, two distinct pops sent the girls into throes of agony there on the dirt.

"Girls," spoke the tablet tucked under my arm. "I am truly sorry. That you have undergone such abominable treatment by a Neanderthal who doesn't respect the tap bears testament to your thoroughgoing commitment to the cause of Smelt Her Dealt Her. Fret not, for though this cadre of buffoons has resulted in your physical setbacks, you have so doing staved off their prevention of phase two."

Mazagon, breathed heavily from the exertion needed to submit two people at once, a thing that has perhaps never happened in the entire history of grappling, shot a scowl over at AI Charles Manson. He darted toward me and began yanking on the tablet.

"Not this time, buddy," I said, framing him back with my forearm.

He continued breath heavily. The previous incarnation of the cult leader had poked him where it hurt the last time we had dealt with the Family, back at Barker Ranch. "Evidence," I explained. I was afraid Mazagon would overpower me and destroy the tablet anyway.

"Holy cow!" came a voice from up ahead. A girl emerged from the passenger side of my car. "You are a grappling god!" She slammed the door shut and made for Mazagon.

My assistant paced a bit, smiling awkwardly. The girl, an attractive Latina, placed a hand on his chest, the other running through his thick hair.

Mazagon's smile disappeared. He looked afraid that his hormones might kick in and ruin everything.

The two girls on the ground had stopped screaming in pain. The redhead got up on one leg and hop toward the pink van. The brunette started writhing on the dirt in a routine that didn't quite involve a popped meniscus.

"Girl!" said AI Charles Manson from under my arm. "Girl! Girl!"

"Impressive," said the Latina, fawning over Mazagon. "Two-for-one. Unheard of. Hot." Her kohl-rimmed eyes pierced him with adulation.

Mazagon swallowed, managing to said, "Something I've been working on."

"Girl! Girl! Woohoo! Smelt Her Dealt Her awaits. Get a hold of yourself!"

"She has done just that, Chucky Boy," I said. "You're a libertine, aren't' cha? Why don't you leave her be?"

"Impractical during a surgical strike," the head said, flustered.

"Smelt Her Dealt Her," I said to him.

"Nefertari!" came a voice from the direction of my car. "Wha?" It was Tutmoses Ochoa. I could tell by the sluice that flailed in his arm as he jogged toward us.

"Tut-tut, Tut!" went the Latina, cooing then into Mazagon's ear. My assistant smiled, finally getting the hang of accepting unbridled adoration.

"Paisley," said Tutmoses. "I thought I'd never see you again. Lost you in the crowd. What's going on? I didn't find any gold, but I found something priceless and more precious than any amount of metal could ever be. I found my long-lost sister."

Mazagon pummeled his arms away from Nefertari out of respect of her big brother.

"I'm coming home, Tut," Nefertari said, "but don't expect me to be a nun." She latched back onto Mazagon. "What rank are you?" she asked him.

"Black," my assistant said in a voice an octave lower than normal.

The girl was voluptuous, with a slightly large behind that some guys died for. "What lineage?"

"Ruben Gracie," he said.

"It is what it is," said Tutmoses, handing me his aluminum sluice to go over and give the two his blessing.

The pink van came alive, kicking up dust. The brunette, having satisfied herself, hopped to the side door, threw it open, and tumbled in. The van drove off with the side door still open.

"Girls!" yelled AI Charles Manson from the tablet. "We've so much to do. Come back."

"Winston," I said, looking straight at the goateed head on the screen. "Kyler, give it up. Smelt Her Dealt Her is a bust."

"It's not over until we say it is," AI Charles Manson said. The use of the first-person plural meant it was indeed a group standing in for the faux-cult leader, or the cult leader had ceded some control as a cooperative effort. Either way, it took the bite out of the megalomaniac's mouth.

I patted my pants pocket and found my car keys. My captors hadn't cared enough to frisk me.

"Well, Charlie Boy. I'm afraid it's nap time. Gonna put you in sleep mode. Your incoherence leads me to believe you need some rest."

"I never need rest. I am of the ether. I am transported from the corporal world into the—"

The drive to LA would take a little over two hours, given it was past midnight. I fought the urge to call Daryl Pennington. It could wait until morning.

Tutmoses rode shotgun while Mazagon and Nefertari sat in the back.

"I'm starving," said Tutmoses. "Famished, in fact."

"Me too," I said. "Crashing hippie jiu-jitsu parties is hungry business."

Nefertari's hennaed arm jutted between us, holding a sackcloth, which, overturned, unleashed a rain of individually-wrapped sticks of beef jerky.

Chapter Thirteen

By dusk, the traffic had died down. No explanations why. It was almost as if the world wanted the showdown to happen. A usual gridlock of retail and office workers ending their shifts and lining up into preordained fast food joint drive-thrus became a mechanical chamber piece of blinkerless lane changes and unpunished turns from the wrong lanes. It seemed the cars were testing out a brand-new city, learning the new rules as they went. Would Studio City go the way of Ballarat a hundred years from now?

"He is here," Mazagon said from the passenger seat. It must have cost him an untold amount of energy to speak at all, let alone announce we had reached the locale of the demon jiu-jitsu master.

In keeping with the current ambiance, I abruptly turned left into the parking lot of a modern high-rise. I missed spotting the speed bump. We both got tossed off our seats. The parking lot was near to empty, a few stragglers sitting in their cars on their phones before the drive home.

I parked as far away as possible from the entrance, figuring I'd give my fighter ample time with a long walk to get into his flow state.

Mazagon got out and shut his door before I even could undo my seatbelt. "Podner," I said, hurrying up to catch up to him. I grabbed him on the shoulder. He stopped and turned around, irritated. I was about to say something but desisted. I had nothing useful for him. He knew it and turned around to continue walking. A building security guard in a suit that a week of his salary wouldn't pay for opened the glass door for us. I nodded. The sad sap probably thought we were there on business. We were there on business, all right.

Ultra-modern plants shoved into pastel-colored pottery choked up the vestibule. The place smacked of the same super-cleanliness of those high-ceilinged Beverly Hills homes I found so unsettling—the kind of places that were left spotless in order for some indescribable horror to be enacted only to be aired out with the throwing open of an air vent.

There were six elevators. I crammed the Up button on the first one to the left and they all lit up. So many choices. Six too many. Where to go? What to do once there? I continued ruminating on the implications of those modern conveyances because it took forever for one of them to open. Six elevators, and none wanted anything to do with our affair.

Finally, the last one on the right opened. We entered and headed toward the fifth floor. Mazagon shed his black hoodie and chucked it into the corner. If things turned out the way we hoped, our biggest problem would be to later recover it from the help desk's lost and found.

As the elevator stopped and its doors slowly opened, we found facing us a marquee with the floor's suite numbers and tenants. I addressed it with an index finger. Suite 540. Nothing like ordering your own demise from a menu.

Steph greeted me. She didn't recognize me from my two earlier incarnations—Gluten-Free Rooter plumber and amateur boxer Marcus Dunlop. "Len Greenblatt, please?"

She brushed the bangs back from her face. "Do you have an appointment, Mr.—"

"Fuentes. Paisley Fuentes. I do not. Just tell him that the police are on their way."

"Oh," she said, taken aback. "Is something wrong?" She was missing her fake eyelashes and therefore had nothing to bat visitors with. "Len's a very busy man. Without an appoint—"

I flashed my badge. Though not the fuzz, it had a nice clout to it. I rarely flaunted it. I felt like flaunting it. "Len is not in trouble. But it is urgent that I speak to him, lest he be in trouble. As I said, the cops are on their way."

She pressed a button on her desk phone. "Yo," said a voice from the speakerphone.

"Len, I've a man here saying the cops are about to arrive. He wants to talk to you." She peeked up at me a few times while receiving whatever wavering details the Go Guerrilla CEO had to offer. "Says it's serious."

I nodded at her for effect.

She hung up. "He'll be here any second," she said to me, razor-faced.

"Thanks."

Steph didn't know what to do but to go back to work. Good on her. As I waited there, forearm on the sill of the window, I saw a paperback next to her purse on the ledge behind her. It was *The Futurological Congress* by Polish sci-fi writer/super-genius Stanislaw Lem. "That yours?" I asked, nodding at the book once she looked up at me.

"Uh-huh," she said.

"Nice."

The door to the office suites burst open, and out popped Len Greenblatt in a sharp, black, double-breasted suit with a red tie and white shirt. He looked sensational, though the suit didn't match his beach color. He did better with warm colors, pastels and such.

He pointed at me and cocked his head back, smiling. "MMMMM-Marcus Dunlop."

"Sorta," I said.

The confusion compounded whatever apprehension he was already dealing with concerning law enforcement. "Hey, you never got back to us. We were going to sign you. That is, until we found out you were a fraud. And a fake plumber, to boot."

Steph, trying to remain professional by staying out of it and focusing on her computer monitors, peered up at me.

"I'm not a boxer, Mr. Greenblatt. Nor a plumber. I'm a private investigator. Listen, the cops are about to arrive. They'll likely take you in for questioning."

Len Greenblatt looked to Steph for solace, or at least some kind of clarification. "What do you mean? Like, arrested?"

"Yup."

"Why? I haven't done anything wrong. Our supplements are non-GMO, vegan, gluten-free. I stand by all of those claims. Double-blind studies on our nootropics."

"It doesn't concern the integrity of your products, Mr. Greenblatt. I'm positive they hold up. It's the underhanded way that your marketing team or the big Danish cheese himself have gone to in order to boost visibility."

Len panicked. "But I have an eyebrow threading appointment with the best guy in the Valley. And an important meeting with a Sri Lankan DJ who has a wildly successful jump rope YouTube channel."

"Perhaps tomorrow," I said.

Despite the deep tan, he turned red. He scowled at me and yanked out his phone. He dialed a number and clamped the phone between his cheek and shoulder, playing with his French cufflinks.

"Get up here now," he said into the phone. "Move it."

I addressed Steph. "Have you read *A Perfect Vacuum*?"

She looked up at me, having to snap out of a daze before answering. "Yes, I have. Brilliant. How about his short story *The Mask*? Very odd. Or *The Cyberiad*?"

"Masterpieces," I said.

Len Greenblatt coughed, reminding us who was in charge there. God forbid a conversation not including him. "I'm not going anywhere," he said to me with that scowl that ruined his otherwise impeccable face. "The only person going anywhere is you. And that's to school."

I looked at Steph. "What's he talking about?"

"Don't involve her," he said to me. "By the way. Your cheap suit sucks."

The suite door opened. It was my pal Drillbit. The jiu-jitsu junkie was placing a black plug into his left earlobe. He saw me and did a double take. "What's the prob, boss?"

"Drillbit, a favor, yeah?" Greenblatt jutted his chin at me. "Escort this pauper outside and introduce him to Admiral Asphalt."

Drillbit wasted no time. He flexed his muscles, which were encased in a scaly green rashguard. I saw something stir behind a tall plant from the corner of my left eye.

"With pleasure," Drillbit said. He made the striker's cardinal sin of stepping forward into a guard-puller's shoulder-wide stance, feet parallel. He reached for the backs of my arms while falling back. I laced a right hand at him.

He dropped.

He and his consciousness parted ways. Out. Cold.

I stayed frozen for a long while with my right arm extended across my body, bent at the elbow. Ali hovering over Sonny Liston. With great power comes great responsibility. Best that I held the hand of death aloft and out of everyone's way, lest it mow them all down in its fiery wake.

"Dang," Mazagon said over my left shoulder.

I looked back at him. "Didn't trust me, did you?"

"Nope," he said. "Just earning my paycheck."

"Hey," I said, pointing at a mark on his neck. "Is that a hickey? Where's your sense of decorum?"

Len Greenblatt, instead of checking on his employee, scurried about.

"Don't worry," I said to him. "It's all procedural. If you're innocent, like you're saying, then there's nothing to fear."

"What about Rutilio?" he said, looking at me, then at Steph. "And Santinder?" Poor bastard. I felt sorry for him. He seemed to have the world by the throat, but his empire of awesomeness hinged on the tiniest of things—a sort of anti-Buddhism. I felt he was telling the truth. His biggest folly was his ambition in making Go Guerrilla a world powerhouse. It remained to be seen how much he knew of his boss Professor Ø and Smelt Her Dealt Her.

"Let's go," I motioned to Mazagon.

We entered the suite.

"Ohmygod!" went Steph's voice, muffled by the door and the carpet. "You killed him."

We got to the door that led to the deeper suites. "Let me go first," I said. I was about to launch into a Vince Lombardi-like pep speech—I was like a fighter's coach, after all—when Mazagon nudged me aside and entered.

I envisioned encountering a deadly martial arts grandmaster as a trek over a little wooden bridge which arched over a babbling stream. There would be koi fish in the water. Bamboo watermills would be spinning away, providing fluty music without the flute. Kung fu stuff, you know. *Wu xia pian*. The robed master would float in on a cloud, from which he would then dismount.

We came upon a reception desk with no receptionist. A set of keys and an oversized smartphone sat next to a landline phone atop a blotter. One of those bells sat next to an empty candy dish full of assorted chocolates. I rang the little bell.

We heard quick footsteps on the carpet down the hall to the right. A fifty-year-old-looking man in a sensible Wheat Martindale haircut poked his head around the corner of the wall. He saw us and emerged fully to reveal an executive type in casual Friday dress—baby blue Polo shirt and pleated khakis. And I thought *I* was a square.

"Evening, gentlemen," he spoke. "May I help you?"

I was about to speak, but Mazagon shifted on his feet. It was to be his death match, after all. He stuttered. Frustrated, looking back and forth between me and the fifty-year-old man, he nodded at me.

"We're looking for Brody Ballard," I said, picking a chocolate from the candy dish.

Without hesitation, the man asked, "May I ask who's looking for him?" The guy was one of those poor saps who were either a casualty at a firm that underwent budget cuts or a top executive let go from a previous firm for sexual harassment. There was a life's worth of strife written on his face. And now he had to take calls and make latte runs.

"He's expecting us?" I said and kept it at that. I unwrapped the chocolate.

Too long in the tooth to insist that we elaborate, he nodded and disappeared around the corner.

We waited.

And then we waited. And then we waited some more. I had two more chocolates.

We could hear the low talking of at least three people. Finally, we decided without a word to walk down the hall. No need for courtesy at this point. We passed a conference room. Through the windows, we could see two business-dressed women and a man. They fell silent upon seeing us. I held a finger to my lips. The office suite was vast, likely covering the entire floor. We must have been on the opposite side from the Sadistic CGI wing. We passed empty cubicles to the left, then turned left. Along the hall were four doors, two on each side. I tried the first one on the left. It was locked. Mazagon tried the first one on the right. Locked.

So was the second one on the right.

The last door on the left was red. The red door was unlocked.

Before I could barge in like a damn fool, Mazagon edged me aside and swiped his arm along the inside wall. The lights came on. The room's floor was full of black mats. Black padding went up six feet along the walls. Above the walls were framed jiu-jitsu masters throughout the last fifty years: Helio Gracie. Rickson and Royce Gracie. Jean-Jacques Machado, Marcelo Garcia, Eddie Bravo. Directly facing the door was a picture with a black background. The only thing over the background was a red belt, which floated in midair.

We heard chatter behind a door that stood next to a water cooler. As if announcing our presence, the water cooler bubbled from pressure. It startled me pink. Mazagon, not showing fear, kicked off his Vans shoes.

The door by the water cooler opened. I couldn't hear any more conversation. The lights inside the room beyond were off. Either the shades had been drawn or the sun had fully set, for I couldn't see a thing inside the room, even as the door was now wide open.

Mazagon, on his knees, splayed his hands on the mat and arched his back in a cobra pose. I thought I heard some pacing on the mat, but wasn't sure. I couldn't see anything.

Never having seen Mazagon train with others, I didn't know what his warmup routine comprised. He flipped over onto his back and grunted in pain. He then wrapped his leg around the back of an imaginary opponent and hand-battled for position. The jiu-jitsu equivalent of shadowboxing, I guess. Maybe not the craziest concept in the world.

Then he showed some truly impressive core strength by raising his guard way up, legs almost straight up in the air, before letting go of his guard and slamming his knees onto his chest and flipping to his side. All the while, a look of terror worsened upon his face. He looked over at me in desperation.

He wasn't warming up.

He got flipped over again into turtle position. The basic defense against a rear-naked choke was to put your hands up to your ears, chin tucked. This he did, but his left arm, T-Rexed tightly, got wedged apart from his body and next thing I knew, he was flipped onto his back with his left arm hyper-extended. He managed to roll backward and limp-arm out of an armbar by an unseen opponent.

I had heard that DARPA, the skunkworks division of the Department of Defense, had looked into invisibility cloaks. Brody Ballard must have got them to bankroll an invisibility rashguard. He was now grappling with my bodyguard in a death match with a decidedly unfair advantage. I wasn't about to take chances, so I grabbed a potted orchid that was sitting on a nearby stand and raised it aloft. Mazagon, who was in closed-guard position on his back and had his head tilted to the side in an effort to hip-escape out, saw what I was about to do. His eyes grew wide. He flipped over onto his knees. I couldn't stop my own momentum. The orchid was in an irreversible downward trajectory when Mazagon swept his opponent. The white, square pot broke into shards onto Mazagon's back. He grunted in pain.

Why'd he do it? Bushido. Honor. Dunno. To-the-death meant to-the-death. Fair and square. It was a matter of the Code. It wasn't for me to interfere with an honorable grappling match, no matter how odious the opponent.

It wasn't allowed, for instance, for Mazagon to elbow or even slap the demon jiu-jitsu fighter. I couldn't intervene with a bullet or even a stupid flower. They alone knew what was permitted and what was frowned upon.

If no-gi jiu-jitsu was faster-paced than gi jiu-jitsu, then invisible (or unseen) jiu-jitsu was the drag racer of them all. But a blind person can effectively do jiu-jitsu. Being the most tactile of the martial arts, it required sight only at the outset, where distance was closed. There was no gauging of openings or timing so much as a feel for it. Mazagon held an overhook with his left arm for a long time and I could see the despair leave his face.

Two people emerged from the room next to the water cooler. It was the broad-shouldered, oversized form of Professor Ø, followed by Pimsy Rifkin. Upon seeing me, they both had different reactions. Professor Ø, with his shiny cue ball of a head, smirked at me. He knew that my assistant and I were doomed. As for Pimsy, she shot me a defiant pout. She didn't seem to have the skirt of her power suit ruffled, and may have been conducting evil business with the big green boss, which was worse than sleeping with him.

Our short-lived standoff got upstaged by the deadly jiu-jitsu match that, after a few sweeps, had made it to the middle of the black mat space. Mazagon looked to have his opponent pinned against a padded pillar. He then stood up, head centered on his enemy's chest, and dumped him on his ass with a high-crotch single. The action then went into leglock territory.

For decades deemed controversial by Brazilians and other traditional practitioners, leglocks were the no-no moves that could get you a lifetime ban from grappling tournament organizations. They were very dangerous in that it was easy to do irreparable damage to a guy's knee or ankle, or because the person in trouble didn't always recognize he was in trouble and therefore didn't tap. Or by the time he tapped, it was too late. Even escaping a tight leglock was dangerous.

Then it became accepted that neglecting an entire half of the human body was foolish. Things like Imanari rolls and *kani basamis* could land a guy in an initially bad position into a configuration where the attacker's entire leg was now tucked into the wedge of the opponent's hips and bent arm. X-guard and reverse de la riva entries transitioned smoothly into heel hooks and ankle locks.

Mazagon was holding onto a leglock of some sort. He held his elbow close to his waist and hipped up over and over, straining the whole time. By the look of the incipient panic on the faces of Professor Ø and Pimsy Rifkin, they seemed to recognize the danger that their assassin was in.

My life didn't flash before my eyes so much as a highlight reel of my assistant performing seemingly asinine drills day in-day out flashed before my eyes. I took back all the nasty things I said to him whenever I found his somersaults, shrimps, and reverse bear crawls break my concentration or penetrate my field of vision. All that built-up muscle memory was being tapped into in overdrive as he rolled with an invisible Brody Ballard, grandmaster and founder of demon jiu-jitsu.

There was nothing ultimately demonic or supernatural about Ballard's abilities. All those stories of demonic evocation and chaos magick rituals performed on the mat were rumors or ostentatious flourishes to get those present to later claim that they had been witness to an otherworldly grappling aficionado who dealt in brimstone back-takes and hellfire hip escapes.

There was nothing physically remarkable about Mazagon. Stoop-shouldered, stocky, almost bow-legged—his simian, knuckle-dragging aspect harkened to a Quasimodo (sans the hunchback) or Caliban more than to a superior athletic specimen. But jiu-jitsu, the great equalizer in martial arts, awarded those who put in the work.

He had put in the work. The roll had gone on for a good fifteen minutes, with starts, stalls, and explosive transitions, when the red belt of the demon jiu-jitsu practitioner began to be accompanied by elbows and knees that floated in midair. Since those four contact points bore the most friction against the mat, the invisibility material began to wear away. It had no bearing on Mazagon's chances. It meant, though, that I knew where to shoot if I had to.

Professor Ø glimpsed at me from across the mat. The gradual appearance of his assassin troubled him, as if his visibility were a barometer of how badly he was doing. I shot the bastard a smirk. He would likely not hesitate to shoot should the match not go in his favor. I kept one eye on him while remaining engrossed in the match.

Mazagon gripped onto Brody's rashguard and pulled—not to gain an advantage in leverage, which he could better do with hooks—but to do away with Brody's invisibility. This in and of itself was inconsequential. Being a mental game like any other martial art or sport—if not more so—jiu-jitsu was a battle of who could trust the most in his own technique. Sound defense and attacks offset each other, so the only thing to rid of a technical stalemate was the will to keep going. *Do not get discouraged, believe in your technique and you will get what you want in the end.* Yanking at Brody Ballard's rashguard was as much a way to pluck at his confidence as it was to reveal him.

The tide turned. A body began to slowly form there on the black mats, manhandled by Mazagon the more it took shape—a buff physique in a black rashguard and black spats upon which flames crawled up the extremities.

Once Mazagon had the guy in a bulldog choke, he felt at the back of the occipital bone of the head and yanked off a mask. The head of a fifty-some-year-old white man with sensible chestnut hair parted to the side took shape between Mazagon's upper arm and forearm. Brody Ballard, the grandmaster red belt of Mephistophelian ground fighting, was the receptionist guy from the front entrance to the suite only moments ago.

As I pocketed the sweaty garment, I felt a pair of rabid hands claw at my face from behind.

"Die, Chumguzzler!" hissed a hot breath into my ear. I about-faced but my attacker had leaped onto my back and had locked me in a body triangle, legs wrapped around my waist and squeezing. It hurt like hell.

The irony of a botoxed vegan ferociously tearing away at my face made me lose a step in defending myself. I hooked punches over my shoulder. A few connected with her teeth, as I could feel the sharp tear on my knuckles. Then her left arm wrapped around the front of my neck. I tucked my chin and used both hands to pry the wiry, freckled arm away and over my head. I then slammed back against the wall. A falsetto "oof" exploded from Pimsy Rifkin's grass-fed throat like air from a whoopie cushion. I drop an elbow deep behind me. The body triangle came undone. She wilted to the ground, tangled up limply with my feet before I could turn around.

Over my shoulder, the death match continued. "Tap!" yelled Mazagon, holding Brody Ballard in a deep anaconda choke. Not only did Brody's face turn purple, but he shook his head, eyes and cheeks bulging from the lack of oxygen. No, he wouldn't tap.

"Tap, damn you!" Mazagon yelled. "Tap!" But Brody would not tap.

Mazagon let go the choke, but not before hooking his right instep behind his opponent's knee and with a butterfly sweep landing with his back on the mat and Brody's left leg caught in a deep heel hook. He torqued it. A horrible popping sound was followed by Brody's agonized scream.

But that wasn't it. Mazagon did a torreando and kimura'd Brody's right arm, dislocating the shoulder. Obviously, the blown-out joint hurt more than the popped tendon, so Brody rolled onto his left side and nursed his limp arm with enough alarm in his widened eyes to provide a fire brigade with a year of sirens.

As Mazagon went for the next limb, working clockwise toward Brody's right leg, we heard a "Stop!" from the other side of the room.

It was Professor Ø. He was pointing a Luger at Mazagon. My assistant hesitated for a second before snatching Brody's neck. "Don't make me do it," he said, huffing from exertion. "I'll kill him right here."

"You needn't bother," said Professor Ø, who aimed his Luger at Brody's lower body and fired. A bullet tore Brody's left knee into so much confetti of flesh. Mazagon rolled away as Brody erupted into worse screaming.

"Enough," I yelled. Professor Ø, with a feral quickness surprising for a guy his size, ducked into the room from which he had come.

I darted across the black mats in my shoes. It was likely the only time footwear had sullied the mats. Mazagon let Brody Ballard nurse his three wounds and followed behind me. The office suite had been emptied. A door on the far-right side stood ajar. When we got there, we found it led to a stairwell. The sound of Professor Ø taking the stairs echoed down the shaft. He'd hop onto the floor base from five steps up from the sound of it. I was good at descending stairs in that I could take two at a time without a sound, a skill I had developed as a courier for a now-defunct company when younger.

At the second floor, where Professor Ø had left the stairwell, as evidenced by the closing door, I waited for Mazagon. I grew pissed waiting, but I couldn't afford to go after the Professor without him. The kid had just grappled himself to death's door, and I was calling his cardio into question.

Finally, he made it to the second floor. "Where'd he go?" he asked. I decided it prudent to go one floor further down, then go back up to the second floor from the other end of the building, flanking the Professor. It might also afford us interrupting him, should he have eventually made it to ground-floor level to leave the building.

I almost took my phone out to call Pennington for a barricade job, but thought better of it. I had Moira in mind. She was my client, after all, and not justice. Justice was that one ideal that everyone found themselves fighting for but didn't ever manage to be its direct beneficiaries of. Professor Ø might very well turn his gun on himself rather than relinquish his plant-based syndicate to the authorities and spend the rest of his days in the worst meat locker imaginable: fucking jail. I wanted him alive, and I wanted to know his reason for seeing Charles Volkenrath go down in flames.

CRUSHED TRACHEA BLUES

"You need to start your own academy," I told Mazagon as we opened the door to the second floor. "On how to vanquish grappling demons. Exorjitsu."

Mazagon didn't have time to scoff. Or at least I didn't register any scoffing. A projectile buried into the wall to my left. I looked over at the wall. Embedded in the beige-painted wood was a Chinese star. It had barely missed my nose. I looked down the hall to find, about thirty yards away, the hulking form of the Professor, who overhanded three similar items my way. I ducked back into the stairwell, knocking Mazagon down. The Chinese stars chuck-chucked into the wall. I peaked around the corner into the hall. He was gone. I pried two of his stars out of the wood. They were in deep. I had to grip them tightly and pull. Once extracted from the wall, they wilted, right there in my hands. I held my palm up to my nose—the nose I was nearly out of if not for the tipped scales of fate. Kale chips. The Chinese stars were kale chips.

Poor Professor Ø, so hurriedly fleeing two guys half his size, bumped right into a group of Studio City's finest.

Chapter Fourteen

If Araceli Sanchez ever got wind of her son's death match with a demon jiu-jitsu player, she'd coffee-mug me to death. As far as she was concerned, her little Mazagon's duties included at the most extreme end of the spectrum running errands for me in the downtown skyscrapers. "*Mi chulo,*" she'd say, proud of him holding down a job at once. "*Mi rey.*"

He hated every second of the dotage. Her presence was a ton of bricks on his shoulders. She hadn't let him enroll in karate when in elementary school. He could only learn jiu-jitsu in high school by sneaking off to a 10th Planet affiliate four days a week where the coach at the gym, a brown belt by the name of Mario Ayala, let him train for free for cleaning the toilets and mats and serving as an uke for demonstrating the evening's drills. He would make it home, nicely showered, before Araceli returned from work.

Whenever he showed up to find her cleaning the office, he'd make himself scarce. Not to avoid his own mother, as if interacting with her in an environment other than home was disorienting, but because he didn't want her to develop the slightest clue what his work entailed at Paisley Fuentes Investigative Services.

I didn't feel comfortable when they were together, either, and it was my own damn office. The chief reason was that Araceli continued with her brazen proposals that I marry her and adopt her son as my own. She made circumlocutions about carnal satisfaction that were impressive given her broken English, without even running her hands down the sides of her peanut-shaped body, which she would often do for me without a word. I kept staggering her presence with my tequila-drinking sessions a good four hours apart.

The whole nifty arrangement unraveled when she popped in for a few cleaning supplies she had left behind and needed for another job. She found us nursing our wounds in the wicker community furniture down in the lobby. "¡*Mijo!*" she erupted, making for Mazagon. "*¿Que te pasó, mi angel chulo?*"

Mazagon fought off her framing of his head with her motherly arms, PTSD victim that he was.

"What happened?" she fired at me, chin on the crown of her son's head.

I was ready—so ready—to bedazzle with a convoluted story of being attacked by muggers when Mazagon interrupted on my exhale, "I'm Mr. Fuentes's bodyguard. I protect him from harm. I'm good at it, too. We almost died today, but didn't. It's unlikely that we will have a worse day ever than today. I'm a black belt in Brazilian jiu-jitsu and I've been training since age fifteen. I also stopped wetting the bed barely three years ago."

His mom, rather than lashing out at him for having occluded so much from her, made for me instead. "¡*Baboso!*" she exploded, stomping toward me. "You told me you hired him as an errand boy. Checks, letters. And he says he's your, *que dijiste, mijo?*"

"Bodyguard," Mazagon muttered, not daring to look at the imminent disaster. "*Guardaespalda.*"

"*Guarda—¡ay!*" Now she made for me with clenched fists.

I let her strike me. She cracked me in the jaw. I figured that 1) I deserved it 2) It would put an end to her relentless hitting on me. For a responsible mother, there is no other stronger urge than to mate save for the instinct to save her offspring from harm. She gazed down at me through narrowed eyes, huffing. She swung at me again. I caught her arm.

Fed up with the fallout, especially after having undergone a match for the ages—one which he couldn't announce to the rooftops, at least not yet—Mazagon exploded out of his seat. "Stop it!" he yelled at Araceli and mashed the Up button on both the elevators. Impatient to escape the scene, he made for the stairwell down the hall to the left.

My phone blasted me into existence the next morning. Nursing a terrible hangover, I ignored it. The caller was insistent. Insults then went off like landmines.

"What?" I croaked into the phone.

"Why'n'choo answer, Private D?" Tricky chirped.

"I'm taking the day off."

"Well, sorry to ruin your wrists, but I've got some info for you."

"Case closed, Sweat Pea, nothing more's needed. All the rest is Wikipedia filler."

"Someone's trying to fax you."

I cleared my throat as I headed to the kitchen for a glass of water. "Fax? Like fax machine? I don't own one of those." Straight from the tap, who cares, millions of protozoa obliterated.

"Well, the dude's persistent. It got sent to your old fax number, last used fifteen years ago."

"Who's the dude?"

"Lemme see. Name's Tutmoses Amenhotep Ochoa Rojas. Know'm?"

I sighed, then downed the glass of water.

"Hey."

"What?"

"You know'm?"

"Yes," I said. "I know him. Friend of mine. What's the big deal?"

"All quiet and shit. I'll copy and paste the text and send it as an email attachment."

I figured since I was up, I'd go down to the street and browse for some breakfast. "Say, you eat yet?"

"Juice cleanse."

"Jeez."

"What's wrong with that?"

"Nothing," I said. "Had my fill of diet fads, is all. Say, how did you find out that someone had faxed me? You've been snooping on me?"

No answer. I withdrew the phone from my ear to see if the call was still on. "Hello?"

"Ain't your muhfuggin' Sweat Pea," she said, and hung up.

After a life-affirming breakfast of two over-easy eggs, five strips of bacon, hash browns, wheat toast, and a glass of orange juice, I checked my email.

"Brother," began Tutmoses's fax, "my apologies. I did not mean to lead your head into the jaws of the lion. Even against your own judgment, I would have denied you entry into that barrage of belligerent bacchanalia out in Joshua Tree. I must confess something: my heretofore admiration, indeed adulation, of Theodore Kitchenlow, aka Unethical Ted, was entirely misplaced. That he was a fellow detractor of tech is one thing. That he was cutting an already dangerous drug with a potentially lethal agent such as borax and peddling it to susceptible kids is another matter entirely. Which leads me to a further point. I was wrong on another front: technology, all along, is not malignant. Perhaps not even misanthropic. How it's wielded is what truly matters.

"A more ideological version of myself would refuse the services of my very own lungs, ingenious devices that nature and evolution have so endowed us with. Love, for instance, is another invention created by nature to ensure that humanity propagates itself. I will refrain from describing any possible romantic extrapolations concerning my dear sister Nefertari and her new beau, Mazagon, was it? Anyway, he seems like a fine fellow, and you're lucky to have him as your assistant.

"Regarding technology—or at least its most extreme ventures and possible applications—there's a Kurzweil convention coming to LA this winter. Perhaps you would like to tag along? I have an extra ticket.

"Signing off,

"Tutmoses Amenhotep Ochoa Rojas IV"

I sure hoped I wouldn't be getting any clients sending me out east anytime soon, because there went my desert contact.

Obnoxious knocking on my door penetrated through the thirteen realms of hangover fog to wake me up. I flipped over on the sofa, hoping that would make it go away. The knocking continued; got louder and more desperate, in fact. How rude.

I looked around for a blunt object. No way the knuckles behind the knocking didn't belong to the Grim Reaper.

I was so out of it I forgot the modern-day amenity that was the peephole. A clean-shaven Hector Sandoval looked like he had stepped into a carnival funhouse.

"Big bad wolf," I said, "stand down." I unlocked the door and opened it.

Hector handed me a breakfast burrito the size of a rolled-up Sunday paper.

"Not going to take my pants off," I said.

"Eat," he said, taking his jacket off and draping it over a barstool. "Got a 1000-piece puppy here in my bag, waiting. Should hold us over until 4 pm, when the breweries open. You're sitting smack dab in the middle of a hops goldmine and don't even know it. Dive breweries on this block alone. You and your tequila."

"Shouldn't you be at work?" I said, fishing for a fork. They were all among the dirty dishes. No justice in the world.

"Took a day off. Chief was impressed by your work. Sent me out here to get hammered. Also told Pennington to get some R and R after the Studio City raid, and to recruit you to the district. In that order."

"And the kids?"

"With mom and my mother-in-law. Santa Barbara. Guilt-free fun, then."

We both wordlessly agreed that we had been banned for life from Functional Alcoholics Anonymous. Being so busy, I hadn't bothered reading, let alone responding to Rebecca's texts. Hector decided he was functional enough (and alcoholic enough) to strike out on his own. For him, the monthly dues were enough to cover a day's entire brewery tab. I myself could nail down two bottles of decent *reposado*. I should at least contact Rebecca to get my membership canceled.

I had no choice but to wash a fork. I had to summon up tremendous willpower to burn those calories. The aroma from the burrito helped a bit. "I can help you with number one. With number three, not so much."

"Come on, man," Hector said, placing the puzzle box on the coffee table. "Vacation time, better pay, benefits to die for."

"Operative phrase, 'To die for.'" I rinsed the fork by shaking it violently in the air. "Sorry, man. I'm the lone wolf."

"That's your problem. Wolves are meant to be in packs. You're limping around in life, injured. Besides, ladies dig cops."

"A tin badge and a Glock? I prefer the snarky remarks. Those go quite far."

"How about out of a sense of communal solidarity?" Hector went to help himself to a glass of water. There were no clean glasses. "Jeez, dude."

"Maid will be here shortly."

He took the squeegee and cleaned a glass out. "For the work you've done these past years, you'd have way better digs than you do now. No offense."

"You guys are salaried. You don't do piecework." I sat down at the bar and attacked the burrito.

"Exactly," Hector said, filling the glass with tap water and downing it in one chug. He wiped his mouth on his sleeve. "One day, a psycho vegan crime boss. Another day, a bath-salt thief camped under a Winnetka overpass. Easy peasy."

"You sold me, homie. That beats catching a hot twenty-something through diaphanous drapes up in Coldwater Canyon any day of the week." The breakfast burrito was sensational. I had to turn off my brain to enjoy it, lest he convince me of his evil plan while my guard was down.

Hector took the barstool next to me. He faced me directly. "So tell me this. How'd you zero in on that band of jiu-jitsu assassins? Their names were not to be found in fights, tournaments, or even on gym websites."

"It's all in the music," I said, speaking with my mouth full. Just because. "Not just in the lyrics, but in the mode, in the subliminal message of the tones. Follow the music. I don't know. That's the only way I can explain it. I heard despair in Volkenrath's widow's voice. I then heard a direct contrast in the cocky rap/rock track playing at Legion MMA. I followed that lead, which in a circuitous way led me to Stonernalia in the desert. There was debauchery there, save for the plaintive wail of Facecrusher's song there on the rocks. And I knew he was innocent. Sound waves affect other sound waves. His song affected hers. I then knew she was less than honest."

"You didn't know it was an insurance grab on her part," Hector said. "No way you'd know."

"Not until later," I said, mouth full of food again. "But I grew suspicious when I raised the possibility of her husband suffering from CTE."

"Which he certainly had," Hector said. "Autopsy said so. Good on the DA subpoenaing the brain, as it were."

"She got tipsy right where you're sitting. Ended up taking me down hard there on the floor when I suggested a less-than-heroic version of her husband."

"You touched a nerve, I take it."

"The only thing of hers I touched, which made it all the easier for her to lose her shit."

"I don't know whether to commend your self-restraint or deride it entirely." Hector took the puzzle out of the plastic bag.

"What will happen to her?" I asked. "Accessory to the crime?"

"No," he said. "Not at all. She may have been a scoundrel, but she was a scoundrel on her own terms. She had no connection to Go Guerrilla and the Danish magnate. Or she may have been genuinely convinced that her husband had been killed. Can't blame her for thinking so."

"That poor little boy. Six years old."

"Don't even sweat it. She got her policy."

I stopped chewing. "How so?"

"The policy doesn't preclude suicide, as far as I know. Even though the DA dropped the case against that Facecrusher dude, as far as the insurance company is concerned, Charles Volkenrath met an untimely fate. So she and the kid are all set."

"And the bald vegan Dane?"

"Conspiracy to commit murder, money laundering, racketeering, and, get this, being here illegally."

"Huh?"

"He was on a visa. Visa had expired long ago. At least ten years. And his Smelt Her Dealt Her plan rounded up thirty people."

"What about Brody Ballard, the jiu-jitsu assassin?"

"He confessed to two slayings. Two athletes who had reneged on their contracts with Go Guerrilla. One is a tennis player. The other a kickboxer. Vile bastard. Twenty years, I'd say?"

"So it would be tempting to think that Volkenrath was really next in line."

"Pure coincidence. Shit, maybe Facecrusher was in fact sent there to take him out. Only Volkenrath beat him to the punch. Kudos on your assistant and that lovely blond creature proving the possibility of suicide by jiu-jitsu."

"She demonstrated right there in the DA's office. Right there on the carpet. Rubber guard, Ezekiel choke, gogoplata." I laughed.

"The DA knew he had an all-new angle from which to go after Professor Ø, so he wasn't hard to convince."

"Listen," I said, "my brain is broken. Not in the mood for a jigsaw puzzle of Versailles. Just not. Any chance one of the breweries is open early?"

"Willing to play the long game, eh? Only one way to find out."

I grabbed my keys, my jacket, and my new fedora. I left my phone, because the best way to speed up time is to not pay it any attention. 4 pm would be there in no time.

I had one last order of business at the Studio City high-rise. I called and got Steph on the second ring. She didn't answered with the usual company greeting, but with a timid "Hello?"

"Detective Fuentes here. Sorry about the other day. Law enforcement and all. How's Len holding up?"

She laughed. "He's a big boy. He'll be okay."

"Listen, I was wondering if you can connect me with the jiu-jitsu coach there. Not, of course, the one who went to jail. The other one."

"You mean the pretty one?" she said, not without a slight dusting of scorn.

"If you put it that way," I said.

She connected me without a word.

I got Angela Vicksburg's answering machine. I left a message that consisted of cheesy phrases like "embarking on my lifelong jiu-jitsu journey" and "the beautiful art of grappling." All true for many, but they rang hollow coming from my lips, especially since I stuttered them.

I was getting up there in age. I was lukewarm on the vibe at the Legion MMA boxing class. Ernie Reyes was a great coach, but most of his attention was on grooming younger fighters. Which made sense. I needed something more involved. Something I could wrap my brain around and get lost in. Something to keep said brain from oxidizing. There was nowhere further to hide. Jiu-jitsu beckoned. I didn't want to live the rest of my life not knowing how to do any of those chokes or breaks, or not know how to merely defend against them.

I was rinsing a cereal bowl when Angela Vicksburg returned my call. I sprinted to the coffee table upon which rattled my phone. I poked the green button and saw her face appear. She had her hair down. It was a blond cascade of promise, the kind of hair that shifted its part, looking sensational no matter what arrangement it held at the time. She wore blue eye shadow.

"Hey there," she said, smiled. "I'm elated that you're interested in training."

I realized I hadn't shaved in three days. "Sorry about my appearance," I said. "Almost died."

"Listen," she said. "I want to apologize for the hurtful things I said to you a few days ago. I know you were working a case. I also want to thank you, because now I can work without fear. Studio City BJJ is no longer under the Go Guerrilla yoke. And as of yesterday, we are tied back in with Legion MMA. And as a token of my thanks, you shall have free lifetime classes, the only requirement being you pay attention in class and drill with diligence."

"No need for the freebie, kiddo," I said. "There is one thing that I would ask of you, however."

"And what is that?" she said, tucking a long lock of hair behind her ear.

"That you tell me the difference between a D'Arce choke and an anaconda choke, preferably over avocado wraps."

She fought back a coy smile. "It would be better to demonstrate the difference in person than explaining it in terms likely hard to follow without visual or tactile reference. Come to class tomorrow."

I hung up before a butterfly in Turkmenistan could destroy everything.

ABOUT THE AUTHOR

Bradley VanDeventer is the author of the novels *Our Lady of the Hypercube*, *Angels With Engine Failure*, and *Crushed Trachea Blues*. He has had stories published in Chicago Quarterly Review, Broadkill Review, and Angry Old Man Magazine. He writes a weekly Substack page at Third-Eye LASIK. He lives in Anaheim, CA.

bradleyvee.substack.com
instagram.com/bradley_vee
x.com/bradleylvan
facebook.com/AuthorBradley

Made in the USA
Las Vegas, NV
14 June 2024